Praise for Jessica Clare

"The residents of Painted Barrel are just as lovely as ever."
—*Publishers Weekly* (starred review)

"[A] steamy holiday confection that equally delivers heart-warming laughs and heart-melting sighs."   —*Booklist*

"Great storytelling. . . . Delightful reading. . . . It's fun and oh-so-hot!"   —*Kirkus Reviews*

"Jessica Clare found a balance in developing the characters and romance with banter, heart, and tension. [She] introduced colorful new characters along with Eli, Cass, Clyde, and the dogs from *All I Want for Christmas Is a Cowboy*."
—Harlequin Junkie

"[Clare is] a romance writing prodigy."
—Heroes and Heartbreakers

"Blazing hot."   —*USA Today*

Titles by Jessica Clare

Wyoming Cowboys

ALL I WANT FOR CHRISTMAS IS A COWBOY
THE COWBOY AND HIS BABY
A COWBOY UNDER THE MISTLETOE
THE COWBOY MEETS HIS MATCH
HER CHRISTMAS COWBOY
THE BACHELOR COWBOY

Roughneck Billionaires

DIRTY MONEY
DIRTY SCOUNDREL
DIRTY BASTARD

The Billionaire Boys Club

STRANDED WITH A BILLIONAIRE
BEAUTY AND THE BILLIONAIRE
THE WRONG BILLIONAIRE'S BED
ONCE UPON A BILLIONAIRE
ROMANCING THE BILLIONAIRE
ONE NIGHT WITH A BILLIONAIRE
HIS ROYAL PRINCESS
BEAUTY AND THE BILLIONAIRE: THE WEDDING

Billionaires and Bridesmaids

THE BILLIONAIRE AND THE VIRGIN
THE TAMING OF THE BILLIONAIRE
THE BILLIONAIRE TAKES A BRIDE
THE BILLIONAIRE'S FAVORITE MISTAKE
BILLIONAIRE ON THE LOOSE

The Bluebonnet Novels

THE GIRL'S GUIDE TO (MAN)HUNTING
THE CARE AND FEEDING OF AN ALPHA MALE
THE EXPERT'S GUIDE TO DRIVING A MAN WILD
THE VIRGIN'S GUIDE TO MISBEHAVING
THE BILLIONAIRE OF BLUEBONNET

The
Bachelor
Cowboy

JESSICA CLARE

JOVE
New York

A JOVE BOOK
Published by Berkley
An imprint of Penguin Random House LLC
penguinrandomhouse.com

Copyright © 2021 by Jessica Clare
Excerpt from *The Cowboy Meets His Match* copyright © 2019 by Jessica Clare
Penguin Random House supports copyright. Copyright fuels creativity, encourages
diverse voices, promotes free speech, and creates a vibrant culture. Thank you for buying
an authorized edition of this book and for complying with copyright laws by not
reproducing, scanning, or distributing any part of it in any form without permission.
You are supporting writers and allowing Penguin Random House to continue to
publish books for every reader.

A JOVE BOOK, BERKLEY, and the BERKLEY & B colophon
are registered trademarks of Penguin Random House LLC.

ISBN: 9780593102022

First Edition: January 2021

Printed in the United States of America
1   3   5   7   9   10   8   6   4   2

Cover image of couple © Stephen Carrol / Arcangel;
farm scene © Wulf Voss / EyeEm / Getty Images
Cover design by Sarah Oberrender
Book design by George Towne

CHAPTER ONE

"Bachelor auction?" Jack stared at his sister-in-law as if she'd grown another head.

They stood in the middle of the kitchen at the Swinging C Ranch. Jack had come inside to grab some water . . . and immediately, he'd been accosted by his sister-in-law.

Now he was trapped.

"Please, Jack? Please? It's for charity and Sage says she's down a bachelor. Come on. You love women. This is perfect for you!" Becca Watson was the tiniest slip of a woman and nice as could be . . . most days. She was also darn stubborn and knew how to get what she wanted from any of the Watson brothers, Jack suspected. She had his older brother Hank wrapped around one of those pretty little manicured fingers.

And Hank probably wasn't the only one. Because when Becca shoved the bright pink paper at him again, Jack sighed heavily and took a look at it. Sage was almost as bad as Becca when it came to wheedling for things. The sweet-natured mayor never took no for an answer when she wanted something. She'd just smile and talk until you somehow found yourself saying yes.

So he glanced down at the paper handed to him. The headline read:

**BACHELOR AUCTION. COME AND BID ON
YOUR FAVORITE BACHELOR!
ALL OF THE PROCEDES GO TO BUILDING
PAINTED BARREL'S ANIMAL SHELTER.**

"What do you think?" Becca asked, clasping her hands under her chin.

He pointed at the paper. "Someone spelled 'proceeds' wrong."

His sister-in-law smacked his arm. "You know what I mean, Jack. Will you do it?" She grabbed the plate of fresh-baked cookies off of the counter and held them up to him, her expression pleading.

Damn, but she was good. Cookies and the sad eyes? No wonder Hank never stood a chance. He looked around the kitchen, desperate for someone to save him, but both of his brothers and his elderly uncle were making themselves scarce like the cowards they were. There would be no escape from a well-meaning sister-in-law. Jack bit back a sigh and took three of the cookies offered. He crossed his arms over his chest so he wouldn't look like he was giving in too easily. "What's it entail?"

Becca gave a happy little squeal, hopping with joy. "You're the best, Jack!"

"I know, but I didn't agree to nothin' yet," he teased. "You gotta tell me what it's about first." Still, he liked seeing her happy. Jack had a soft spot for women, even if she was married to his big, rock-headed brother.

"Okay, well, it's going to be super cute," Becca gushed,

and inwardly, Jack cringed. There were hearts all over the pink flyer, so he could only imagine what this was going to entail. "Cute" had better not mean him dressing up like a fool. "We've asked for volunteers around town to show up as our bachelors, and we're going to auction you off to the highest bidder. All the ladies of the Painted Barrel Animal Helpers Committee are going to be there, bidding on the men, but of course it's open to the public."

"The what what what?"

"Painted Barrel Animal Helpers Committee. PBAHC. It's the committee Amy and I and some of the other girls in yoga made to help out with the animal population. You know the city doesn't have an official shelter, but if we can raise ten thousand dollars, Sage is going to put in a request to have the back of the city hall converted to make a shelter big enough to hold ten animals. It's a great cause, and it'll make you look like a great guy." Becca pushed another cookie his way as he polished his off. "And you're the only one that's still single."

"Doc's single," he pointed out over a mouthful of chocolate chips.

"He's busy that day, unfortunately," Becca told him. "We actually had a bunch of guys lined up, but with scheduling conflicts, we moved down to twelve. Then Mr. Hammond had heart surgery and so he can't volunteer."

Jack tilted his head. "Did you say Hammond? Tom Hammond?" The man was eighty if he was a day, and skinny as a nail. "He's doing this?"

"Like I said," Becca repeated slowly. "It's for a lot of the club ladies and some of the women in yoga. You should expect the average age to be geriatric. Like, bingo-and-retirement-home age." She hesitated and then added, "Though it is open to the public."

Jack bit back another groan. He knew all about the public in Painted Barrel. For all that the town was bigger than most of the ones he'd been in over in Alaska, there didn't seem to be a ton of single women. They all seemed to be married or ancient. Becca had a cute friend that wore glasses, and he'd tried to get her name . . . but every time he'd looked in her direction, she'd given him an utterly disinterested glance, so he figured she wasn't into cowboys. Jack knew when he wasn't wanted, so he hadn't pushed things.

Even so, he had a limit. "I'm supposed to date someone?"

"No, not exactly." Becca shook her head a little too quickly to make him comfortable. "Like I said, it's for charity. You show up in your cowboy gear and anyone that bids on you is bidding on your services. You can mend fences or milk cows or whatever it is cowboys do." She waved a hand in the air.

Milk cows? He tried not to laugh. Jack wondered if Becca even knew what Hank did all day long. "You . . . do know we have beef cattle here, right?"

She shrugged. "It's for charity, Jack. And you're so cute. The girls will eat you up." She set the cookies down and clasped her hands under her chin again. "Please? Sage is desperate."

He pointed down at the paper. "This says it's a Valentine auction. You sure it's not supposed to be romantic?" Much as he liked women, he drew the line at a twenty-year age gap. Or thirty. Or fifty. He shuddered at the thought.

"Like I said, they're buying a big hunky cowboy and his services. That's all."

"So why can't you get Caleb to do it?" His brother was serious with his girlfriend, Amy, but it wasn't like they were married. And if it was true that it was just an auctioning of skills, he didn't see why it had to be him.

"Because Caleb will say the wrong thing," Becca exclaimed, snatching the paper back from him. "You know how he is."

That he did. Jack still liked to tease Caleb about all the

ways his tongue seemed to trip him up when it came to women. Or people in general. Or the public. Caleb was just . . . shy. Which made no sense, but there it was. He still liked to tease his older brother about how he'd accidentally called one of Jack's old girlfriends "loser" instead of "Louisa" because his tongue just didn't work right when Caleb got shy.

It was amazing that the man had found someone as understanding (and pretty) as Amy.

Now Jack was the lone unattached Watson brother and it wasn't a situation he was used to. Normally he was the one with the endless string of girlfriends, the one that always had a phone full of numbers and plans for a Friday night. Even in the remote wilds of Alaska, he always had girls waiting for him to come back to town, and he was never lonely.

Painted Barrel was different, though. Jack had been so focused on helping Uncle Ennis get the ranch running that he hadn't really spent too much time in town this past year. Wouldn't do any good to get attached to town life—not that Jack was the type to get attached anyhow—when they'd just be heading back to Alaska in a few months. But then Hank had met Becca. And Caleb had fallen for a school-teacher.

And suddenly no one was planning on going back to Alaska except Jack. But seeing as all his family was here, going back to the lonely, one-room cabin in the middle of nowhere seemed pointless. Jack was a people person, and if there were no people, he'd go stir-crazy in a week. Before, he'd always had his brothers.

So now Jack was looking at staying in Painted Barrel and in Wyoming.

He wasn't sure how he felt about that just yet, but he'd given himself some time to think, and he was thinking maybe he'd get a little land of his own, start ranching on his own. Hank and Caleb were content to work with Uncle Ennis and run the Swinging C, but Jack liked the idea of having his own place. He'd eyeballed some land in the area but hadn't come to any decisions yet.

It seemed like a big move to make, and he wasn't sure he was ready to do it just yet. He supposed it'd be smart to get to know the townspeople, and he guessed that showing up at an (ugh) auction and volunteering might be a good way to do it.

"You owe me," he told Becca.

Her eyes widened and she clapped her hands together. "If you do this, I will totally owe you. We just really need twelve and having you as our hottest bachelor will be a total coup, I promise."

Jack wasn't so sure about it being a coup, but he'd take the compliment. He pocketed the flyer. "So what, you just need me to show up in some chaps and swagger around? Romance the ladies?" He grabbed her hand and mock-kissed the back of it.

Becca giggled and let him kiss her hand. "I'm going to tell Hank you did that."

"And let my brother kick my ass into next week? Why, Becca, I'm hurt. I thought you liked me." He clutched his chest.

"Oh, I do. I just like Hank more." She beamed at him. "And thank you so much for doing this. I promise I really do owe you."

"I already know how you can pay me back."

"You do?"

Jack nodded. "You still cut the hair of that real estate lady? Gimme her card. I've got some questions."

He might as well see what was for sale around Painted Barrel.

CHAPTER TWO

"Annnnnd we're going to ease into pigeon pose," the yoga instructor cooed to the class in a smooth, easy voice. "Let's stretch those hips, ladies. Get them opened."

Layla was such a dork, she always snickered quietly to herself at the double entendre of "opening her hips" every time she came to the pigeon pose. Not that she was great at the pigeon pose. Her hips did a lot of things—banged into walls, squeezed into too-tight jeans—but they did not open like the instructor's did. Instead, Layla's pigeon pose was more of a dying pigeon. Possibly a turkey. She chortled at the mental image.

"Shhhh," Amy hissed at her from the mat at her side. Amy, darn it all, was able to do a remarkable pigeon pose. "Everyone can hear you laughing," she whispered.

"Sorry," Layla said, though she wasn't all that sorry. She tried to lean forward to force her muscles to open up a bit more, but all it did was remind her that she had a bit of a tummy roll and her workout pants exacerbated the issue. "I think my hips aren't very open. They're more 'Fort Knox.'"

One mat ahead of her, Becca giggled.

Amy put her finger to her lips, but she was twitching, trying to hold back a smile. It was like this with every class. Layla was absolutely terrible at yoga and all things physical, so she tended to cut up and make jokes through the class so she wouldn't feel so very awkward. Plus, she liked making her friends laugh. She'd have quit the class weeks and weeks ago if it weren't for Amy and now Becca. It was nice to have friends. Layla had been in Painted Barrel for three years now and it had taken her this long to make friends, and how sad was that? But she just wasn't good with people.

Like the yoga instructor, who was glaring quietly at her and not looking very Zen.

Layla closed her eyes and tried to sink into the pigeon pose—she really did. When they switched legs, she gamely did so, even though she accidentally kicked Amy in the side. She knew she was hard to take in sometimes. She was an accountant, which wasn't exactly a thrill-a-minute career. She lived in a small town, alone. And most of her hobbies were, well, they were dorky compared to what most women her age liked. Single women in their late twenties liked dancing and going out to clubs, didn't they? Or shopping and getting their hair and nails done. Layla liked crafts—the more ridiculous the better—and video games. And board games.

Basically, she was a nerd, and it was awful hard to meet other nerds sometimes. Nerds didn't run in packs. Nerds were lone wolves. Thus, Layla had been lone-wolfing it around Painted Barrel for far too long.

But she'd met Amy, and Amy was the sweetest—and somehow most clueless—woman the accountant had ever met. She'd come out of a bad, controlling marriage without a clue of how bank accounts or finances worked. Layla had felt sorry for the schoolteacher and gave her her personal cell phone number so she could ask questions without coming in to Layla's office, and though most of the questions had started out with things like "How do I pay my water bill?" it had turned into a genuine friendship. Through Amy, she'd spent more time with Becca, too. Funny how she'd done Becca's taxes for her hair salon for two years now but they'd never talked for more than five minutes. Now they were friends, going to yoga classes and getting drinks together twice a week, and Layla no longer felt like the saddest lone wolf alive.

Her mat squeaked as her foot moved across it, sounding like a fart, and Layla snort-giggled again.

Less lone wolf and more rabid, mangy mutt, she decided.

They moved from pigeon pose into a few resting poses, and then the class was done. Layla immediately leapt up. "So, are we going for drinks? It's my turn to buy."

Amy lay flat on her back on her pink mat, her cheeks flushed and her thick bangs sweaty. "We doing alcoholic drinks or coffee drinks? Because I definitely want something cold."

"Becca?" Layla asked. "What do you prefer?"

Becca had a crafty look on her face. "Let's go down to the café and get some iced cappuccinos. Amy and I have to talk to you anyhow."

Uh-oh. That sounded ominous. "Great?"

Turned out, it wasn't so great. No sooner had she sat down at the table with Amy than Becca hurried off to order their drinks and Amy gave her a knowing look. "So . . . what are your plans this weekend?" Amy's voice was far too chirpy.

"Um, taxes?"

"Really?" Amy furrowed her brows. "In February?"

"Well, I start shaking down the really disorganized clients mid-February for their receipts," Layla admitted. "The more I nag them, the better chance I have of getting everything on my desk before midnight on April fourteenth. But these particular taxes are my mom's." Not that her mom would turn them in, but Layla would at least try. She gave her friend a weary look. "And trust me, she needs the head start. Mom's a train wreck."

Amy tucked a damp lock of hair behind one ear and managed to look delicate and ladylike while doing it. It wasn't fair that she could be sweaty and still pretty and delicate, Layla mused. Here Layla had barely managed a single pose in class and she still came out of it looking like a sweat hog. "Your mom's the one always starting businesses, isn't she?"

Layla nodded. "That's how I got into accounting. I had to help her with her books, and she was so terrible at it that I eventually took over." She didn't point out that her mom also liked to fudge numbers a little too much and Layla had always been more than a little terrified of her mom going to prison for tax fraud. "But that's a whole story that needs more than just a few drinks, trust me."

Becca sat down with three icy, frothy confections and Layla shot her a grateful look. "It's on me," Becca proclaimed.

Amy immediately spoke up again. "What about Saturday lunch?"

Layla frowned. Free drinks? Amy wanting to hang on the weekend instead of being with her smoking-hot boyfriend? Something was definitely up. "Are you guys ditching me for someone cooler? Because this is a small town and I know where you live."

Becca snorted. "You're going with us to the bachelor auction on Saturday. That's what she's trying to work up to saying."

"Wait, I am?" Layla stopped short of taking a sip from her straw. "Why am I doing something as awful as that?"

She knew they'd mentioned it several times in the past few weeks, but each time she'd claimed to be busy. Bachelor auctions really weren't her thing, and considering that the average age of said bachelors was in the sixties, she thought it was sweet but kinda pointless. All the so-called bachelors were mostly small business owners in the area who were going to be bid on by their girlfriends or ladies they knew at bingo. Layla had planned to avoid the entire affair like the plague, given that it'd just remind her that people her grandparents' age were still finding love and here she was, perennially single.

"We just need you there as emotional support," Amy promised, reaching over to squeeze Layla's hand. "That's all."

"And if you happen to slip up and bid on Hank's youngest brother, then it happens," Becca added in.

"What?" Layla screeched.

Everyone in the café turned to look at them, which made Layla all the more aware of her Pokémon workout shirt and leggings, and the frizzy mess of her post-workout ponytail.

She ducked her head and then frowned at her friends, pitching her voice lower. "What? Are you guys setting me up?"

"No, of course not," Amy said quickly. "It's just that . . ." She bit her lip and looked over at Becca.

"He doesn't want to do it," Becca added.

"So he's smart," Layla butted in.

Her friends gave her an exasperated look. Amy continued. "He's subbing in because Tom Hammond had that heart procedure and had to drop out. We'd have been down to eleven candidates and we're worried that the fund-raiser won't hit the goal with just eleven. Becca asked Jack to step in and he offered to do so."

"But we need to make sure someone bids on Jack, and he doesn't have a girlfriend we can rope in."

"Because he's so hideous?" Layla joked. She'd seen Jack

around town. The man looked like something from those old-timey cigarette ads for the Marlboro man—all rugged masculinity. And then she'd seen his face and he had the softest eyes and the prettiest smile she'd ever seen. He was like a damn model, and he'd smiled at Layla.

Who'd promptly looked over his shoulder, pretended to be disinterested, and never made eye contact again. Guys like him didn't look at nerd girls like her. It wasn't that Layla was hideous. She just wasn't his type. He needed someone classically beautiful—like he was—to hang off his arm and so they could wow everyone with their Ken and Barbie looks and raise a bunch of creepy, too-pretty porcelain doll–like children.

Layla was . . . messy. She dressed up if she had to, sure, but she didn't wear much makeup and her hair tended to land in a pencil-stuck bun after five minutes. She had big-framed glasses that were utterly necessary and made her look like an owl. She wore jeans and nerdy T-shirts and crocheted. She carried fifteen extra pounds and had a food baby that showed in tight clothing. So, no, she wasn't his type.

He was the star-quarterback type. She was the nerdy-younger-sister type, the one that was supposed to blossom into some sort of beauty but never had.

For heck's sake, she was an *accountant*. They were punch lines for a reason.

"It's for charity, and we'll front you the money," Becca said, reaching out and squeezing Layla's other hand. Layla wasn't sure if it was meant to be encouragement or to keep her from running away. "And you don't have to win. It's just we need insurance in case no one else bids on him."

She pried her hands out of their grips. "Are you both crazy? Have you seen Jack? Someone will bid on him if they have eyes."

"It's just an insurance policy," Becca said, her expression bright. "Since Amy and I are organizing, we're not allowed to bid. That leaves you."

Layla groaned as if pained. The last thing she wanted to do was spend her Saturday watching elderly bachelors strut across a Valentine's Day stage to impress their equally elderly girlfriends. "Must I?"

"We could really, really use the help," Amy said gently. "We've been pushing so hard for this addition to the city hall and to have all these people back out at the last minute is incredibly discouraging."

The sad note in Amy's voice clinched it, but Layla wanted to drag her feet a little more. "Let me go through my desk and see what I can put off until Monday. And don't front me the money. That's ridiculous. Let's stick to one embarrassment at a time."

Because if they fronted her the money, she'd really have to come through. If she didn't take it, she could still get out of this.

Theoretically.

When she got back to her office, her inbox had a few notes from clients who were late filing their federal unemployment returns, but nothing that needed to be handled immediately. She emailed her usual suspects, reminding them to send over any receipts for the prior calendar year, and then played a match-3 game on Facebook to pass the time.

The nice thing about being her own boss was that if she was lazy, no one could call her out on it. If she didn't get enough done during office hours, she'd just take her work home and pick through it while watching Netflix, her computer in her lap and her cat, Sterling, tucked against her side.

Somewhere on round sixteen of her current game, Layla's mom called.

"I have a date for you, my baby," Janet Schmidt sang into the phone. "I met a doctor and his son's a pharmacist. He works at a hospital and they have fantastic benefits, baby. Let me give you his number and you can call him. His name is Arthur Junior."

Ugh. "Mom, I don't want you to set me up on a blind date." She pinched the bridge of her nose. Her mother always did this. It was like it was personally killing her that her daughter wasn't the fashionista that Janet was, or the dating maven, and so she was trying to constantly "fix" Layla. Even though Layla was twenty-nine, her mother still bought her clothing and constantly tried to fix her up on dates.

"It's not a blind date if you guys exchange photos first! Take a picture of yourself and put it on Facebook. I'll send him your profile."

"Mom, no. Don't make me pick out a shallow grave for you in my backyard."

"Don't be vulgar, Layla. Men don't like a woman with gallows humor."

Well, her mom had that right. Layla shrugged to herself. "If he's not going to like me, why don't we skip this whole charade?"

"Get a pen," her mother said in a take-no-shit voice. "Write down this number."

"Writing," Layla lied. "Got a pen right now."

"You're not. You're lying."

Layla sighed and picked up a pen for real. Her mother was far too good at that. "Fine. Read it off."

Janet rattled the number off twice, and Layla wrote it down, fully intending to never call the man. She was pretty sure Arthur Junior the pharmacist wanted nothing to do with glamorous Janet's far-less-glamorous accountant daughter.

"You'll call him?" Janet prompted.

"Yup."

Her mother sighed. "You're lying again."

"I *might* call him," Layla hedged. "We'll see."

"Still lying. You know I do so much for you, Layla-belle. Your mother works so hard, and what are the thanks I get? Nothing."

She rolled her eyes. She'd long ago gotten used to the fact that Janet was a narcissist who thought of herself first and others as a very distant second. She loved her mother, but she was also familiar with her mother's bullshit. "Thank you, Mom. I appreciate you looking out for me."

"I just think our lives would be easier if you married a nice rich man."

And there it was. It wasn't that she wanted grandchildren or longed for Layla to be happy. No, she wanted her daughter to marry a "nice rich man" so she'd have someone to borrow from when she got into financial hot water . . . as she always did. "I'm doing just fine on my own, Mom, but thanks. I'll keep that in mind. Did you send over your receipts like I asked?"

"I'll get to that, I promise." Her mother paused and then giggled girlishly. "Did I tell you I'm going to go into business with a friend?"

Layla's lip curled in silent horror. Oh god, not again. "What now?"

"Don't 'what now' me," her mother continued. "I met a guy and he's going to help me flip my properties. You know, all those properties I bought that you said were terrible investments? Well, I showed them to him and he thinks I'm sitting on a gold mine."

Of course he did. Anyone that flattered her mother could get just about anything they wanted out of her. Layla face-palmed silently and took a deep breath. How many times had she gone through this with her mother? How many get-rich-quick schemes would Janet Schmidt fall for? How many times had she shown up, asking Layla to cook the books "just a little" so she could apply for another loan she didn't need? Her mother was terrible with money and lived in a state of perpetual debt. It was amazing that she found anyone willing to partner with her—and more amazing still that these people usually found a way to squeeze even more money out of her mother.

"Mom, no—"

"This one is different," Janet said firmly. "I promise. And remember that Sinclair land on the edge of town that I got for a song?"

"The floodplain?" Layla tapped a pencil impatiently. Her mother had spent a small fortune buying up several hundred acres from a rancher on the edge of town and hadn't bothered to ask why the land was so cheap. She'd found out later on that it was dirt cheap because it turned into a mud pit almost every spring and was practically un-usable as pasture.

"See, that's the thing. Marco thinks if I can get a surveyor to reassess it and get it marked as hundred-year floodplain instead of normal floodplain, we can sell it for three times as much. He knows a guy that can work with me."

"Why are you telling me this? It sounds illegal—"

"Because I'm going to need you to notarize some documents for me, darling. Can I bring them by Saturday morning? I'm at the spa for the next few days and can't head your way."

"You were supposed to send your taxes over this week-end," Layla reminded her.

"Busy," her mother said. "So you'll have plenty of time to do this other paperwork for me."

Layla cringed. If she notarized something, she was put-ting her official stamp on it, and she didn't want to touch any of her mom's crazy schemes. But Janet was impossible to say no to. She'd bully and whine until she got her way. It was better to just avoid her altogether. "I'm busy Saturday morning."

"Doing what?" Her mother sounded openly skeptical.

She thought for a moment and then the perfect answer hit her. "I'm going to a Valentine's bachelor auction with some friends. There's a cute guy I'm going to bid on."

"Layla-belle! That's wonderful! Tell me about him!"

"He's just a guy I met, Mom. Chill. It's not like we're engaged." And she wasn't really going to bid on him, but at least this would keep her mom occupied for a while. "Listen, I've gotta go—"

"But my documents—"

"My two o'clock is at the door," Layla lied. "I'll talk to you later."

"You're lying—"

Damn, her mom was far too good at that. "Bye, Mom! Love you! Kisses!" She hung up and rubbed her face. How long had it been since the last scheme? Not long enough. And Layla didn't trust anyone who told her mother she could "flip" the properties she'd been buying and make a fortune. That was a lie. Her mother had gotten a windfall—somehow—of an inheritance from a distant relative and had then proceeded to spend every penny buying up random properties she found on the cheap as "investments." She'd listened to a few seminars and thought she knew of a "grand way" to make some cash.

Turned out she learned the hard way that sometimes properties are cheap for a reason. Like the house that was a meth lab once, and she couldn't sell it without disclosing it was a prior meth lab, so no one was interested. Or the "gorgeous pasture" that was a mud pit. Or the murder house she'd bought in Kansas that still had the chalk outlines on the carpet.

Janet was not great at reading the fine print, and it always came back to bite her in the ass . . . and Layla, too, because she tried to help, she really did, but her mother was far more interested in what paperwork Layla could "smooth over" for her instead of doing her taxes properly.

It was a constant bone of contention between the mother and daughter. Janet wanted Layla to massage numbers. Layla refused, and it inevitably led to fights.

It was one reason Layla turned to chocolate. And cross-stitch, because crafting calmed her mind when her mother stressed her the hell out. She broke a chunk off of the Hershey's bar on her desk and popped it into her mouth, then opened the bottom drawer of her desk and pulled out her latest cross-stitch project. It was a glorious square border of bright flowers and ribbons, and in the center there was a saying that read SNITCHES GET STITCHES. It made Layla laugh to create detailed, beautiful works of art with terrible sayings on them, so she did it, even if everyone looked at her like she was crazy.

Maybe she was, just a little.

Because now that she'd told her mother she was going to a bachelor auction, she kind of had to go. She wouldn't put it past Janet to show up on the doorstep of Layla's office to check in on her.

So . . . now she had plans on Valentine's Day. Damn it all.

CHAPTER THREE

W ell, ain't you the prettiest sight," Hank drawled as Jack showed up at the barn that morning. The oldest Watson brother pulled a dollar out of his pocket and held it up. "Can I bid on you, Prince Charming?"

At his side with a pitchfork, Caleb snickered.

"Shut the hell up, both of you," Jack grumbled. He rubbed a hand over his jaw, feeling a little self-conscious. "I just came to tell you two that I'm heading out and I'll be back later."

"Did you shave for us?" Caleb teased. "You shouldn't have. I like my men hairy."

"I'll be sure and tell Amy that," Jack shot back. In fact, he had shaved. Was feeling a little foolish about it, too. It was just . . . he knew he had a pretty face, and in the last while, he'd let his beard get bushy. He figured if he was going to be in a bachelor auction, he'd let his vanity take over.

Jack Watson was gonna be the best-damn-looking Valentine charity bachelor Painted Barrel had ever seen.

So, yeah, he'd shaved his face clean of the big, hairy winter beard even though it was still cold out. He'd put on his favorite black cowboy hat. Put on a tighter-fitting black button-up and some tight jeans that hugged his ass. Boots. The works. Was it a little vain? Sure.

Did he look amazing and ready to break some elderly hearts? Absolutely.

"You're just jealous that you don't look as good as me," Jack teased his brothers, tipping his hat back. "Besides, I have to look like I'm worth at least a couple hundred bucks to the ladies that are showing up at this thing. I can't have Clyde beat me in the bachelor auction."

Hank stared at him. "Old Clyde? From Price Ranch? Isn't he married?"

"Yeah, but he wanted to participate anyway."

His big, bearded older brother stared at him. His mouth twitched, and then he snickered. "I can't believe Clyde's your competition."

"Oh, believe it." Jack shrugged. "Word is that Hannah's bringing her wallet and gonna spend a fortune on him."

"And you're dressing up for this?" Caleb asked, a dubious look on his face.

"Well, yeah. Amy and Becca asked me to do this. I might as well go all out." He pointed at his brothers. "And you two owe me big."

Hank scowled in his direction. "Why the heck would we owe you anything?"

"Because it's your damn girlfriend"—he pointed at Caleb—"and your wife"—he pointed at Hank—"that are running this ridiculous show. They're the ones that guilted me into doing this instead of helping out around here."

"Maybe you'll get lucky," Caleb offered. "Maybe some local angel with nice boobs will bid on you."

Hank just looked as if he was trying not to laugh.

Jack was pretty sure that the odds of any local angel showing up to this Valentine's auction were pretty slim. Or his angel would be gray-haired and old enough to be his nana, not his date.

Now that he was thinking about it, maybe he shouldn't have shaved. Jack rubbed his naked jaw again. *Charity,* he reminded himself. *This is for charity and for your sister-in-law and for Amy. You aren't doing it because you're expecting to score.*

It's charity. Nothing more.

I can't believe you brought your crochet to the auction," Amy hissed at Layla as they sat at the numbered table.

"Believe it, sister." Layla hooked another loop in the scarf she was making and shrugged. "Mrs. Kilpatrick brought hers."

"She's ninety."

"So? She's still here to buy a bachelor. Like me."

"Yes, but . . ." Amy protested, and then sighed. "It just seems weird, that's all."

"The weirder it is, the more I like it." Layla did a few more loops, concentrating on her project. In a way, it helped her calm down. She was incredibly nervous—and sweaty— at the thought of having to bid on a guy at the auction today. She knew she was the backup plan and hopefully it wouldn't be necessary. Maybe several ladies looking for love would show up with fat wallets and make this charity shindig a success.

Layla had her suspicions, though.

For one, the room wasn't more than half full. The Painted Barrel Animal Helpers Committee had decorated the gymnasium at the high school in all manner of construction paper hearts and pink garlands. There were pink and red flowers at every round table and white tablecloths to add a touch of romance. There was a volunteer DJ (who looked like he was fourteen) putting on romantic music, and pink balloons filled the room. Each table had cute stationery and glitter stamps so you could write a love note for your valentine. There were heart-shaped cookies with bright red frosting and Layla had already eaten two of them. It was all really adorable.

Problem was, no one was there.

Oh sure, the elderly bingo-hall folks had shown up, but they hadn't quite come in the numbers that Amy and Becca had expected. Maybe word hadn't gotten out. Maybe there was a football game on. Maybe people were wanting to do other things with their Valentine's Day than bid on a bachelor, but whatever the reason, the situation was looking pretty grim.

Layla hooked faster, her hands sweaty and nervous. "So how many bachelors did you end up with?"

Amy looked miserable. "Eleven. We had another last-minute drop. Turned out his girlfriend lost her dentures and didn't want to come out in public without them. Not that I blame her, but it just means less money for the charity." She twisted her hands in her lap.

"We could both buy a bachelor," Layla suggested. "I can spot you the money."

"I think we have bidders for the others," Amy said, her gaze roaming the curtained stage like the most impatient stage mom ever. "But if we don't hit our goal, you might have to buy two."

Layla glanced around. "Where's Becca?"

"She's coordinating props and making sure they're all fed."

Do . . . what? Layla wasn't entirely sure she'd heard that right and meant to ask, but a woman with a frosty white beehive and an absolutely glittering dress pushed her walker up to their table and sat down. She smiled at them. "Hello, girls."

"Oh man, I love your dress," Layla told her sincerely. "Were we supposed to dress up?" She glanced down at her worn black cardigan over a gaming T-shirt and jeans. Her hair was in her usual bun and she wasn't wearing makeup other than a slick of tinted lip gloss. Maybe she should have dressed up, but she was trying to throw a vibe into the universe: if she didn't look like a hot piece, she wouldn't need to win a man at auction.

"Honey, when you're my age, you take any excuse to put on fancy clothes," the woman said, chuckling. "I'm Cora."

"Layla," she said, offering her hand. "This is Amy."

Amy smiled at her. "Thank you for coming, Cora. Do you have your eye on anyone in particular?"

"All of them," Cora said with a sassy wink, and Layla decided she wanted to be Cora when she grew up. She patted her little spangly coin purse. "I'm going to bid on all of the bachelors because no one should go home alone."

"That's amazing." Amy clutched at her chest.

"Total baller cougar move," Layla agreed, and Cora just chuckled and waved a hand in the air.

The lights flashed and went down and the music stopped. A microphone clicked on, and when the lights flicked back up, Sage Cooper-Clements came out onstage. She was wearing a bright red sweater dress and beamed at everyone. "Thank you so much for coming out to support the Painted Barrel Animal Helpers Committee. This committee was founded in order to provide our town with a place for stray animals to stay in safety. As you all know, since we're on the small side"—she paused for the inevitable chuckles—"we don't have very many municipal buildings. Our library is in the water department, as is city hall and my office and . . . well, pretty much every city job imaginable." She grinned, dimpling. "But if we raise enough money today, we're going to add on to the municipal building and make a place for our furry friends. To show you just who we're building this addition for, each of our bachelors is going to come out with a dog that is currently being housed with volunteers until we can find him or her the perfect forever home. So you can not only bid on a bachelor today, but you can bid on a dog for adoption, too."

Polite applause filled the room.

"But I don't want to stand up here and talk to you all day. We're here for the men, right?"

More polite applause.

Oh god, Layla was secondhand embarrassed for poor Sage, having to try to pep up this mostly empty room. Seriously, why were there so many tables? Painted Barrel wasn't a huge town, and if half of the residents had shown up, Layla wasn't sure if the gym would be full then. This seemed like a lot for just eleven bachelors to be auctioned.

As if she could read Layla's mind, Amy leaned over, a worried look on her face. "We were supposed to team up with another town to do this, but they fell through on us." She bit her lip. "I can't believe it's been so hard to pull a charity together."

"I know, you'd think people would want the tax deductions, am I right?" Layla joked.

Amy batted at her arm. "Very funny."

Well, to Layla it was.

"We'll start the bidding at five dollars for each guy," Sage said. "And we'll go in increments of fives until there's a winner. You're bidding on each gentleman and his particular skill set. The person that wins their bachelor will coordinate with him for the 'date' of their choosing. Good luck to all the ladies out there." The music started again and Sage exited off the stage and went to a podium just at the edge. "We'll start with bachelor number one . . . Garvis Newsome!"

The music from *Magic Mike* started playing—"Pony" by Ginuwine.

Layla groaned and picked up her crochet again. "I am *sweating*, Amy. This is so mortifying for these men."

Garvis strutted out onto the stage. He had the skinny, bowed legs of a man that had spent most of his life in the saddle, and a weathered face with a white handlebar mustache that Layla had only seen in memes. She knew a lot of people in Painted Barrel, but Garvis was not one of them. He tipped his cowboy hat back and then started to do a little dance. She wasn't sure if it was the Cabbage Patch or a dab, but it was making her incredibly uncomfortable. As he strutted forward in his red-and-black-plaid shirt and leather vest, he carried the leash of a very confused copper dachshund. The wiener dog gamely trotted after the cowboy and sat the moment they hit the middle of the stage and scratched at his ear.

"Garvis is a much-in-demand farrier," Sage called out in a chirpy voice. "Do your horses need a little TLC? Do you need a little TLC yourself? Then take a good look at Garvis! He's our first bachelor for the day. Let's start the bidding, shall we?"

"One dollar!" Cora called out in a reedy voice.

There was a ripple of laughter. Sage smiled and then leaned into her microphone. "The bids start at five dollars, everyone."

"Two dollars!" Cora yelled.

Layla leaned over to Amy. "I am totally going to nervous puke right about now."

"Oh god, I am, too," Amy whispered back. She clutched at Layla's hand, making it impossible for Layla to do more crochet. Not that she could, anyhow. Her hands were so clammy from secondhand embarrassment that the yarn was losing all tension. She set it down on the table for now and let Amy squeeze her hand in support.

"Five dollars," someone called out.

Garvis clapped his hands with delight, startling the dog

at his side. It barked at him, and the crowd laughed once more.

Amy buried her face in her hands.

"Surely someone can bid more than five dollars?" Sage asked, a worried smile on her face as she gazed out at the crowd.

"Two dollars," Cora called again. No one laughed this time.

Oh god. Here was where Layla took one for the team. She squeezed Amy's hand and then raised her free one into the air. "Two hundred dollars," Layla called.

The room erupted with noise. Layla thought Sage was going to come over the podium and kiss her with gratitude.

"All right," the mayor called happily. "We have a bid for two hundred dollars! Sounds like someone needs a big handsome farrier to come over for an afternoon!"

Onstage, Garvis flexed.

"Two hundred fifty," called another voice, and Layla breathed a sigh of relief. She wasn't even sure what a farrier was, but if it had something to do with horses, he was out of luck. Layla had a house cat and that was it.

Luckily, the bidding started to rise in earnest, and there was a lot of laughter and good spirits as the money slowly escalated. When it hit seven hundred fifty, the bidding came to a standstill, and an elderly woman jumped up with glee when she was announced the winner. The people at her table cheered, and even Garvis looked thrilled. Layla remembered that Amy had mentioned something about most of the bachelors being "bought" by their girlfriends anyhow. Even so, it looked like everyone was having fun. Garvis bounded off the stage and handed off the wiener dog's leash, exchanging it for a bouquet of bright red roses, which he presented to his new date.

That was a little disappointing. Layla had kinda been

rooting for the wiener dog. He looked so small and confused up on the stage next to the cavorting cowboy.

"Okay," Amy breathed. "Seven hundred fifty isn't bad.
That's not bad at all. If they all go for that much, we just
might hit our goal."

Layla leaned over, the accountant in her taking over.
"Actually, you'd still be seventeen hundred and fifty dollars
short—uh, never mind." She bit off her own words at Amy's
frustrated glare. Boy, nobody had a sense of humor when it
came to this auction.

At the other side of the table, poor Cora looked de-
pressed and Layla felt so bad for her. Maybe she hadn't
heard the rules and that was why she'd bid so low. Layla
reached out and touched the other woman's arm. "Don't
you worry, Miss Cora. We'll get you a bachelor today, I
promise."

Cora giggled. "I was bidding on the dog."

A woman after Layla's own heart.

CHAPTER FOUR

The auction rolled a little more smoothly after that. The next few bachelors all sold for several hundred dollars each, though not as much as Garvis. Each man came out with a cute dog and strolled around the stage while Sage extolled their virtues, and then the auction would begin in earnest. Cora bid a dollar each time, and Layla wasn't sure if Cora was just the world's oldest troll and having fun at their expense, or if she genuinely thought her dollar bid was legit.

Layla bid two more times herself, when no one was quick to bid right out of the gate. Once for Mr. Johnson, who she always ran into at the grocery store. And then she bid for old Mr. Hill, who mowed lawns, because he got peed on by the puppy he was holding, and because, well, Layla's lawn could use a little work. And it was all for charity anyhow.

She figured if she was having to buy her love, she might as well get some weeding out of it. But she was quickly outbid on him, and really, that was fine.

Cora turned and looked at Layla with a pitiful expression. "You and I aren't having much luck today, are we?"

"It's okay," Layla told her reassuringly. "We're bound to get lucky at some point. Did you have your eye on someone in particular?"

"Well." Cora thought, then sighed. "I still keep thinking about the fat wiener from before."

Layla blinked.

"The dog," Amy whispered behind her hand, trying to hold her smile.

Oh riiight. The wording was just too perfect. Layla bit back a snicker and cleared her throat. "You know, Miss Cora, we can check in after the auction and see if the dog is available to adopt. That's supposed to be the point of this whole thing—to find homes for stray animals that need some love."

Cora brightened. "Do you think so, dear? I've been saving all month and I'd love a companion." She fingered her two wrinkled dollars that she kept bidding over and over again.

Layla's heart broke a little. Was that all that Cora had as her savings or was this just more of her confusion? Or her trolling? Either way, she vowed that she would make sure that Cora had a dog in her arms by the time she left, even if Layla had to pay for it. She glanced over at Amy, but Amy was chewing on her lip, writing numbers down on a napkin and desperately trying to do the math as the next bachelor came out onstage. Layla had done the numbers in her head, and they were still close to three thousand dollars short of the goal. That had to be disappointing for her friends, who'd worked so hard to pull this together. There were still two bachelors left, with the second to the last being bid on right now. He had a pit-bull puppy in his arms and his girlfriend was bidding on him . . . but it wouldn't be enough money. Even if Layla bought the last bachelor due to lack

of bids (which didn't look as if it'd be the case given how
the other auctions had gone), it wouldn't be enough. Maybe
Layla could do some research, look up some tax incentives
for the city that might make up the difference—

Amy grabbed her arm as the bidding continued. "Don't
look now," she hissed. "But your mother is here."

Every bit of Layla went cold. Janet Schmidt was here?
At the auction? This day was going from bad to much,
much worse. "Please tell me you're joking."

"She's near the door. Looking for you." Amy patted her
arm. "I'd tell you to hide in the bathroom, but we both
know she'd probably find you."

She would. Janet had been known to peek under stall
doors looking for Layla in the past. "She thinks I'm here to
bid on a boyfriend," Layla whispered as her mother caught
sight of her and waved.

"Lucky for you Jack is up next," Amy said, patting her
hand.

Oh lord. And all the "bachelors" so far were more Janet's age than Layla's. Her mother would sense a plot for
sure, and then she'd get bombarded with all kinds of nag-
ging and guilt and her weekend would be ruined. Layla
glanced over and Janet waved even harder.

"Are you bidding, ma'am?" Sage asked from the podium.

"I'm just here to see my daughter. She's going to bid on
a man," Janet called out loudly, trotting over to Layla's table
in ridiculously high heels.

Cringe. Cringe twice. Layla kept smiling even though
the urge to flee was running rampant through her system.
Why did Janet always do this to her? Janet was the mom
that showed up in the skintight bandage dress at Layla's
school dances. She was the mom that flirted with the teachers. The mom that always made sure the attention was on
Janet and not Layla.

Of course she'd show up to a bachelor auction to try to

nose in and see what her daughter was up to. Part of it was Janet being an overbearing mom. Part of it was Janet being bored. And part of it was Janet wanting a slice of the action. Her mom would absolutely not be above flirting with a guy that Layla was interested in. She'd done it in the past. Was it shitty? Yes. Was it something Layla expected at this point? Also yes.

So she shouldn't have been surprised to see her mother. Yet somehow, Layla always was. She always expected Janet to be a bit more . . . mom-like. Never happened.

"There you are," Janet cooed. She thumped into the empty chair next to Layla and set her Birkin bag on the table, blocking Layla's view of Cora entirely. "How goes the bachelor hunting, Layla-belle?"

"It's just fine, Mom. What are you doing here?" God, even her tone sounded sulky and petulant, like she was fourteen again.

Janet licked her thumb and tsked, reaching forward and smoothing a flyaway hair at Layla's temple. "Honey, did you even fix your hair this morning? I thought you were trying to get a man."

"It's fine, Mom."

"Is it?" Janet gave her a wintry little smile that said she didn't agree. She glanced over at Amy and cooed at her. "Hello, sweetheart. Are you bidding on a man, too?"

Amy just chuckled. "No, my boyfriend's working today."

"Look at that," Janet said in a low voice, leaning in toward Layla. "She's got a boyfriend *and* her hair looks fantastic. What a coincidence!"

"Ugh, Mom. Please. Just stop it."

Janet raised a beringed hand in the air. "I'm just saying, Layla-belle. You know I just want you to be happy."

"Do we have any more bids?" Sage called. When no one else answered, she banged her gavel on the podium. "Sold, for five hundred thirty dollars. Congratulations, you two!"

Everyone at the table clapped politely. Layla noticed that Amy added that to the math on her napkin, but it wasn't enough. Unless the final bachelor pulled in twenty-five hundred dollars, it wouldn't be what the city needed to make the project a success. And no one had gone for more than seven hundred fifty that day.

Janet leaned over to Layla, still clapping. "That last one was a bit gray. Are they all older?" She gave her daughter an interested look. "Should I find myself a sugar daddy? Are any of them rich?"

"Mom," Layla groaned.

Amy just laughed. "I don't think any of them are exactly wealthy, Mrs. Schmidt. Everyone's bidding on the total package—the dogs, the skills the bachelor can provide, and for charity."

"Well, that's disappointing," Janet said brightly, then leaned over to her daughter. "Besides, I already have a sugar daddy."

Layla groaned again and buried her face in her hands.

"Oh, stop being such a baby," Janet said. "I'm allowed to have needs."

"It doesn't mean I want to hear about them."

"Well, who else am I going to tell?" She sat on the edge of her chair, peering at the stage. "So where is your man? Which one is he?"

Amy shot Layla a curious look.

Right. She'd told her mother she was going to be bidding on a guy she liked here. Looked like she was going to have to bid on Jack Watson either way. With luck, someone would outbid her quickly and she could feign disappointment and then this whole sordid mess would be over. She'd take out her feelings on some pastries and an evening of cross-stitching pithy sayings about narcissists and feel better by morning. "He's coming up soon."

"Well, while we're waiting, I brought you something."

Janet tossed her bright red hair and reached into her purse. She pulled out a folder of papers and slid it toward Layla, then offered her a pen. "You said you'd notarize these for me, right? I thought I'd bring them over."

"I didn't say I'd notarize anything, Mom." Janet was a master at the art of pushiness. She pretended like you'd already agreed to something, hoping you'd forget and cave. "What is this?"

"Just those documents that we talked about. For the property."

Layla flipped open the folder. There were maps, weather charts, and discussions about flooding. Pictures of the land. A long, detailed letter explaining that to the party's best knowledge, no flooding had occurred since ownership had transferred to Janet Schmidt's hands. Well, that was a flat-out lie. Rather than create a scene, Layla closed the folder again. "I'll look at it later."

"Just do it fast," Janet said brightly. "I want to get that property on the market quick. If I sell by summer, I'm going to take a European cruise."

Layla opened her mouth to protest, but the microphone whined with feedback, gathering everyone's attention. A dog howled somewhere offstage.

"Sorry about that," Sage chirped into the mic. "Are we ready for our final bachelor? He's a good one!"

Amy grabbed Layla's arm in silent terror.

Right. This was the moment she'd promised she'd bid if no one else did. Janet grabbed Layla's other arm, no doubt thrilled to get a good look at her daughter's "man." Layla felt a little like she was trapped between two opposing forces.

The music started and the lights flickered. This time, the song was "Where Have All the Cowboys Gone" and a tall man strolled onto the stage with the same dachshund from before.

"One dollar!" Cora bellowed.

"Oh my," Janet murmured as Jack Watson swaggered onto the stage. Layla didn't say anything. Her tongue was glued to the roof of her mouth.

Because Jack Watson was an utterly gorgeous dream of a man. It had been months since she'd seen him, and so Layla had forgotten just how intimidatingly perfect he was. He was tall, with broad shoulders, and seemed to take up half the stage with his sheer presence. His cowboy hat and clothing were entirely black, giving him a sinister, sexy vibe. He had the wiener dog tucked under his arm like a football and scratched at the floppy copper ears with a big, work-hardened hand.

He'd shaved, too. Layla had remembered a scruffy beard—so incongruous with a man as gorgeous as him— but it was gone now. Instead, she could see his chiseled jaw, the full lips, the perfect nose that led up to thick, equally perfect brows, and gorgeous dark eyes. He grinned out into the crowd, and his teeth were as perfect as the rest of him.

"I'll bid on his package," Janet murmured, fanning herself.

"Mr. Watson is a ranch hand at the Swinging C," the mayor called out, as if reading a bio. "He's a Virgo and a bit of a romantic. Want to ride horseback into the mountains for your date? This is your man. He's also good at helping repair fences and working in the barn if that's more your thing. Bid on him and you can discover what you've been missing in your life without a big, strong cowboy."

"I know what I've been missing," Janet commented.

"Mom!"

"What are we bidding for our cowboy?" Sage asked. "Shall we start?"

"One dollar," Cora bellowed, disgruntled from her tone of voice.

This would be so funny to Layla if she didn't have to be part of it. As it was, the room got quiet, and her stomach dropped. She remembered that Jack was a last-minute volunteer and had no significant other lined up to start the bidding on him. Surely that was criminal. A man that perfect should have legions of women lined up to bid on him. As it was, she sucked in a deep breath and raised her hand.

"Five hundred dollars," Janet cried, bidding before Layla could get the chance.

What the hell?

CHAPTER FIVE

Janet looked over at Layla with a little shrug. "What can I say, Layla-belle? You have great taste."

"Mom," Layla hissed. "This is not cool, okay?" How could her mom be such a jerk? If she thought Layla truly liked the guy, why was she doing this?

"Oh, it's all in fun, sweetheart. Lighten up. You said it was for charity, right?" She gave an exaggerated wink to Amy.

Layla glanced up at the stage. They weren't far away from it, and she was close enough that she could see Jack's gaze meet hers. He seemed to be watching them with amusement, and as she stared at him, he lifted the dog in his arms and kissed one floppy ear.

Damn it, and there went her ovaries, melting like butter.

"Do we have any other bids?" Sage called.

Layla flung her hand in the air. "Thousand."

Janet gasped, and Layla couldn't tell if her mother was delighted or annoyed. "Eleven hundred!"

"Why are you bidding against me?" Layla whispered angrily. "I thought you wanted me to date."

"Maybe I'm just nudging things along!"

Or maybe you're being a jerk, Mom, she bit back, didn't say it aloud. She never did. It was no good with someone like Janet. And Layla was competitive. And stubborn. And she really, really hated when Janet pulled this crap. Scowling, she glanced at Amy's napkin, ignoring her friend's gaping expression. They still needed about twenty-five hundred to make the auction a success. All right, then. Layla raised her hand in the air again. "Two thousand six hundred."

A low cheer went up. Under the table, Amy grabbed Layla's knee. "You don't have to do this, Layla."

Oh yes, she did. Her mother was a textbook narcissist, and most of the time, Layla was fine with it. She tolerated it because everyone had their flaws. But this irritated her for some reason. Why was it that everywhere Janet went, she made it all about her? This reminded Layla all too much of graduation, when her mother had spent hours fixing Layla's hair and makeup, and then when they got to the ceremony, she'd promptly told Layla that she looked like a whorey sausage in her cap and gown. Her mother had apologized later and said she'd been drinking, but Layla knew the real reason.

It was because all of the attention hadn't been on Janet, so she'd torn Layla down. It happened at weddings. Family get-togethers. Holidays. It had beat her father down so much that he'd divorced Janet and then moved halfway across the world to get away from her.

And Layla was tired of it.

So maybe she was spending a little too much on a bachelor auction. Maybe she'd regret cleaning out a large chunk of her savings later, but darn it, right now it felt good to stick it in her mother's face. Layla cast a triumphant look in Janet's direction. She'd done her mother's finances in the past. She knew Janet didn't have the money. Five hundred? Janet could squeeze it on a credit card somewhere. But a couple of grand? Wasn't gonna happen.

And they both knew it.

Janet's perfectly lipsticked mouth flattened, just for a moment. Then she shrugged lightly. "He's all yours, Layla-belle. I just hope you know what you're doing with a man like that."

Implying that she didn't. "Thanks, Mom," Layla said.

"Any other bids?" Sage called from the podium. She looked around again and then banged the gavel. "Sold! To Layla, for two thousand six hundred, the largest amount in the auction!"

The room was filled with polite cheers, and Layla's cheeks flushed with a giddy sensation. She looked up at the man on the stage, and he was smiling at her. It wasn't a friendly, nice-to-meet-you sort of smile. It was a slow curve of perfect lips, a knowing look in those dark, liquid eyes, and a hint of a smirk that told her he wasn't displeased with who'd bought him. In fact, he was busy looking her up and down as if she was the one onstage.

That made Layla blush. Hard.

Dear lord, she'd just bought a date. With a gorgeous man that was way, way out of her league. When was the last time she'd gone on a date? College? Oh god, was it really college? She was such a loser.

She watched, thunderstruck, as he trotted off the stage. Instead of handing off the dog, he grabbed the bouquet of flowers he was supposed to hand his winning date and carried them both over to her, a grin on his face. Layla could feel her face heating with every step that he took toward her, and the blood was pounding in her ears.

"You're one of the best friends ever," Amy told her, hugging Layla before running off to find Becca and Sage and share the good news that the bachelor auction had been a success. It didn't give Layla a chance to tell her that it wasn't that Layla was a good person at all. She was a stubborn mule and her mom was a jerk, and so she'd bid.

And bid. And bid.

Her "date" came up to her. Smiled and held out the roses. She took them with a trembling hand and he jiggled the little dog in his arms. "I know I'm supposed to give him back, but Oscar gets scared if someone puts him down. Couldn't stand to see the little guy shaking, so I swapped him out for the dog I was supposed to carry. Hope that's okay."

Layla reached out for Oscar's long nose to pet him.

The dog snapped at her, barking.

"He's named after Oscar the Grouch," the cowboy said helpfully.

"Wish you would have told me the context before I reached for him," Layla muttered, rubbing the hand that he'd snapped at.

The cowboy chuckled again. "I'm Jack. No grouch."

"I know. Layla." She gave him an awkward little wave and then wanted to smack herself. Waving. At her date. Who did that?

Dorks like her, she supposed.

"Well," Janet said loudly. "I can see the romance flowing between the two of you already. I'm glad my little matchmaking ploy worked."

Layla rolled her eyes.

Jack bit back a grin and looked over at her mother. "Was it a ploy? Very clever."

"My daughter told me that she'd been waiting to bid on you," Janet said, moving up to him and patting his arm. She patted his biceps for a little longer than a normal person would, then shrugged. "You'll notarize those papers for me, Layla-belle? You know what my signature looks like."

"I said I would look at them," Layla corrected. And she sure wasn't going to forge her mother's signature.

Another flash of annoyance crept across Janet's youthful face and she shrugged, looking Jack up and down. "Be good with my baby girl, will you? Romance her right. She's still a virgin so she's going to be awkward around a handsome man like you."

Layla knew Janet would say just about anything to get attention, but that was really a low blow. She gaped, stunned, as her mother picked up her expensive purse and swanned out of the room, leaving Jack staring at her.

W ell, this had quickly turned into a mess.
    He'd had an idea of how this would all go. Jack had thought about it as he'd approached the stage, holding the far-too-bitey little dog in his arms. He'd turn on the charm for whoever won his auction, maybe dip the winning lady, kiss her hand, and flatter the hell out of her. He'd initially been reluctant to do this, but after seeing the enthusiasm of the elderly women as they bid on their equally elderly beaus, Jack had been caught up in the spirit of things. He loved women, young or old, and there was nothing wrong with showing someone a good time. He'd been thinking this was going to be romantic, when it was all really just for fun and for a good cause. For the "date," he'd take someone out horseback riding, maybe, show someone his uncle's age a good time, and that was it. Bring a little bright spot into a dull day or something.

The first bidder had alarmed him, though. A dark-haired woman of about forty to fifty years old, she'd given him such a lascivious look as she'd bid that he'd immediately hoped she wasn't the winner. She was expecting a much different kind of date than he'd have to offer.

And then the woman right next to her had bid a thousand. And then twenty six hundred. And he'd gone back to smiling again.

Jack recognized her as the cute accountant friend of Becca and Amy. The one that always stared past him when he ran into her. She was the youngest bidder at the auction . . . and the highest. Maybe she wasn't so disinterested in him after all.

Valentine's Day was looking up.

He'd gotten off the stage and grabbed the flowers, then headed over . . . and felt as if he was walking into an argument. The dog in his arms bit at Layla. His new "date" was squabbling with the cougar, who turned out to be her mother.

And then the cougar flounced in the most dramatic of ways. *Be good with my baby girl, will you? Romance her right. She's still a virgin so she's going to be awkward around a handsome man like you.*

A look of horror had crossed Layla's face, and Jack had frozen. Because what the hell did you say to that? They both stared at the woman's retreating back, and everything grew silent and uncomfortable.

Jack was the first to clear his throat. "Your mom is something else."

Layla recovered, the tension in her shoulders easing slightly. She pushed her glasses back up on her nose and shook her head. "She's a textbook narcissist."

"Ah."

"It's okay." She sighed, crossing her arms over her frumpy sweater. "I've had years and years of therapy to learn how to handle it. In fact, I should probably schedule my next appointment right now."

He chuckled, because she was funny. That was a plus. He liked a woman with a sense of humor. "She always make such a dramatic exit?"

"As far as Janet Schmidt exits go, that one was a seven on a scale of one to ten for dramatic exits."

"Damn. I'd hate to see a ten." He couldn't imagine having a mother like that. Now that he stood next to Layla, he could see some of the resemblance between her and the other woman. They had the same face shape and full mouth, but Layla's face was hidden by glasses and her figure by a sweater over a T-shirt. Her hair was dark and thick like her mother's, but instead of big, bouncy waves, Layla's was twisted into a knot. She looked as if she'd be an easygoing sort to hang out with. The type that wouldn't spend two hours in the bathroom to get ready just to go to a movie. Ironic that he found that so appealing, because Jack was vain. He was the one that would be the bathroom hog if they were a couple.

Not that they were a couple, but it was fun to imagine.

She grimaced. "It's not pretty."

"Did you come here just for me? Or am I the backup prize because someone else stole your Prince Charming?"

He watched, fascinated, as a flurry of emotions moved over her face. Her cheeks grew pink and she tucked a strand of hair behind her ear, then glanced up at him. "I was told to bid on you if no one else did."

"Ouch." Jack clutched his chest, wounded. "So then you decided to empty the whole wallet?"

"No . . . that was me wanting to win." She gave him a rueful smile, looking nervous and uneasy. Her gaze flicked to his mouth repeatedly, and she blushed. He suspected she liked looking at him, and that made him want to flex. "Besides, it's for charity."

"That's why you bid against your mom? Doesn't have anything to do with this?" He struck a Superman-like pose, chin in the air, a hand on one hip, dog tucked under the other arm.

She snort-giggled, a sound that he found endearing. "Okay, now you're just fishing for compliments."

"Damn. How'd you guess?"

Layla gestured at the door. "I can recognize narcissism from a mile away."

"Do you think I'm a narcissist, then?"

"No, I think you just know that you're hot."

Not cute. Not charming. Hot. His grin widened. Well now. Things were getting mighty interesting.

Layla fidgeted in place, as if uncomfortable with the silence that fell between them.

"So . . . about our date," Jack began, but someone came up to Layla and whispered something. She nodded and pulled out a checkbook. Right. This was for charity. For a moment, he'd almost forgotten because he'd been so pleased to see her. She was the one girl around here that he'd had his eye on, and seeing her up close and talking to her just cemented his fascination.

It had almost distracted him from the fact that her mother had announced to the entire room that Layla was a virgin. He didn't know what to think about that. He lifted a hand to pet Oscar, and the dog snapped at him. He winced and pulled back, wondering what the hell the dog's problem was. Sometimes he was loving and affectionate, and sometimes he was a damn asshole.

"Hands," came a thin, reedy voice.

Jack looked over. There was a thin woman with a walker next to Layla, her hair teased into a snow-white helmet atop her head. She wore a bright glittery dress and looked as if someone's nana was heading out for a night on the town. "Ma'am," he said politely, offering her a smile.

"It's your hands," she told him. "That good boy is afraid of hands. Someone probably hurt him in the past. Just don't wave them in front of his face and he won't panic."

She had a wistful look on her face as she eyed the dog, and he sat down next to her and held Oscar out. The little dog immediately began to tremble, but the woman was careful and cradled him against her chest. She kept her hands out of sight and petted his head, and sure enough, Oscar calmed down.

"You're a real genius with animals," Jack mentioned. "You have several at home?"

"No." Her voice took on a sad note. "My last dog died a few years ago. Didn't realize how much I missed him until now." The woman continued to hug the dog, a smile on her face. "I bid on you, you know."

"I know you did," Jack said, grinning. She'd bid a dollar on everyone.

She looked up and gave him a sharp look. "Not you. The dog."

His brows went up, and he laughed. "Sorry. I misunderstood." Damn, but he liked this fiery nana. She reminded him of his before she'd passed on when Jack was ten.

Layla sat down next to the woman and glanced over at him again, a hint of a smile on her face. "I'm sorry I bid against you, Miss Cora. I just saw Jack and had to have him for myself."

"It's okay, dear. You're young." She stroked the dog's head, careful to keep her hands out of his face. "I don't need a boyfriend. I have too many of them already."

He noticed Layla's lips twitch with amusement as she glanced over at him. "The dog's up for adoption," she pointed out. "And he seems to like you, Miss Cora."

Cora considered this. "Do you think I should?"

Layla exchanged a look with Jack, one full of sympathy and sweetness. "Well, since I outbid you, maybe it's only fair that I get you the little man you came for." She reached for the dog, and Oscar bared his teeth.

"Hands," Cora said calmly, patting the dachshund's fat sides.

"Right. Why don't you pet him and I'll get the details worked out?" Layla got to her feet, wallet in hand again, and brushed past Jack and Cora.

Jack watched her go, following the sway of her hips.

"She's a nice girl," Cora said. "You'd better lock that down if you're interested."

He grinned over at her. "Of course I'm interested. I have eyes, don't I?"

Cora just hmphed again. "I know your type. You're a pretty man who thinks the world should kiss his feet. You're no good for her, but if she likes you, it's because she's dazzled by your charm."

Was he getting a dressing-down from Cora? Jack fought back an amused smile. "So you think I'm charming?"

"I think that you think you're charming," Cora pointed out.

Jack laughed. Well, damn. "That cut me right to the bone."

"All I'm saying," Cora continued, patting the dog's fat sides as it nestled in her arms, "is that that young lady paid a lot of money to spend an afternoon with you. I only bid a dollar, you know." She sniffed. "Not sure you're worth more."

"You're breaking my heart, Miss Cora."

"Oh please. You'll get over it." She rolled her eyes. "Just don't go breaking her heart. She deserves better than that."

He suspected he'd never win this argument, so best to bow out gracefully, considering that he wasn't even sure why they were arguing. "Yes, ma'am."

Layla returned with a leash and paperwork a short moment later, smiling. "He's all yours, Cora. I hope the two of you are very happy together."

"Why, thank you, dear. You're a lovely girl. You deserve the best." And she gave a sharp look to Jack that had him twitching to laugh again.

Layla looked uncertain for a moment, so Jack pulled up the chair next to him and offered it to her. "Won't you sit? We were just talking about Oscar."

"Oh, of course." She glanced at Amy, but Caleb's girl-friend was busy talking to Becca and another person. Layla pulled out her phone and looked over at him. "Maybe we should—"

"Time to give the dog back, Miss Cora," a firm voice said, and a stout woman arrived, keys in hand. "The bus is about to leave."

"Five more minutes," Cora demanded, holding Oscar tightly.

"No, I'm afraid we're leaving now." She pulled out Cora's walker. "Come on. Party's over."

"Oh, but we got the dog for her," Layla said, a hint of a frown on her face. "Oscar's going home with her."

The newcomer frowned at them both. "No, he's not. There's no pets allowed at the assisted-living facility."

Assisted living? There was a place on the edge of town, Pine Tree or Pine Grove or some pastoral name like that for a square, soulless-looking building. Cora lived there? Layla was clearly shocked, too.

Miss Cora, however, had a sly look on her face. She got to her feet and handed the dog carefully back to Jack. "I can have visitors on Tuesdays and Thursdays," she announced. "Bring my boy by to see me."

"We'll see, Miss Cora," the nurse said in a firm voice. "These nice people might be busy. Come on, now."

Cora winked at him, turned and put her hands on her walker, and then let herself be led away. "I'm coming, I'm coming," she muttered.

Layla looked at him, her mouth slightly open. "I thought she was just a little bit spirited and having fun. I didn't realize . . ."

"Oh, I'm pretty sure she was having fun," Jack drawled. "Something tells me she played us exactly how she wanted."

"Maybe so." Layla's expression softened and she reached for Oscar, careful not to flash a hand in front of his face. She scratched the back of his ears, leaning in toward Jack. "So what do we do now?"

"Figure out a way to share custody of our new grouchy child?"

She chuckled, and the sound was husky and low and like magic. "I have a cat. I can't have a dog."

He could. No one at the Swinging C would care if he added another dog to the mix, even if it was as odd a breed as the dachshund. His uncle—and the Swinging C's owner—was a veterinarian. Another dog wouldn't be a problem . . . but he didn't want Layla to know that. He wanted an excuse to see her again.

More than one excuse, really. Sure, they had a date to schedule, but he couldn't stop looking at her. At the way her mouth pursed with consternation as she rubbed Oscar's ears. At the small hands and long fingers. The way her glasses slid down her cute nose. The way her thick hair escaped its haphazard bun. There were a lot of things about Layla that weren't "his type," but on her, he liked the look.

In fact, he liked everything. And he liked it more and more the longer he was around her. So, yeah, he'd push some dog sharing on her if it meant seeing her again.

He suspected Layla was skittish. She was nervous as she talked to him, as if she wasn't entirely sure what to say. She fidgeted in place. Glanced at the doors and other people as if she was looking for a way out . . . and yet he suspected she liked him. She watched his mouth a lot. Blushed. Leaned toward him. He knew if he agreed to the date she'd paid for and nothing else, he'd see her that afternoon and then never hear from her again.

He had to corner her, it seemed.

Jack pulled his phone out, and immediately Oscar started to snap at it and his hand. He grimaced, handing the phone in her direction. "Uh-oh."

She took it, chuckling. "How dare you move a muscle and scare our child?"

He tried to put a hand on Oscar's back to comfort him,

but the dog was worked up and snapped at his fingers again, yapping sharply. Jack winced, letting the dog maul his fingers as he nodded to Layla. "Can you put your name in there for me? And your number?"

She waved the phone at him. "I don't have your password, friend."

"I'll give it to you." He recited it and she unlocked his phone, then arched a brow in his direction. "What?" he asked.

"You're awfully trusting. How do you know I'm not going to log on and clean out your accounts or dig through all your emails?"

"Maybe I don't mind you digging through my life," he teased, then bit back a curse when Oscar nipped a little harder.

"You are a terrible flirt, and I'm already regretting the money I've spent." But she said it while smiling, and she typed on his phone with those fascinating long fingers, her movements far quicker than his when he tried to type on the damn thing. "Okay, my name and phone number are in there."

"Great. I've got your number now, so there's no backing out."

She rolled her eyes, her smile wider. "What, you think I'd spend twenty-six hundred dollars to ghost you?"

"Absolutely."

Layla laughed at that, shaking her head. "Am I that obvious?"

"I'd raise my hand to signal that you're maybe a little obvious, but, well . . ." He glanced down at the dog mercilessly chewing on his forefinger. Lucky for him, they weren't aggressive bites, just annoying.

"Okay, I'm texting," Layla began, her concentration on his phone.

"Here, put this in there," he interrupted.

"Didn't realize I was a secretary," she grumbled.

"To the beautiful woman who won my hand and my

heart this day," he began in a lofting voice, watching her reaction. She flushed, not looking up from the phone, but her smile grew wider. "I'm very glad you won me and would like to meet over coffee to discuss our future date that you won, and the custody of our child."

She flicked him an amused look over the phone but went on typing. "Anything else, Shakespeare?"

He liked that some of her twitchiness was giving way to a relaxed ease. That her smiles were wider with every moment they spent together.

"Just one thing," Jack said, and winced as the dog snarled and bit down again. "You won my hand, but you might have to pry it from Oscar's mouth."

She looked up and, with a horrified giggle, set the phone down and took the dog from him. Oscar, the darn dog, immediately quieted in her arms, and Jack noticed she was careful to hide her hands this time.

They were both learning, it seemed.

CHAPTER SIX

Jack took Oscar the dog home with him when he left, and Layla said a quick goodbye to Amy and Becca, who were being swarmed by people wanting to just chitchat; both promised to text her later. Sage grabbed Layla and full-on hugged her, ecstatic that the auction had been a success, and it was all because of Layla's checkbook.

"You're such a vital part of this community," Sage gushed.

"Of course I am. I do your taxes."

"No, I mean it. It really shows just how much you care at moments like this." She smiled and squeezed Layla's hands again. "Anything you need, you let me know."

"I need twenty-six hundred dollars," Layla teased, but when Sage got a frozen look on her face, Layla immediately added, "I'm joking, I'm joking."

"Are you sure?"

"I'm positive," she reassured the mayor. "Jack's worth it."

At least, she hoped so. It was a good cause and she hadn't totally cleaned out her savings . . . and it was a tax write-off. Even so, it was a large chunk of cash . . . for a date. And Layla didn't date. It wasn't that she didn't want to date. It just didn't seem to happen for her. All her online matchups fizzled out. There wasn't a big pool of locals with similar interests. Anytime Layla had expressed interest in someone in the past, there had been crickets . . . or her mother had swooped in and ruined things. Eventually Layla had stopped trying. Why date when it was just going to turn into a shit show anyhow? She'd bought herself a battery-powered boyfriend and left it at that.

Today, though, she'd more or less been pushed into this, and Layla was definitely feeling out of her comfort zone. What if Jack found her irritating? Or weird? What if he didn't like being around her? What if he didn't call? Ugh.

Problem was, now she was invested. It wasn't just the money—though, sure, that was a huge chunk of the situation—it was that Jack was incredibly handsome. And charming. And funny. And he liked animals. And because of all of that, her heart was fluttering like she was a teenager with her first crush.

He was just doing this as a favor to Becca and Amy, she chided herself as she drove home. *Don't get too caught up*.

But he'd flirted with her. With *her*. And he'd laughed at her jokes. She'd felt a connection when looking at him. .

It was probably all in her head and she was in too deep already, but, damn it, she was excited. He'd have to text her first, because she knew if she did, she'd really look desperate and needy and—

Her phone buzzed with an incoming text.

Layla almost swerved off the road and sideswiped a bush. She pulled over, heart pounding, and checked her phone.

It was her mother.

MOM: Are you mad at me, sweetie?

Ugh. Now came the apology tour after the public humiliation. Because it was all about Janet and her need for attention. She didn't like it when people were mad at her, because she craved love and affection . . . and even more attention. She knew she'd embarrassed Layla, so now she was going to backpedal and swear she didn't mean it and basically whine until Layla forgave her with gushing reaffirmations of how great Janet was and no, no, she wasn't mad at all.

So Layla ignored it.

After all, therapy had taught her that the best way to get under a narcissist's skin was to ignore them. She put her phone on silent, tossed it into the passenger seat, and drove all the way home. Once she got to her house, a tiny little two-story a few streets over from her office, she took her shoes off, peeled off her winter coat, and made herself a cup of coffee in the kitchen. Sterling was draped over one of the countertops, exactly like he wasn't supposed to be, and she scooped him up and set him down on the floor. Even the cat didn't listen to her, she mused, but at least the cat loved her. Well, she was reasonably sure he did. Maybe not as much as he loved licking his own butt, but surely Layla was somewhere on the hierarchy.

Once her coffee was done, she grabbed the cup and moved to the living room, hauling her laptop onto her crossed legs. It was Saturday night, which meant it was online gaming night, but that wasn't for several hours. She poked around on her email, scanned over a few work documents, and then futzed on the internet, killing time.

When she could ignore her phone no longer, she finished her coffee and crossed the room to get it, moving back to the couch. Sterling jumped into her lap, wedging himself next to her laptop, and began to knead, his claws digging tiny pinpricks of pain into her skin.

"Ow, buddy," she whispered, clicking on her phone screen.

The cat didn't move, just kept on purring and making biscuits, and she couldn't really be mad at that. Layla stroked his ears while she flipped through the texts. There were a bunch more from her mother that she didn't want to process right now so she refused to look at them and scrolled past, searching for other names.

Amy had texted her and Becca both in a group chat.

AMY: I was sweating so hard that the auction wouldn't be a success. Did you see how many chairs were empty? Did you see what Mr. Peppridge wore on the stage? But it's done and it happened and I'm so happy!! You're our rock star, Layla!

BECCA: Omg, yes! We can't thank you enough, girl. When we asked you to pony up, we didn't mean like that. We were just nudging. You know, a friendly nudge. I didn't mean for you to bid your entire savings on Jack. ☹ Now I feel like a terrible friend!

AMY: I feel guilty, too. It's so much money!

BECCA: Do we need to talk? Are you mad, Layla?

AMY: Also god, your mom is the worst.

AMY: Can I say that? Is it mean? Because wow. SHE IS THE WORST.

BECCA: Did I meet her?

AMY: Count yourself lucky if you didn't. She would smile very nicely and then just say something to cut Layla off at the knees. I can't believe she bid on Jack even after she knew you were there to bid on him.

BECCA: Wait, was she the one that bid on Jack before Layla?!?!

BECCA: How the heck did I miss that?

AMY: I told you earlier!!

BECCA: Before or after the dog peed on my sweater?

AMY: Might have been during. Lol.

Seeing the perfectly normal (and, okay, completely supportive) wall of texts from her friends eased some of the tension zinging through Layla's body. Yeah, her mother was a jerk, but no one was going to look at Layla weird for it. Her friends had her back and that was all that was important. She lifted her hand to text and Sterling immediately shoved his head into her grip, forcing her to type a response one handed while she scratched the pushy cat's ears.

LAYLA: Sorry I'm so late to respond, my mom was texting and I turned my phone off for a bit. I'm not mad at you guys, my savings isn't cleaned out, and yes, my mom is a jerk.

AMY: Your savings isn't cleaned out? I think this means drinks are on you next time. ☺

LAYLA: What kind of an accountant would I be if I wasn't good with money?

BECCA: You're still a rock star. We owe the success of this all to you.

BECCA: Did you really adopt a dog, too?

LAYLA: Kinda? I didn't mean to. Jack and I got hoodwinked by Cora.

AMY: The sparkly woman at the table?

BECCA: The one that kept bidding one damn dollar!!!

LAYLA: Ha, that's the one. Either she was a little confused or a master manipulator.

LAYLA: She loved Oscar and so I offered to buy him for her. Turns out she lives at an assisted-living home and can't have pets!!! So now he's mine and Jack's and Cora wants us to bring him to visit her on Tuesdays and Thursdays.

LAYLA: And I'm just enough of a softy to do it.

AMY: Omg!

BECCA: Waaaait back this truck up.

BECCA: You're sharing the dog with Jack?

BECCA: How's that going to work out?

LAYLA: I don't know. He took Oscar home. I haven't talked to him since the auction. I guess I'll wait and see if he contacts me? If he doesn't, that's okay too.

BECCA: Do you want me to have Hank make sure he contacts you?

LAYLA: Oh god, no. If he doesn't want to, I don't want to force him to, you know? It's just supposed to be lighthearted fun. It's not lighthearted or fun if he's being harassed.

LAYLA: Really it's no big deal.

Another text came in from her mother, pinging through the stream of texts she was sending her friends.

MOM: I know you're ignoring me because you're mad

MOM: For some reason

MOM: But please look at those papers I put in your purse and get back to me? The Realtor has a potential buyer and I want to get things moving.

Had she taken the papers with her at the auction? Layla couldn't remember. Frowning, she moved Sterling out of her lap and went over to her purse. Sure enough, the blue folder was in there, tucked next to some ear buds and a ball of yarn (Amy liked to joke that Layla was a pack rat). Curious now, Layla pulled the folder out and began to flip through it.

There were lots of maps, which stymied her at first. She was an accountant. She knew balance sheets and deposit slips and quarterly tax filings. Why was she getting maps? But the more reading she did, the more it became clear.

The land that her mother had bought was listed in a FEMA flood zone. She was requesting that a recent survey be discarded as "irregular" and wanted notarized statements confirming this. She was going to pay for a new survey "at her discretion" and attempt to get the floodplain classification overruled.

It was absolutely a floodplain. Layla knew that like she

knew water was wet and the sky was blue and Janet was selfish. All Layla had to do was notarize that Janet swore she was telling the truth on her statement, but because this was Janet, she also wanted Layla to forge her signature for her.

Well, that sure as shit wasn't going to happen. Layla scowled down at the offending paperwork. The sheer nerve and utter gall of her mother. Layla wasn't her personal notary. And if she abused her notary powers, her stamp could get taken from her. It'd be damn hard to run an accounting business without being able to notarize anything. Disgusted, she tossed the folder aside. Sterling immediately moved to the paper and sat on it, then began to lick his butt.

"There you go, buddy. Good cat." Layla chuckled.

She texted with Amy and Becca for a little while longer, then turned on some mindless television and worked on amending W-2s for a while.

Her phone pinged again.

Layla clenched her jaw and picked it up from its spot on the couch next to her. If it was her mother, she was going to block her for a week—

It was a photo. In the photo was a long, boopable snoot and big liquid eyes on a copper-colored dog with floppy ears. Oscar, with his head down on a flannel-covered chest. It looked like he was in a bedroom.

Jack's bedroom.

JACK: Your son has your eyes.

Her belly fluttered with nervous excitement. He was contacting her already? Granted, it could be because the dog was a bit of a problem, but she hoped it was more than that. She gazed down at the picture, biting back a smile, and then finally texted him back.

LAYLA: If I say he has your nose am I a bad parent?

Jack's response was almost instant, which told her that he was on his phone . . . waiting for her response. The thought made her toes curl.

JACK: As long as you don't tell me we have the same build, I think we're good.

She laughed. How could she not? Damn it, why did he get to be so good-looking *and* funny? Some people had all the luck. It was inconceivable that this fantastically hot man was text-flirting with her. Heck, maybe she was the lucky one.

Then again, she'd bought that attention. It wasn't like it was legit. That burst her bubble quickly. With a little sigh, she texted him back.

LAYLA: How's Oscar doing?

JACK: I learned a few things about him today.

LAYLA: Oh?

JACK: He is apparently scared of cattle. And horses. And hands, but we knew that.

LAYLA: Oh dear.

JACK: Not to worry, he's calm now.

JACK: I spent most of the day holding him. Now I know how women feel when they have a purse.

She giggled at the mental image of that, picturing the big, burly cowboy walking around the ranch with a wiener dog tucked under his arm, purse-like.

LAYLA: I should say I'm sorry but I'm laughing too hard.

JACK: Poor little fella. I feel bad for him. Something bad must have happened in his past life to make him so scared of everything.

LAYLA: I appreciate you taking him for the time being. Maybe we can work with the city and see if we can foster him until we can find him a new home?

She watched her phone, waiting for the three little dots to show that he was texting a message back, but a long moment passed with no response. Then another.

Her phone rang, startling her.

CHAPTER SEVEN

"Hello?" Layla picked it up without checking the number, then inwardly winced. If it was her mother . . .

"How dare you," came Jack's playful, rumbling deep voice. "We're not rehoming our son. A family is forever."

Layla broke into another fit of giggles. "Yeah, well, I'm not sure how I feel about that. Oscar's sibling Sterling won't be a fan, I can tell you that right now. The cat barely tolerates me as it is."

"I find that hard to believe. I thought you were extremely tolerable."

She made a little sound of derision. "I'm starting to see why you're single."

He chuckled, and she heard a little growl come through the phone. "Sorry, Oscar," Jack muttered. "Hands. I know, buddy."

"He's still with you?"

"In bed with me, actually. He's the little spoon."

She laughed at that mental image and, for a wistful moment, wanted to be there. Curled up with a big, gorgeous cowboy? Yes, please. "You're too nice, you know that? Most people wouldn't put up with holding a dog all day long."

"Eh, he was so scared all day I just felt bad for him. I'd put him down and he'd start trembling like a leaf. Seemed easier to just hold him. Uncle Ennis said a ThunderShirt might help, but he didn't have one to fit this little sausage of a hound, so he's checking with a friend of his that has a dog-training service down the road."

"I have no idea what a ThunderShirt is," she admitted. "And I still think you're very kind." She smiled into her empty living room. "You got a lot more than you bargained for when you signed up for this mess."

"Oh, I didn't sign up. I was enlisted, remember?"

"Me too. Becca and Amy strong-armed me."

He paused for a moment. "And you still shelled out that much to go out with me?"

"Not to go out with you," Layla admitted. "To win."

She heard him laugh softly. "There goes my inflated ego."

"I sincerely doubt that very much," she teased. "I think it'll take more than one reality check to get that hot-air balloon back under control."

"Damn, you're cold." She could hear the grin in his voice. "How do you know I have an ego?"

Because you're utterly gorgeous and you know it. But she wasn't going to give him more fuel. "It's in the way you walk."

"Bowlegged like any good cowboy?"

Now she was the one laughing. "Sure."

"So . . . what are you up to on this fine Saturday night? Clearly not living it up in the Painted Barrel nightlife."

"I am in my pajamas, amending W-2s as I sit on my couch and watch Netflix."

"Is that . . . accounting dirty talk?"

Layla snickered. "No. If you wanted to dirty talk to an accountant, you'd talk general ledger."

"A what?"

"Never mind. Nerd joke." She felt shy and curled her legs under her on the couch. "What about you? Isn't it early to be in bed with the little spoon?"

"Maybe." It was quiet for a moment, and she mentally suspected he was shrugging. "Kinda used to early nights in bed. I have to get up early for work most days. Cattle aren't big on sleeping in, you know. And when I lived in Alaska, there wasn't a whole hell of a lot to do at night. Our cabin was kind of rough, so it wasn't like we spent all day watching Netflix or something. We just kinda hung out with one another, played cards, shot the shit." He chuckled. "And went to bed and got a good night's sleep."

Now she felt guilty for sitting in cozy pajamas with an episode of *The Office* running in the background while she worked. "I think Becca mentioned Hank came from Alaska. How long have you been in Wyoming?"

"Too long," he muttered.

She laughed, because she could relate. Sometimes Painted Barrel felt very small.

"You?"

"Me? Oh, I'm not from here. I'm from Kentucky. I moved out here after college and was originally going to settle in Casper. No state taxes here, you know. That was a big plus for me as an accountant. Less paperwork, but also less hassle." She shrugged. "I drove around one weekend when I first got to Wyoming and just did some sightseeing, and I liked this place. Saw my office building had a vacancy and kinda saw myself in it."

Layla had also very specifically not seen her mother in Wyoming, especially a place as small as Painted Barrel. It had been a place to get away, to start over fresh, to start a life that didn't involve catering to Janet Schmidt's constant need for attention.

How wrong she'd been. Janet had followed her out here

less than six months later. Sure, she was living just outside Casper, so they weren't completely neighbors, but it was still closer than Layla preferred.

"You ever think about going back to Kentucky?" he asked her.

"Never. You ever think about going back to Alaska?"

"All the time," he admitted, and there was a sigh in his voice. "But family's staying here, so I guess I'm going to put down roots, too. Buy some land, make a ranch of my own."

"More cattle?"

"Dunno. Maybe cutting horses."

"What's a cutting horse?"

"How is it you live in Wyoming and don't know what a cutting horse is?" he asked, amused.

"Uh, because I've never sat on a horse in my life? You are talking to one hundred percent city girl right here."

"Well, now, I can fix that." His voice took on a flirty tone. "You give me half a chance, and I'll get you all saddled up."

And didn't that sound incredibly dirty. "You assume I want to be on a horse."

"You bought yourself a cowboy. Of course I'm gonna assume you want to be on a horse."

And Layla laughed again. How was it that he could make her laugh at everything? Normally she was the one that joked around. She was the "funny" friend, so it was nice to tease and have someone tease back.

"Did you call me tonight because you wanted to talk me into riding a horse for our date?" She shut her laptop and tossed it aside. Even after this phone call was over, she suspected she wouldn't get a thing done. She'd be too busy replaying every moment in her head to concentrate on numbers. "Or are you trying to get out of our date? Because if you are, just say so. I'm no cruel overlord to force you to go on a date with me just because I bought you."

"Actually, I was calling about the date."

Damn it. She knew it. It was always too good to be true. Fighting back disappointment, she forced a smile to her face so he could hear it in her voice. "Go on."

"I was wondering if you wanted to meet up tomorrow to discuss a custody agreement for our son? I was thinking a nice long walk, and by walk, I mean me holding Oscar as I walk around."

Layla laughed. "A custody agreement, huh?"

"Yeah, at some point I'm actually going to have to put him down and get some work in. I was hoping we could trade off. Not that I don't love having him bite at my hands every time I reach for something, but the other guys here on the ranch might get a little ornery if I don't start pulling my share."

Her face was glowing with excitement. She could feel it . . . or maybe that was a blush. "So you're not trying to bail out on me?"

"Absolutely not. This is actually a shameless attempt to get to see you again before we have our official date. Is it working?"

"It might be."

"So . . . does tomorrow work for you?"

"I think I can spare a Sunday." Because she worked for herself, she picked at tax returns, amendments, and emails all weekend long. She never really took an entire day off. Not that she needed the whole day, but getting out of the house on the weekend for fun? For a date? It felt like a treat.

A double treat if she was going to be spending it with a hot guy.

"Is it gonna be a problem?" he asked. "We can do another day—"

"No, no, Sunday's great."

"What is it you do again? Something nerdy?" He sounded like he was teasing.

"Nerdy" wasn't the worst thing she'd been called. "It is hella nerdy. Accounting."

"Right. You told me that, didn't you?"

"Probably. But I don't blame you for not remembering. It's not like I wear an accounting hat like you wear a cowboy hat." Oh god, she was flirting back and she was so damn awkward at it. Inwardly, she cringed at her own words. Accounting hat. For fuck's sake. Why was she saying such dumb stuff?

"Nope, just big glasses, right?"

"I have contacts. Just never wear 'em. None of my clients will recognize me if I wear them," she joked.

"I'll recognize you."

That made her get all flustered all over again. "At any rate, accounting is far less exciting than being a cowboy."

"Sometimes being a cowboy isn't all that exciting." His voice sounded sleepy, or maybe just relaxed. "There's a lot of poop, a lot of pregnant cattle, and occasionally there's an auction."

"A cattle auction?"

"No, a bachelor one. I hear that's how you meet the prettiest girls."

That made her roll her eyes. "Man, you are a hard-core flirt."

"It's because I can practically hear you blushing. It makes me want to flirt even more. I like it when you blush. It's like catnip for me."

"And yet you're a dog person." Man, she really was terrible at this flirting crap.

"I'm an everything person. I like cats and dogs. And cat people. And accountants."

Layla groaned. "Now I know you're lying."

He laughed, the sound so full of joy that it made her feel warm. "You mean to tell me that accountants aren't a hot commodity?"

"Only at tax time."

He laughed again, and she felt warm all over. He thought she was funny. That was good, right? Unless this was going to turn into one of those "funny friend" situations, where she'd be great to drink beer with but not so great to date. Ugh. She wished she was better at this.

"So when is tax time?"

She'd go with a serious answer, not a funny one. "Not now."

Her answer was flat and unfriendly, and inwardly, Layla winced. Instead of sounding strong and confident, she just sounded like a jerk.

Jack paused, then spoke again. "Is . . . this a bad time? We don't have to talk about the date, if you'd prefer not to. It's just a friendly sort of thing. Doesn't have to mean anything."

Oh great. Now he thought she was trying to blow him off? This conversation was taking a rapid downhill turn. Layla cleared her throat delicately. "Can we start over? Hi, I'm Layla. I like long walks in the woods, bidding absurd amounts on random strangers at charity auctions, and hiding my feelings with humor."

There was a long, tense moment, and then he laughed again. "Hi, Layla," he said, taking up the conversation where she'd left it. "I'm Jack. I like hanging out on stages holding puppies and meeting cute accountants, but I think we covered that part."

She smiled into her phone. "Hi, Jack. I guess it's a good thing we met after hearing our common interests."

"Isn't it?" he teased. "Speaking of the auction, can I ask you a quick question?"

Oh no. Here was where he asked her about her virginity. Layla tensed, waiting for the worst. "Go ahead."

"Your mother . . . is she always like that?"

Relief flooded through her. This was a question she

could answer truthfully. "So one of the things with a narcissist is that they'll use information like a bat and club you with it out of nowhere. My mother deliberately picks things to say that will garner attention for her and make people remember her. It's kind of classic, really. I've gotten pretty used to her zingers." Well, "used to" wasn't the right term. Maybe "braced for disaster" was. The disappointment didn't slap as hard when your expectations for someone were already incredibly low.

He grunted.

"But am I surprised she did it? No. She wasn't the star of the moment so she did it to save face. I'm the nerdy, unsexy daughter and she reminds everyone that she's the glamorous, beautiful one."

"Wait, wait."

"What?"

There was a rustle of blankets on his end of the phone, and a disgruntled yap. "Oscar, hush. Here, chew on my finger." A tiny growl, and then Jack sighed. "Okay, sorry. I think I must have flashed him a hand or something. Your mom always tears you down in front of others?"

"Not always. Like I said, just when she feels threatened or overshadowed. She has to remind everyone who the hot one is." Like Layla had ever forgotten. She had nightmares of school trips when her mom had showed up in short sequined miniskirts to take them to the museum. Of summers in the community pool and her mom in a red string bikini next to the other moms wearing floral, skirted swimwear to hide their thighs. Janet Schmidt made sure everyone was aware of her presence, and if she couldn't get the attention she craved with flash, she'd do it in other ways.

"I think that's pretty fucked up," he admitted.

"It is—"

"I mean, she's clearly not the hot one."

Layla opened her mouth and then snapped it shut again.

A half-strangled squeak came out of her throat instead of a clever answer.

"Did I make you blush again?"

"A little."

"You know you're hot, right?"

That threw Layla for a loop. "I am?"

"Are you kidding me?" He gave another sultry laugh that made her toes curl. "I don't know what your mom's been filling your head with, but allow me to point out that you are absolutely in my spank bank and I would definitely touch unmentionable parts of myself to thoughts of you."

Well, now this conversation was making her squirm in all kinds of ways.

"Before I list out all the ways I find you hot, I should probably point out this is not a conversation we should have in front of our bitey son or else he might remain an only child for life."

She chuckled at that mental image. "Thanks for sharing that. You should probably stop letting him chew on your finger."

"If he's biting on my finger, I know the rest of me is safe. So . . . tomorrow? Or have I scared you off with my heavy-handed flirting?"

"Please. You can't scare me," she bluffed.

"Good. Because I want to see you."

And then she was blushing all over again. They set up a time and said an awkward good night, and then Layla put her phone down. She immediately picked up her crochet, just to give her restless, frantic fingers something to do.

She had a date. Tomorrow.

With a hot, flirty cowboy . . . that she'd paid for.

Layla decided that she'd focus on the first part and not the latter.

CHAPTER EIGHT

Did she think she was going to get any work done this weekend? Layla had clearly underestimated just how distracted she was going to be at the thought of going out with Jack. She poked at an amended tax return, filling in deposit information on the Schedule C. The problem was, she wasn't really concentrating on the return and it wouldn't balance. Instead, she googled Jack Watson. She googled what the name "Jack" could possibly be short for. She googled Alaska. She googled cowboys.

She looked for Jack on Facebook. And Twitter. And Instagram.

Eventually, she gave up on tax returns. She curled up with her phone and watched animal videos and thought about Jack and obsessed over her upcoming date.

They were taking the dog for a walk.

What exactly did one wear to take a dog for a walk? Layla went to bed pondering this, and it was the first thing she wondered when she woke up. Luckily, the weather saved her from having to consider dressy clothing. It was chilly, with a stiff breeze, so she pulled out her favorite *Space Invaders* sweatshirt and jeans. She put on a little bit of makeup, flat-ironed her hair so it was loose and wavy around her shoulders, and then sat on the couch and tried not to feel self-conscious. Did she look like she was putting too much effort into things? Or just enough? She wished she knew.

Her phone rang, and the screen said "unknown caller." Could that be Jack? Did he have more than one number? Layla hesitated and then answered it. "Hello?"

"So you're not dead."

Her mom. Groan.

"No, Mom. I'm not dead. I just didn't feel like talking to you yesterday."

"Are you still mad at me?" Janet sounded utterly surprised. "Honestly, you're so sensitive, Layla. You get upset over the tiniest things."

For a moment, she felt guilty; then she remembered that no, she wasn't sensitive. It was just another one of her mother's subtle attempts to make her question herself. "What's up, Mom?"

"Well. I was calling to see if you'd mail that paperwork back to me. I don't feel like driving all the way over to Painted Barrel to get it."

"I'll send it back to you, sure, but I'm not signing anything, and I'm sure not notarizing it."

"What? Why not?" Janet's voice was shocked. "Is there a problem with them?"

"You're asking me to sign off stating that you told me that you're completely unaware of any sort of flooding since the purchase of the land. We both know that's not true."

"Oh, FEMA doesn't care," she said lightly. "It's just a formality."

"It's not a formality, and I'm not going to sign off on it so you can make your money back. I told you not to buy land unless you knew the market, but you didn't listen to me, Mom. I'm not going to lie for you. Not when it could cause me to lose my notary license."

"Oh please. You're such a worrywart."

"No."

"Don't be such a baby—"

"If FEMA really doesn't care if the land is in a flood-plain or not, why not just go to them directly? I'll pay for you to get someone else to notarize these documents for you if money's a problem."

"Oh, good lord. If you're going to be like this, forget it. I have a friend that will help me out."

"Good!"

"I just don't see why you're being so stubborn. You owe me one."

That made Layla sputter. "Excuse me? What on earth do I owe you for?"

"Oh, how about the fact that I raised you?"

Layla tried not to roll her eyes hard enough that she'd strain something. "It's called parenting. I'm pretty sure most mothers don't look at it as a favor to their child."

"How about that man I got you yesterday? You wouldn't have stepped in and bid on him if I hadn't nudged you in that direction."

Nudged her? Was she serious? "Yes, I would have."

"No, I know you, Layla-belle. You'd make some silly excuse and back out at the last moment, and then you'd be disappointed. I knew you wanted to buy yourself a boy-friend and so I showed up to help things along. Really, you should be thanking me."

It probably all sounded completely logical in Janet's head, but it was utterly infuriating for Layla to hear. "You shouted to everyone in the room that I was a virgin, Mom."

"Well, I can see it's clear that you're going to hold a grudge." Janet sniffed. "You won't notarize the documents for me?"

"Still no. Nice try, though."

Janet sighed. "Just FedEx them back to me, then. I know a guy. I'll tell him my stubborn, ungrateful daughter wouldn't do the tiniest of favors for her poor broke mother."

Tiniest of favors, her ass. More like break the law. Commit perjury. "Just sell the land like it is, Mom, floodplain and all."

"But then I won't make my money back."

"Not my problem."

"Can I just borrow your notary stamp—"

"Goodbye, Mom. I have to go."

"Got a busy weekend of watching television—"

She hung up. Sometimes Layla felt bad about hanging up on Janet, but sometimes her mom made it easy. Today, she didn't feel a smidgen of guilt, just irritation. How much easier would her life be if she didn't have Janet and her drama to deal with?

Layla picked up her cross-stitch basket from the end table and glanced at the clock. Still several hours before she was scheduled to meet the cowboy, and she needed a distraction. She picked up her project from where she'd left off—this was a colorful, pretty wreath that looked like flowers from a distance, but when you looked closely, the flowers were actually dancing aliens and the phrase THE TRUTH IS OUT THERE was artfully stitched in the middle. This was going to be a birthday gift for one of her gaming friends, provided she finished the project in time. Layla plucked out a few red stitches, trying not to think about the irritating phone call with her mother.

You owe me. You know you wouldn't have bid on him if I wasn't there.

The sad thing was, Janet had been right about that. How

many times had Layla chickened out on dates that her mom wanted to set her up on? How many times had she pulled excuses out of her ass when she knew a "potential date" would be showing up at a family get-together? Layla was good at avoiding romantic conflict . . . probably because she'd spent so many years trying to extricate herself from her mom's constant life of conflict.

Maybe going out on this date with Jack was a mistake.

She stabbed at the fabric. *Don't be ridiculous,* she chided herself. *This isn't even a date. You're walking the dog and discussing who's going to take him for the week. He might just be trying to pawn the dog off on you. It's probably not romantic, no matter what he said last night.*

After all, a guy as hot as Jack Watson? All he had to do was give her a smile and flutter those long, thick lashes at her, and she'd be putty in his hands. It was entirely possible that she was about to be played, and that made Layla anxious.

Maybe not, though? Just because her mother was a raging jerk didn't mean that everyone was . . . did it? Layla wasn't sure if she had a special knack for just finding them. She sure hoped not.

CHAPTER NINE

Layla showed up at the bakery early. To be fair, she'd left her house a few minutes ahead of schedule to get gas, but even with a pit stop, she was still ten minutes earlier than their meeting time and feeling a little overeager.

The bakery was empty, at least, so that was something. Painted Barrel was too small to have a fancy coffee chain set up here, so the local bakery had tables and served as the latte and snack shop of choice. Layla came in far too often for a nice brisk espresso, and usually on weekdays, there was someone sitting inside with a laptop.

"Did you want to order?" Megan, the teenager behind the counter, asked her.

"I'm waiting for someone."

She grinned at Layla. "Girls' lunch?"

"Something like that." Oh god, did no one think she'd date a man? Was she that pathetic? Why didn't she say it was a date? Or would that seem like bragging? Layla kept smiling even as she watched Megan swipe the counters

clean. Even to a teenager, Layla was perpetually single.
That was . . . painful.

The urge to sit down and text—so at least she'd look
busy—was overwhelming, so Layla headed for one of the
tables and shrugged off her jacket. She sat down on one of
the tall chairs. Immediately, she knew it was a mistake.
Something cold and wet was seeping through her pants.
With a feeling of horror, she got back up again and immediately headed for the bathroom.

Sure enough, the remains of someone's iced latte was
soaking through the pale denim of her jeans, because of
course it was. With a frustrated sound, she glanced around
the small bathroom. One stall. Okay, then. Layla glanced at
the door and saw it had a lock on it. She locked the door, then
stripped off her jeans and began to scrub the wet spot.

As she did, she grumbled to herself. Good thing she was
early, or she'd have had to turn around and go home to
change. She also might have grumbled about the job Megan
was doing keeping the café clean, but it was fine. It was
fine.

Everything was fine.

She was able to clean off most of the brownish stain, but
it meant a much larger wet spot covered the backside of her
jeans, along with a pink tinge from the cheap hand soap. It
was getting worse the more she fucked with it, and so Layla
gave up. She turned on the hand dryer and held her jeans
under it, but it didn't seem to be doing much drying.

Her phone rang.

Shit. That had to be Jack. Layla groaned and let it go to
voicemail. If he asked, she'd just say she was freshening up
or something. She cranked the dryer again, smacking the
button, and when it finally turned itself off, the wet spot
looked no smaller than before. Crap.

Why was this happening to her?

A hysterical giggle escaped her. Was this the universe

telling her that dating was a bad idea? It was entirely possible.

Best to just accept defeat, wear her jacket over the stains, and laugh about it . . . someday. She put her jeans back on, grimaced over the sensation of the wet denim against her butt, and slipped her shoes back on. When she grabbed the door, though, it didn't budge.

Layla frowned to herself, tested the lock, and tried again. Sure enough, she'd unlocked it but the door still didn't budge. She knelt down by the locking mechanism and flipped it again. The lock "moved" to unlocked, but there was no click of the mechanism inside. Something was stuck. She pressed her face against the handle, smothering the hysterical laughter bubbling in her throat.

Okay, she had a wet diaper, and she was now locked in the bathroom. What else could possibly go wrong?

Her phone pinged with a text message. Because of course it did.

JACK: Here.

She set it back down and stared at the door. Okay. Did she confess to her hot date that she'd somehow locked herself in the bathroom after she'd sat in a drink? Or did that all sound incredibly stupid and fake? It was utterly humiliating, but she also didn't know what to do. Call a locksmith and ask him to spring her from the can?

The thought made her snort with more panicked laughter.

Megan's voice drifted through the door. ". . . can't . . . dog in here . . ."

Jack's rich voice rumbled through the bakery, but she couldn't make out what he said. She could hear him chuckling, though.

Fuuuuuck because of course he'd come in looking for her. Megan was probably flirting with him, too. Layla groaned and grabbed the door in a panic, shaking it. Didn't budge. Didn't even make enough noise to get anyone's attention, because she could hear Megan's high-pitched giggle in the other room as she talked to Jack.

After a few more moments of fiddling with the lock, she came to the realization that she could either stay trapped in the bathroom until Megan noticed she was here . . . and Jack would probably think she'd flaked . . . or she could suck it up and point out where she was.

CHAPTER TEN

With a sigh of defeat, she scooped up her phone and texted.

LAYLA: So you're not going to believe this

LAYLA: I have locked myself in the bathroom

LAYLA: Can you please let Megan know so she can let me out?

There was no answer, but it did show the message as read. She tugged on the door again, fretting. Had he already left? Was he embarrassed at her dorkiness and changed his mind about the date?

A knock came at the door. "It's Megan," chirped the too-happy voice on the other side. "Did you lock yourself in?"

"Yes!" Layla tugged on the door again. "It won't open."

"Yeah, the building's settled and the lock sticks. Let me get a knife and I'll jimmy it for you."

"Sorry," Layla called out, wanting to wring her hands. She clutched her phone tightly, imagining what Jack must think of her.

Five excruciating minutes later, Megan jimmied the lock and the door opened. Layla let out a sigh of relief and practically hugged the teenager. "Thank you so much."

"Yeah, I keep telling the boss to fix the lock, but he never does." She shrugs. "So the guy outside. That the one you bought at the auction?"

Layla, who was busy tugging her sweater down over her ass, paused. "What?"

"You paid a shit ton of money to snatch up some hot guy at that dippy bachelor auction, didn't you? That's what I heard from my mom. Everyone's talking about it."

"Are they?" Layla felt faint. "I just . . . love animals. That's why I bid that much."

"Uh-huh." Megan smirked. "He's really hot. You'll have to let me know if things don't work out for you two."

"He's too old for you," Layla snapped, grabbing her coat and shoving her arms through the sleeves. The inside of the bakery wasn't empty, of course. There were customers patiently waiting in line for Megan to get back to the register, and Layla wanted to sink into the ground when they all stared at her. None of them were Jack, though. She glanced out the bubble-lettering-covered windows, and sure enough, there was a man wearing a cowboy hat outside, leaning against the glass, a doggy butt perched under his arm.

Waiting for her.

She didn't know whether that made her happy or not.

Layla shoved her hands in her coat pockets and grabbed her purse, then headed out the door. The wind was bitterly cold—especially on her wet ass—and blew her hair in her face, and she felt like an even bigger idiot for wearing it down.

Jack glanced over at her. He looked gorgeous, of course, wearing a dark plaid shirt, a cowboy hat, and a puffy vest jacket to ward off the cold. He had a backpack casually slung over his shoulder and the dog under his arm, and a huge grin on his face. "Well, hello."

"Hi." She gave him a meek wave.

He said nothing. She said nothing. For a moment, she wondered which of them would break first. Was he going to comment on her being locked in the bathroom? Or would she give up on her dignity and point it out herself? They both knew the truth. With a little sigh, she crossed her arms over her chest. "So in addition to the buns, the locks are also a bit sticky."

"Were your buns sticky, too?" His mouth twitched. "You might be sharing a little too much info."

She smacked his arm, and the dog snarled. Layla took a step back and ignored his little smirk. "Sticky buns are a pastry, you doofus."

"And part of a bad joke, apparently." He reached carefully around Oscar's back and patted the dog's head. "Poor Oscar thought you bailed on him."

"No, I was just busy panicking in the bathroom, because I got here early and sat in someone else's drink. It's all been downhill from there."

"All your hopes and dreams flushed away?" he asked innocently.

She glared.

His mouth twitched again. Then hers did. Then, they were both laughing, and all the tension was gone. "It's so bad," she giggled. "There was this big horrible stain on my pants and then, and then"—she gasped for air between choked laughs—"the door wouldn't freaking unlock! Why me?"

"I wasn't sure what to think when Megan told me you were spending so long in the bathroom."

"She didn't!"

He chuckled. "Oh yeah. She ran her mouth like there was no tomorrow. I'm sorry, but I'm afraid most of this town is going to know that Layla got trapped in the bathroom while on a date."

She groaned, burying her face in her hands. "This is the worst day ever."

"Does that mean you want to call off our date?"

"Is it a date?"

"You tell me." His smile remained, but it was less easy. "I'll understand if you want to head on home."

"Now? After all that I've endured?" She snorted. "If you don't mind me having a soaking-wet ass, I'm more than happy to hang out with you and our son."

"We could get drinks and move on?" He tilted his head at the little bakery. "If you want to hold Oscar, I'll order for us and bring them out here. Megan was not a fan of you know who." He whispered, inclining his head toward the dachshund.

"I can hold him." She took the dog from his arms carefully and noticed that Oscar was bundled up in a sweet little doggy coat, but it didn't seem warm enough for his tiny legs. She unzipped her jacket and tucked him in against her sweater as Jack headed inside. She carefully petted his head and glanced around. The weather was incredibly brisk, so there weren't many people on the street, the edges of the sidewalks heaped with snow. Perhaps a walk today wasn't the best of ideas. She didn't want to cancel, though.

Now that he was here with her and looking mighty gorgeous—and she'd gone through the bathroom ordeal—she'd put up with a little bit of a chill.

Oscar seemed content to be in her jacket, and Layla

hummed to him while she waited. The coffee seemed to be taking a while, and she turned around and glanced back through the window. Sure enough, Jack was at the counter, smiling, as Megan chatted with him. As Layla watched, Megan flipped her hair and licked her lips, giggling.

Oh god, Megan was flirting with her date. Seriously? She wanted to bang on the window, but there was a family sitting and eating pastries at one of the tables, so she watched through the window, glaring, as Megan finally turned around and went back to making the coffees. Jack glanced in her direction and discreetly glanced at his wrist, rolling his eyes. Okay, so he knew Megan was taking her sweet time. Layla watched a little more closely as Megan offered the first coffee up and tried to hold on to it, pausing to talk some more. Jack's smile was polite but strained, and he took the coffee from her anyhow, gesturing at the door. Megan's smile faltered a little and she made the second coffee faster than the first, and then Jack was finally free.

He joined her outside, holding out the two cups of steaming coffee in a cardboard carrier. "That was awkward."

"You're welcome to go back in there and spend your date with her if you want."

"Why would I want that?" He made a face. "She offered me her number twice."

Layla glanced at the cups in his hand. Sure enough, her number was written there, too. "Three times."

He groaned. "Jesus. I made sure to point out several times that I was on a date."

"But it's not a real one because I bought you, right?" She could guess what Megan said to him.

His grimace told her that she'd guessed the truth. "I told her I wasn't interested. Payment or no, I'm on a date with you."

Well now, she wasn't sure how she felt about that response. He made it sound like an obligation, and the last thing Layla wanted to be was someone's obligatory date. She got enough of that with her mom and the blind dates she was constantly flinging Layla's way.

Oscar shivered in her arms as the wind picked up again, and it reminded her that today seemed cursed, despite everything. "Maybe we should call everything off."

"Nope," Jack said easily.

"It's kind of cold for a walk—"

He gestured down the street, still holding the two coffees. "Is that your office?" When she nodded, he grinned at her. "I'd like to see it, if that's all right. And we could get Oscar out of the cold."

She hesitated, but it sounded so reasonable that she couldn't refuse. "Don't get your hopes up too high. It's just an office." But he gave her another one of those heart-stopping grins and Layla bit back a sigh. It was so unfair that he was so, soooo pretty. Just being around him made her brain short-circuit. She knew she was being defensive and sniping at him, but it was just so she didn't get her heart broken too badly when this didn't work out.

And when it didn't, she'd just be that crazy accountant that paid too much for a hot guy at a bachelor auction. Oh god. Under her coat, Layla began to sweat.

She hadn't thought this bidding thing through in the slightest.

They walked over to her small office and she unlocked the building. It was an old house—as many of the office buildings were on Painted Barrel's main street—that had been converted to a suite of five or six private offices with a shared lobby. Inside, it felt uncomfortably warm after getting out of the snow, and she led Jack down the hall toward the small room she called hers as she juggled Oscar under her arm. The window looked professional enough, she supposed, with LAYLA SCHMIDT, CPA, CPP, NOTARY PUBLIC emblazoned on the window. Inwardly she cringed when she unlocked the door and the extent of her dorkiness was unleashed.

Her office was craft central. A crocheted blanket was tossed over the love seat against the wall, and a crocheted pillow was tossed into the visitor's chair. Her desk was covered in paperwork of all kinds, but there was a sewing basket and thread organizer next to the garbage can. The walls had her framed certifications, sure, but they also had her cross-stitch projects all over them. Stitched floral murals proclaimed things like NOT MY CIRCUS, NOT MY MONKEYS and I CANNOT BE HELD RESPONSIBLE FOR WHAT MY FACE DOES WHEN YOU SPEAK and STITCH LIFE.

"Huh," he said, looking around.

"Have a seat," she told him, pulling out her latest cross-stitch project (a banner that read OFFICE, SWEET OFFICE for one of her neighbors) and emptying her craft basket. She tucked a soft, crocheted blanket in there and gently set Oscar down. The dog looked up at her, tail thumping happily. "You, uh, want some coffee?"

Jack held out the two coffees in his hands.

"Right. Sorry if my office is a little dorky." She'd always liked all the personality that her small office showed. After all, most accountants did boring work and most offices were boring, but not hers. In front of a date, though? That was a very different matter.

He set her coffee down on her desk and then slowly walked around the room, gazing at the frames all over the walls. "It's not dorky. It fits you."

"Because I'm dorky?"

"Because you're cute." He glanced over his shoulder at her, grinning.

Okay, she'd take that. "I'm sorry if I've been snappish at you today. I know I seem cranky." She sipped her drink and pulled out a package of peanut butter cookies that she kept in her drawer for that certain time of the month. Carefully, she broke one in half and offered it to Oscar, who snarled at her hand and then gently bit down on the cookie as if he were the most delicate of animals.

"You've had a hell of a day," he commented, his boots clomping on the old wooden floors as he moved to peer at another frame. "I'd be in a terrible mood, too, if my ass was wet in this weather."

"It's not the most pleasant feeling I've had on my ass. Not that my ass has experienced tons of feelings," she hastily added, and then wanted to sink through the floor when he flashed her another grin.

"It's not fun when you're meeting someone, I imagine."

"It's not."

"One time, back when I was in Alaska, I flirted with this one girl at the fur shop for months. Talked a huge game, made it sound like I was a real Casanova. Finally she went out with me, and so I bought all these nice, new clothes to impress her. Of course, I tried to play it all casual-like. I took her out and she immediately asked me if I'd gotten new clothing. I said no. She reached over and pulled a size sticker off my leg. One of those long ones that you don't see until you put the jeans on, and she peeled it real, real slow. It made the loudest noise and I remember just cringing inside and dying." He chuckled. "For some reason, she never went out with me again."

"Her loss," Layla defended. She liked that he was trying to make her feel better about her day by sharing a story like that. It was sweet. "And that's not nearly as bad as locking yourself in the bathroom."

"So you say." He gestured at one of her certificates. "What's a CPP?"

"Certified Payroll Professional. I can process payroll for small companies, do reporting and tax returns." She shrugged. "That probably doesn't mean a lot to you."

"It doesn't," he admitted. "But it sounds smart." And the

look he gave her was impressed. He gestured at the walls. "You do all these?"

"No, I mugged old ladies and forced them to give me their craft projects."

Jack stared at her and then threw his head back and laughed. "Okay, I deserved that one."

"You kinda did," she teased back. "But seriously, yes, they're mine. When I was a kid, I was stressed-out a lot. My parents were divorcing and my mother was, well, my mother. So I went to a lot of therapy. My therapist suggested that if I had something to focus on, a small project of some kind, it would help me relax, and a smaller project would give me a sense of accomplishment when it was finished. So I started to crochet scarves, and then blankets, and then I started cross-stitch. I like the silly sayings more than serious things, though. A lot of cross-stitch projects are just sweet puppies and kittens and flowers, and I like things with a bit of an edge on them. Unexpected sayings."

And some of the sayings on the ones she had at home were utterly filthy.

But he grinned and gave one last look to a sampler that read 99 PROBLEMS BUT A STITCH AIN'T ONE and then sat down across from her. Oscar finished chewing his cookie, got out of the basket, and immediately went to Jack's leg, pawing at it.

"Traitor," Layla muttered. "Who fed you?"

"Can I help it if he knows I'm a sucker?" He scooped the dog up and settled him in his lap, resting a big hand on Oscar's back.

She smiled, offering the rest of the cookie over to the dog, but he only watched her hand warily. After a moment, Layla gave up and sighed, setting the cookie down at the edge of the desk. Sure enough, Oscar wiggled over to it and began to chew, getting crumbs everywhere.

She glanced up at Jack, and he was watching her with

that unreadable look in his eyes, a hint of a smile on his face. It made her want to squirm, because she didn't know what he wanted from her . . . or this date . . . or anything. Did he just want her to schedule the whole "date" for the auction thing and get it over with? Or was he here because he genuinely wanted to spend time with her? Or was he just trying to figure out what to do with Oscar? She didn't know.

Layla bit her lip and pulled another cookie out of the pack, breaking it in half. "Sorry if this isn't much of a walk."

"I don't mind. I can walk anytime."

"I'll understand if you want to call things off—"

He tilted his head, the brim of his hat making the movement seem that much more exaggerated. "Layla, can I ask you something?"

"Sure . . . ?"

"Why do you keep trying to get rid of me?"

She flushed. Dropped the cookie on the edge of the desk and sat back in her chair. "I'm best with numbers and patterns. I know exactly what's expected of me with those. I'm not that great with people. I'm really, really not that great with the opposite sex."

"And?"

"And all I'm saying is that I know I paid a lot at the auction, but it was mostly because I wanted to make sure that the project took off because Becca and Amy worked so hard on it, and I liked making my mom lose, and my feelings won't be hurt if you call this thing off—"

He raised a big hand in the air to silence her.

Oscar immediately snarled, lunging at his hand.

Grimacing, Jack hid his hand again, rolling his eyes. "This dog. Okay, Layla. You want me to be bluntly honest with you?"

"That would be wonderful, actually."

"I thought I was the other night, but allow me to be even

more blunt." Jack gave her a heavy-lidded look that made her breath catch in her throat. "I've wanted to get to know you from the first moment I saw you. In fact, I wanted to ask you out then, but you deliberately avoided looking in my direction, so I figured the interest was one-sided. Then you strolled on into the auction and bid on me, stepping on your own mom to do so, and you think I'm not gonna find that incredibly sexy?"

"I'm more dork than sexy—"

He raised a hand in the air, silencing her protest, and Oscar yipped. Jack grimaced and then continued. "You think being unique means you're not sexy? I like a sense of humor in a girl. I like a woman that knows when to laugh. And I sure like a smart woman." Jack gave her a frankly assessing look. "I like most everything I've seen so far, and I want to see more. So you're not gonna chase me off. This isn't for charity. Or at least, it might have started off as charity, but I'm here today because I wanted to see you. Talk to you."

"I thought you were here for Oscar."

He pointed a finger in her face. "Take a compliment, woman."

She mock-snapped her teeth at it and grinned.

Jack threw his head back and laughed. "That's better."

She tucked a lock of hair behind her ear, feeling flustered, yet unable to stop smiling. "Okay, I think I get the idea now." Whatever it was that appealed to him about her, she'd do her best to just roll with it. It was unprecedented territory for her, but also . . . kind of exciting. "You know you're the first man I've ever bid on."

"What, there's not a string of bachelors in your bidding past? You don't go to all the charity bachelor auctions and try to snatch up men?"

Laughter bubbled in her throat. "Believe it or not, no, I don't. I'm very boring."

"I can see that from your office," he deadpanned, pointing at one of her wry cross-stitch projects of a T. rex trying to use a pencil. "So, Miss Boring, you bought the cowboy experience. When do you want it?"

Well, didn't that sound dirty? "And what exactly is the cowboy experience?"

"You know, some horseback riding, maybe a tour around the ranch. I could mend a fence or chop some wood and show off my guns." He lifted an arm, flexed, and kissed his biceps.

She rolled her eyes, fighting back another laugh. "Thrilling as that sounds, you do know I didn't buy you because I had a deep and abiding need to ride a horse?"

"I figured as much." He lowered his arm carefully, mindful of Oscar, and scratched behind the dog's ears. "Which is why I thought we could get together today and talk about things."

Layla gave him a skeptical look over her glasses. "That's the third excuse you've given me for wanting to get together. First you blamed Oscar, then you said it was because you liked me, and now it's because you wanted to have a barn date?" She leaned forward over her desk, as if imparting a secret. "Which one is it precisely?"

Jack put a hand on his chest. "Me, personally, I think every person should get to experience a nice horseback ride once in their life. And you bought a cowboy, so I figured you should get a little cowboy action in there. I'll even wear spurs if you're so inclined, and chaps." He moved his hand to the side of his mouth, whispering, "Ladies love the chaps."

She chuckled.

"But if that's not your thing, I understand . . . if you're chicken." He smirked.

She narrowed her eyes at him. "Is that a dare?"

"It is absolutely a dare." He gave her a challenging look.

Leaning back in her chair, Layla crossed her arms over

her chest and studied him. "Well, if we do something that's your element, don't you think we should do something that's mine?"

"If that's your way of getting me to agree to two dates, I accept," he said immediately.

Layla sputtered. Okay, she laughed, too. She was cornered, wasn't she? "It's obvious I'm going to have to think of something sufficiently evil to drag you to for my date."

"We could always go somewhere fancy. Dinner and a movie? Dancing?"

"Dancing? That sounds dreadful."

"You pick." His big hand went to Oscar's back and he patted the dog.

Such big, strong hands, tanned by work. His nails were blunt, his fingers thick, and lord if she didn't find that fascinating. "When did you want to do this?"

"Which one do you want to do first?"

"Not the horseback riding, that's for sure."

At the disgust in her voice, he laughed, his shoulders shaking with amusement. "But what if that's what I've got my heart set on?"

"Paper rock scissors?" she offered.

"You're on." He carefully picked Oscar up and set the dog on the floor, with an apologetic look to her. "Just in case we scare him."

"Very thoughtful." She rested a fist atop her palm and waited. Layla couldn't believe she was going to do paper rock scissors with a man about a date. It was just bizarre enough that it somehow fit in with the rest of this day.

He mimicked her movement, and they counted off. One, two, three. She threw paper, he threw scissors.

Layla groaned, flinging herself backward in her chair. "Noooo," she cried dramatically. "Best two out of three!"

"Nope. I won."

"Cheater."

"You're just salty because I beat you, and because you're gonna have to get up close and personal with a horse. Don't worry, little darlin'," he drawled in a fake John Wayne accent. "I'll wear the chaps for you."

"This is a disaster," she grumbled. "I can't believe I'm going horseback riding in February."

"We can have our date when you bring Oscar back to me."

"Bring him back?"

Jack reached over and scooped up Oscar, who, she realized, had his paws up on Jack's leg and was eagerly waiting to be picked up again. "You've noticed he's a bit clingy?"

She pinched her fingers indicating "just a little."

"I can't exactly do my job if I've got him all day long, and he shivers and cries if I put him down."

Oh dear. "But he loves you."

"It's because I'm so lovable," Jack agreed, holding Oscar up to his cheek. The dog licked it happily, his little tail thumping, and her heart melted a little bit more.

"But . . . I have a cat."

"Oscar promises to play nice."

She sighed, knowing she was a big softy and was going to end up taking the sad little wiener dog home with her. Not just because Oscar had sad eyes, but because Jack did, too, and she was an idiot. "For how long?"

He shrugged, lowering the dog carefully back to his lap. "Today's Sunday . . . We could trade off on Wednesday?"

"Wednesday? But—"

"And we can have our date then."

She pulled open her planner, flipping through her calendar. As luck would have it, her Wednesday was open. February was slow for her, the calm before the storm. January was a mess because of W-2s and 1099s, and April was when things picked up again. February and March were nice and simple. She could take Wednesday off. Layla bit her lip. "I guess I'll pencil you in," she grumbled.

He grinned at her. "And then we can switch off again on the weekend. You want your date to be Friday night or Saturday night?"

"Two dates this week?"

"I'm worth it." He winked at her.

Layla arched an eyebrow. "Should we pull another chair in here for your ego?"

Jack just laughed. "Your cheeks get pink every time I say something outrageous. It makes me want to say more." He shrugged, rubbing the dog through his ridiculous little jacket. "And if you don't want to go out this weekend, I'll understand."

"I didn't say that." Damn it, her cheeks really were hot, weren't they?

"You want cocktails and a fancy dinner somewhere? It'll be my treat since I'm making you ride a horse."

It was sweet of him to offer, but she did the payroll for a few of the ranches around Painted Barrel and knew most of the cowboys weren't exactly swimming with money. And besides, she wasn't the type to fuss about that sort of thing. "Let's just make it something relaxed and easy. No sense in going to a ton of effort."

The smile slid off of Jack's handsome face. "No? Why not?"

"Because . . . I don't know. Because it's not a real date?"

"Who says it's not real?"

Layla gave him an exasperated look. "We both know I'm not the kind of girl you date."

Jack leaned in as if he was about to share a secret. "Maybe that's why I'm still single."

Ooh, he was smooth.

CHAPTER ELEVEN

After they finished their coffees, Jack transferred Oscar to her lap and gave her a backpack of supplies—dog food, chew toys, the works. When he left, she locked the office back up again, Oscar tucked under her arm, and then she went home.

She didn't know what to think about her flirty, not-quite date with Jack. He said all the right things, flattered her into making it sound like he was sincere . . . and yet there was just a hint of too much playfulness that made her wonder if it was all a joke. If Jack took anything seriously or if he just coasted through life being cute and charming and getting his way.

Probably the latter.

For a dog that liked to be held, Layla had to admit that Oscar was very well behaved . . . other than the hand thing. Sterling's bluish-silver tail fluffed to three times its usual size the moment he smelled the dog, but Oscar was so meek and shivering that Sterling soon got bored and lost interest, lurking on the back of the couch so he could watch the dachshund. Oscar trembled every time she set him down, so Layla ended up sitting her laptop on her legs, tucked Oscar against her thigh, and put a heating blanket on his other side to give him the idea that he was being held. He slept like a baby, then woke up and trembled and gave her a sad look until she figured out he had to use the bathroom and took him outside. Once he did his business, she gave him a can of food and some water and let him eat in the kitchen while Sterling prowled around. The moment he was done, Oscar returned to her feet, shaking and waiting.

It really was sweet and sad at the same time. It was like poor Oscar was terrified of being left alone, and she couldn't imagine who would abandon a dog like that. Layla worried that Sterling would get jealous, but the cat didn't seem too bothered.

When she crawled into bed that night, she brought Oscar with her, tucking him against her chest. Sterling liked to sleep at the foot of the bed, so she hoped the cat wouldn't feel too neglected. She was just about to drift off to sleep when her phone pinged.

JACK: How's our son?

She smiled into the darkness, picked up her phone, and texted him a picture of Oscar, sound asleep against her sweatshirt, tucked under the covers with her.

JACK: Damn it, he stole my spot.

The man was an incorrigible flirt. What on earth was she going to do with him? Why did it make her smile so damn much?

* * *

Layla thought the next day at the office would really be business as usual. Clearly, she was an optimist.

She walked in a little after eight with Oscar tucked under her arm, her coffee in hand, and smiled at Phyllis, who ran the front desk for the building.

"There you are!" Phyllis beamed at her as if she'd solved world hunger, and immediately, Layla's hackles went up. "The talk of the town."

Uh-oh. "Oh? Why's that?" She kept her voice deliberately light and easy. Oh sure, Phyllis wouldn't even mention that Layla had walked in with a sausage-like sweater-clad dog under her arm. Which meant that she was about to be bombarded with something far more juicy.

"Miss Big Winner at the auction." Phyllis giggled girlishly. It was a bit of an alarming sound coming from a woman older than her mother. "You bought yourself a fine-looking man."

"Um, it was for charity."

"Well, I hope with all the money you paid, he treats you right." Phyllis gave her an exaggerated wink.

Layla smiled awkwardly and headed back to her office. Okay, that was weird and somewhat unnerving. Phyllis made it sound creepy, like Layla was some sort of basement-dwelling monster that had somehow emerged into the light to buy a man for sexually deviant purposes. She knew it was a small town. Knew that people were going to gossip. That was what they did. But she hadn't really thought too much about it when she'd bid so much. In that way, she was just like her mother—plowing ahead without thinking.

Ugh.

She settled Oscar into her office, put down a bowl and some food, and let him walk around on the floor for a bit.

He gave her hopeful looks as if wanting to be picked up again, but she wouldn't be able to get a thing done if she held him and tried to type. Eventually she relented at his sad expression and sat down on the floor with her laptop. He immediately put his head on her leg and curled up against her, and she petted him between answering emails, mindful of her hands.

And because she was that person, she checked her phone constantly. Just in case Jack texted her. So far there was nothing, and she had to admit it was playing with her nerves a little. Not that he had to text her constantly, but it would have been . . . reassuring. Now that she'd taken the dog from him, there was always the slight worry that he'd ghost her.

A knock at the door made Oscar jump.

"Come in," Layla called.

A big man stuck his head inside her office. It was Carl, who did insurance down the hall. He was twice her age, balding, divorced, and sometimes a little too friendly for her tastes. Now was one of those "too friendly" times. "Heard you had a wild weekend."

She managed a smile. "Not so wild."

"If you're that hard up for a man, I'm available. Free, too." He laughed at his own joke.

Layla managed to smile weakly.

It went like that for most of the morning. Layla would get some work in, and then someone would inevitably drop by her office to try to gossip about the auction. For an event that hadn't been all that well attended, everyone in town sure seemed to know about it. They knew she'd bid an extravagant amount on Jack. They knew she'd bid against someone else, who'd stormed out. And everyone seemed to think she'd bid on Jack because she was lonely and desperate.

After all, she was a single woman, so she clearly had to

have a biological clock that was ticking like a time bomb, right? No one seemed to grasp that Layla was perfectly fine being just Layla, not Layla-plus-one. Was dating Jack going to be fun? She hoped so. But it didn't change who she was . . . and it made some of the shocked and titillated reactions of her co-workers in the office kind of irritating.

Her inbox flooded with emails, too. All the clients she normally had to chase down for receipts and documentation? They all seemed to be emailing today, attaching the needed files and asking casual questions about how her weekend was and how did the auction go, and she ignored them all. She gave up on getting any work done, pulled up a crochet pattern online for a dog sweater, and managed to make a blue Superman sweater with a red cape attached to it for Oscar, who endured having it tugged over his head with the patience of a saint.

"You're a good boy," she cooed at him, and was rewarded with a whippy little wag of his tail.

At lunchtime, she took Oscar out for a walk and handed off her mom's paperwork package to Phyllis. "Can you overnight that out, please?"

"You leaving for lunch?" Phyllis asked, fascinated. She leaned forward on her desk. "If Jack calls, what should I tell him?"

Like Jack would call her office. Phyllis was bored and fishing for details, and she was being totally obvious about it. She wanted to make a joke. *Yes, please tell Jack I've gone and bought a ton of latex for tonight.* Or *Tell Jack that his gimp costume is ready and I'll only respond to the name Dr. Mistress.* But it would fly right over Phyllis's head and only add to the rumors. "Just . . . send him to voicemail," she choked out, and left.

She went for a long walk, taking Oscar to the playground at a nearby church.

Why did everyone have to stick their noses in and ask

about her and Jack? They weren't anything yet. They hadn't even gone on a date. They'd literally talked for five minutes at the auction and had coffee yesterday. A handful of texts. That was it.

The more people made a big deal out of things, the more skittish it made Layla feel.

Oscar delicately picked through the icy grass, did his business, and immediately went to her side and put his paw on her leg, asking to be picked up. "You're such a diva," she grumbled, even as she scooped him up.

Her phone pinged with an incoming text.

Heart pounding, Layla took a deep breath and checked her screen.

Amy. Oh. Not that she was disappointed to hear from her friend . . . but it wasn't Jack, was it?

AMY: You are all that the teachers here are talking about today!!

AMY: Small-town celebrity status achieved!

Layla wanted to throw up.

LAYLA: Don't remind me. Everyone at the office won't leave me alone.

AMY: They're just bored and love having something to gossip about. It'll die soon.

AMY: Don't take it to heart. People just love a fairy tale!

LAYLA: It's not a fairy tale if we haven't even gone out on a date yet.

LAYLA: I'm tempted to call the whole thing off. You know I hate this.

LAYLA: You guys can keep the money but I just want to be left alone.

Long years of experience had taught Layla that attention inevitably brought with it bad feelings. She didn't like being scrutinized. She didn't like everyone nosing into her business. Maybe because it reminded her of her mother far too much, and inevitably she was waiting for someone to trot her flaws out for the entire town to see. You know, like her mother did.

Painted Barrel had felt safe and comfortable because it was quiet. Anonymous. Sure, she was the local quirky accountant, but every town had quirky people. That wasn't weird.

Now she was the weird single lady that had bid far too much on the hot guy. Now everyone was talking about her.

She wished she'd never gone to the stupid auction. She wished she'd told Becca and Amy that she was busy.

AMY: No! You cannot back out. You and Jack would make such a cute couple, I promise.

AMY: Just ignore everyone, okay?

Layla didn't respond. She rubbed Oscar's head and thought about going back to work. She could answer some of those emails that had come in over the weekend, but it felt strangely tiring to try to put on a normal face when she was feeling so out of sorts. In the end, she decided to grab her laptop and work from home. She returned to the office, put the OUT OF OFFICE sign on her door, and beat a hasty exit.

Even there, she couldn't escape all this date stuff, though. She'd no more than walked in the door when her phone pinged again with another incoming text.

JACK: Amy says you want to cancel?

JACK: Did I do something to offend you? If so, I apologize.

JACK: Can I call? Not a fan of texting.

Layla groaned. She set Oscar on the couch, and the dog sniffed worriedly at Sterling, who was sprawled on his favorite spot on the cushions. The cat growled low in his throat, tail flicking. "Behave, Sterling," she told the cat, and for a moment, she could relate. Sterling just wanted to be left alone. Layla just wanted to be left alone.

Oscar wagged his tail uncertainly, looking from her to the cat.

"We're pretty growly at first but I promise it's all bluster," she soothed the dog. She patted his head one more time, gave Sterling equal love, and then turned to her phone.

Before she could decide if she wanted to text Jack back, she had an incoming video call.

Oh shit. Unfair.

She inwardly winced at the thought of her messy bun, answered the phone, and glared at him. "You can't just video call someone without a heads-up."

"Why not?" His phone bobbed and she realized he was on horseback.

"Where are you?"

"Out in the field. Moving the cattle to a less muddy pasture. Where are you?"

"At home." She headed into the kitchen, intending to

make herself a cup of coffee. "The office was getting on my nerves."

Even from this angle, he was unearthly beautiful. Most people would look bad from a chin-up angle, but it somehow only highlighted the fact that he had a godly-looking jaw. Scruff was growing in, which only added to his sexiness. At the edge of the screen, she could see hints of the sky and the brim of his cowboy hat. His picture bobbed back and forth, and she could just imagine his hand resting on the pommel of his saddle, holding the phone.

"Amy says you're bailing out on me."

"I didn't say that," she grumped. "I just don't like how utterly fascinated everyone suddenly became in my love life."

"You made a big, public gesture. Of course it's going to follow you around for a few days."

"A few days?" she asked skeptically. "You sure it's not a few months? Longer?"

"I'm sure," he said, all confidence. "They'll get bored and move on to something else. You still want to bail on me?"

Layla sighed. "No."

"Good. Else I was going to have to come over there and spank you."

She sputtered. "You would not."

"You'd like it, don't worry."

"Oh my god, you're incorrigible."

"So I've heard."

Another voice boomed over his phone. "Can you quit flirting with your new girlfriend and get back to work?" One of his brothers, she guessed.

"Why?" Jack shot back, grinning. "The cattle don't care if I talk to her."

"Yeah, but Caleb's gonna vomit if he has to hear you giggling with her about spankings."

For the first time, she saw Jack scowl. "I'm not giggling."

"Giggling," came another voice.

Layla chuckled. "This is what happens when you take a personal call while at work. I can let you go."

"Not yet. Not until you say we're still on for Wednesday." He peered into the phone.

"I said we were, didn't I?" She felt shy.

"Okay, then." He paused. "And how's my son?" One of his brothers groaned, and he ignored them. "He doing okay?"

"He's doing great, and he can't wait to see Dad again on Wednesday."

"All right, then. Give him a big hug and kiss from me."

"You know he's a dog, right?"

"Okay, fine, I'll save the hug and kiss for you when I get there."

"I'm hanging up now." Mostly so he couldn't see her blush.

He chuckled. "See you Wednesday." He pointed at the screen. "I'd better."

"Yes, sir." She gave him a jaunty salute and hung up.

Well . . . she supposed that was that. He wasn't going to let her chicken out of their date after all. That made her feel good. Nervous, but good.

CHAPTER TWELVE

For some reason, Jack figured the days must have gotten longer. Someone out there in the universe had added several hours to every day, and an extra three days in before Wednesday. That must have been the reason why the week was crawling by so slowly. Didn't matter how much he threw himself into work, how many extra chores he did around the ranch; time seemed to crawl past.

Jack wanted to text Layla.

Often.

He didn't, because he didn't want to seem like a crazy person, but, man, he sure wanted to. He wasn't obsessed. He just . . . liked talking to her. Liked hearing her thoughts. She was the most charmingly fascinating person he'd met in a long, long time. He liked that she was alternately shy and yet somehow brash. That she was unafraid to be her own person despite her humdrum job. He liked that she had a sharp sense of humor and she was able to laugh at a situation, no matter how bad or strange. Jack had known a lot of girls that would have retreated after the bathroom mishap and gone home. Layla had stayed and laughed at her own predicament, even though he'd known she was embarrassed. She just wasn't embarrassed enough to let it ruin her day.

That was what he liked about her. He liked that she chose to have fun despite the hand that fate dealt her . . . and so he wasn't going to let her wiggle out of their date.

Jack had texted her casually throughout the last few days, just to check in on the dog. He was sure the dog was fine; it was just pretense. He wanted to talk to her. Hoped she'd send some cute photos of her cuddled up with the pup.

She'd played it cool, though. Cooler than he had, and Jack didn't like that. He was losing his head to a smart mouth and sparkling eyes, and he wanted her to fall with him. It was no fun if you fell in love alone, after all.

Not that he was in love . . . but the falling sure was fun.

Now it was the day of their scheduled date. The one he'd anticipated all week, had thought about more than he probably should have, the date she'd paid twenty-six hundred dollars to go on . . . and she was late.

That made him antsy.

Jack checked his phone for the time yet again, pacing near the barn. He'd given her the address. Confirmed that she'd be coming by this afternoon. He'd saddled two horses for them—the gentlest gelding they had for her, and his horse, Rocket, so he could ride alongside her. There was a bundle of snacks in a saddlebag—sure, it was February, but romance knew no season and she had a thick jacket, right?—and a thermos of cocoa. He'd shaved this morning, too. He'd wanted to grow his beard back out, but the scruffy four-day growth didn't look like date material in his eyes, and Jack was vain enough to want to look good for her. So he'd shaved clean and endured the joking of both Watson brothers. He'd ribbed them when they'd found their ladies, so he supposed it was only right that they tease him.

He paced around the barn, and when his nerves started to make the horses stomp, he headed out to the main house. Maybe by the time he got a coffee, she'd show up . . . unless she'd ghosted him.

The thought had no sooner crossed his mind than he was dialing the phone.

She picked up immediately and didn't even offer a greeting. "I'm almost there!"

Jack laughed. "I thought you might have done a runner on me."

She snorted, all prickly irritation, and he liked that. "No."

"Okay, good."

"Okay, *bye*." She hung up on him and he grinned. Oh yeah, she sounded thrilled to go horseback riding. Just *thrilled*.

Five minutes later, she pulled her car down the long gravel driveway leading to the ranch and parked it next to the row of pickup trucks out front. He wasn't entirely surprised to see she had an SUV (practical) in bright, neon green (not practical) with a bunch of bumper stickers plastered to the back.

She hopped out of the car as he approached, her hair pulled up into a bun, her glasses dominating her small face, and she wore a sweatshirt that looked like it was covered in bright pink and green dinosaurs.

"Nice car," he commented.

"I can find it in a parking lot at all times," Layla shot back. "Unlike you and your bright red truck that screams you're making up for other inadequacies."

He laughed, because he absolutely did have a bright red truck. "I can safely say that *that* is not the reason I have a bright red truck and I'm happy to show you proof."

"Cool it, Romeo. I have to get our son out of the back seat." But she tossed a grin in his direction, and his heart swelled a little. She didn't mind his outrageous flirting. Just rolled with the punches and didn't take him seriously.

Oh yeah, Layla made falling for her a lot of damn fun.

He approached as she opened the back door of her SUV and pulled the dog out. Oscar's little wiry tail was thumping overtime, and he wiggled with joy at the sight of Jack. Damn dog was melting his heart, too. He held his arms out and when she handed over Oscar, the dog was beside himself with joy, licking Jack's face.

"I think he missed you," Layla said. "He never greets me like that."

"He hasn't left your side in the last few days. He had time to miss me." He glanced over at her. "And you? Did you have time to miss me?"

Her cheeks flushed a pretty pink. "Absolutely not." But she smiled as she said it.

"I think one of us is lying," he confided, and was rewarded with a chuckle and a light batting hand at his shoulder.

"Oscar's been doing good," she told him. "Strangely enough, he likes my cat and Sterling tolerates him. I found them curled up together this morning, and I'm wondering if maybe Oscar just needs a buddy instead of constant carrying."

"Hmm. Maybe." He studied the little dog as he licked his face again. "Is this your way of telling me that you want full custody?"

"Not at all. I just . . ." She shrugged, tucking a lock of hair behind her ear. "Want to make it easy on you. I have an office so it's a little easier for me to take care of him during the week."

"So what I'm hearing is that weekends are mine."

That bright smile broke across her face. "I figured I could take him to visit Miss Cora tomorrow."

"I'm sure he'll love that." He rubbed the floppy ears and studied the gaudy sweater on the dog's body. "Is that a Wolverine costume?"

"It is, actually. I made it for him." She tugged at the bright yellow jacket and then pulled the little hood over the dog's face. Oscar growled at her hand but didn't snap, and she soothed him with a little touch. "Most of the dog sweaters are terribly ugly and without personality."

"He looks fantastic." Jack was in awe of her creativity. "I'm gonna have to get you to make me one."

She pretended to look distressed and leaned in, mock whispering. "I don't think you're the same size."

Jack threw his head back and laughed. Man, he loved her sharp tongue. "Come on. I'll introduce you to Uncle Ennis and then we'll get you on horseback."

"Oh goody, I can hardly wait."

Uncle Ennis loved Layla. That was no surprise, as she was damn adorable. She chatted with him as he checked over Oscar, doing an impromptu vet appointment as Layla talked things like taxes and bookkeeping.

"I wish I'd been using your service. You know I got audited last year? Had to pay a penalty, too." Uncle Ennis shook his head. "Animals, I'm good with. Taxes, not so much."

"Do you want me to take a look at your books?" she asked earnestly. "I'm happy to give them a glance over. For free, of course. I'd be a jerk if I tried to drum up business while on a date." She gave Jack a small smile.

"I would love for you to look them over," Uncle Ennis began.

"No," Jack said firmly. "She's stalling because she doesn't want to get on horseback."

"Busted," Layla agreed, grinning. "But I really will look at your paperwork. Just get it together for me and I'll take it home. It's a slow time of year for me and I can use a project."

His uncle nodded. "You're mighty kind." Uncle Ennis smirked. "And that means you probably deserve better than Jack."

"Busted," Jack joked, and sent her into a fit of giggles. "Now, come on. You'll watch Oscar for us, Doc?"

"Of course."

Jack put a hand to the small of Layla's back and steered her out of the veterinarian's office attached to the main ranch house and toward the distant barn.

"Why do you call him Doc?" Layla wanted to know.

"Everyone in town calls him Doc. He was here before the first doctor showed up in the area, so when people had a medical emergency, Uncle Ennis was sometimes called in. Name stuck, I guess."

She smiled up at him. "Sometimes I forget just how small this town is." Her smile faded. "Other times, it's impossible to forget."

"They still giving you grief in town?"

Layla shrugged, but he could tell it bothered her. "Just people being nosy. Asking far too many questions, not letting things go, the usual."

"Just being people, then."

She glanced over at him and gave him the briefest of smiles. "I guess so."

"Don't let it get to you. They're only fascinated because I'm so incredibly fine."

Laughter bubbled out of her at that. "Right. Okay."

He put a hand on the small of her back. "You know what will relax you?"

"If you say horseback riding, I'm going to kick you," she warned.

"Horseback riding," he agreed, feigning innocence.

Layla scowled over at him, and it was delightfully cute. *She* was delightfully cute. And he was absolutely loving this.

Jack escorted her to the barn, noting that she'd dressed appropriately for their date. She'd pulled a coat out of the car and some gloves, and while she wasn't wearing cowboy boots, her heavy combat boots would protect her all the same.

"I have to say," Layla began as they entered the barn. "I don't feel I'm getting my money's worth."

He looked over at her in surprise. "Is something wrong?"

"You're not wearing spurs or chaps." She shook her head, tsking. "Very un-cowboy of you."

That made him grin. "I'll wear them for our weekend date, deal?"

She held up her smallest finger. "Pinky swear?"

He hooked his in hers. "Pinky swear." Jack might have found the only woman as irreverent as he was, and his heart wasn't gonna survive this.

Layla's playful demeanor lasted until they got into the barn and he introduced her to the horses. She petted their noses and they fed them apples, but when he gestured that they should mount up, an uncertain look crossed her face. "I've never ridden a horse before."

"I'll help you mount. You can do it."

She bit her lip, glancing up at Rocket. "It's just . . . they're awfully . . . big from this angle."

"You say that to all the men you buy at auctions, don't you?"

That earned him a laugh, and he got a mounting block and set it next to her mount, Cameo, the most docile palomino he'd ever seen, and Uncle Ennis's favorite horse. Cameo was unflappable and remained perfectly still even as Layla nervously took his hand and stood atop the mounting block.

"Swing your leg over," he instructed her, and when she tried and her leg wouldn't go all the way, he quickly put his hands on her ass and hefted her all the way up into the saddle. Layla squealed a protest. "You have to get on right away or it confuses the horses," he explained. "Trust me, if I just wanted to grab your ass, there's easier ways to go about it."

"So you say." Her voice was wobbly and her hands were glued to the pommel. She listed to the side, her shoulders hunched. "I feel like I'm sliding."

"You're not sliding. Grab the reins."

"I'm sliding!"

She was, in fact, sliding. He watched as she inched over, falling a little too far on the opposite side, and he hurried over to Cameo's other side to grab her before she dropped onto the floor of the barn. No sooner did he move into place than she slid right off the saddle and into his arms.

Layla let out a little choked cry and flung her limbs around him, squeezing him like an octopus. Jack coughed, staggered just enough to keep his balance, and managed to somehow stay upright.

"How the hell do you fall off a horse?" he asked, curious. Even people that weren't naturals in the saddle didn't immediately slide off the other side.

"Maybe . . . maybe the saddle's loose."

"The saddle isn't loose," he promised her. "You were leaning over too far."

"Because it felt like I was going to fall off!" She pushed her glasses up her nose and frowned up at him. "I've changed my mind. I don't want to go horseback riding."

Oh no, she wasn't going to get away from him that easily. He'd been around enough inexperienced horse riders to know when someone was afraid to ride. Jack rubbed a hand up and down her back. "How about we ride together? You can just hold on to me and I'll handle everything else."

She relaxed. "I'd like that."

CHAPTER THIRTEEN

A short time later, both of them were on Rocket, and the horse ambled along at an easy pace instead of racing off into the hills like his name proclaimed. Layla was still nervous atop the horse, even though she sat in front of Jack on the saddle with his arms around her and they were more or less crawling, speed-wise. The cattle were in one of the nearer pastures, so he opened the gate and headed in that direction.

"Why are we going in with the cattle?" Layla asked, tense.

"Just to ride around. Giving you the full cowboy experience and all." He shut the gate, noticing she was slumped forward and clinging to the pommel again. It was like her bones deserted her the moment he dismounted. Biting back a laugh, he mounted again behind her, ignoring her indignant squawk when the saddle jostled. "Come on, this is fun, isn't it?"

"Board games are fun. Watching Netflix is fun. Playing *Animal Crossing* is fun. This? It's very . . . outdoorsy."

Jack laughed. "That it is."

"It's not terrible, I guess," she offered as he guided the horse forward. The cattle mostly ignored them, moving around Rocket and casting hopeful looks after the horse. "Why are they all so fat?"

"The cattle? They're pregnant. They're gonna have calves right around the beginning of April."

"Tax season. Busy for everyone, I suppose." She wrinkled that cute nose of hers, and for a moment, he thought the glasses would slip off her face entirely. "So these are all girl cows?"

His mouth twitched. "They are. I guess they left their skirts in the barn."

She giggled and smacked his leg. "Hush. I told you I don't know anything about cows." Layla craned her head, watching them wander past. "They're close."

"They're gonna follow us because they're hoping to get fed," he pointed out to her. "Just ignore them. They're harmless."

"No boy cows in here?"

"No bulls, no. They're a lot more aggressive."

"Huh." Layla was quiet for a while, and he enjoyed watching her process the sights. She eyed the cattle and the snowy landscape. She watched the horse and gazed at the distant mountains, and her nose wrinkled again as they passed by the muddy watering hole. They left the herd behind—once the cattle figured out they weren't getting fed—and headed further out. "Where are we going?"

"Just up the next ridge," he promised her. "The view's nice. It's not too much further."

They rode along for a little while longer before Layla glanced over her shoulder at him and spoke. "They make this a lot sexier in the books, you know."

"What books?"

"Romance novels." She arched an eyebrow at him. "Don't you dare judge."

"Not judging anything. They talk about being a cowboy?"

"No, I meant riding on horseback. There's even a book where the main couple make love on the back of a horse and it's all very dramatic and romantic." She shifted in her seat. "The reality is a lot more irritating to the ass."

He snorted with amusement. "I can think of a lot of places to make love to a woman, and on horseback is not anywhere on that list."

"No?"

"Nope. If I'm holding on to the reins, I'm not holding on to you. Pass."

She giggled. "You're ruining all my fantasies."

"Well now, if it is a fantasy of yours, I'm happy to give it a try, uncomfortable or not. Do I have to wear my spurs? Is that in the fantasy?"

Her laughter grew louder. "I've never given it much thought."

"I'm disappointed in you. Here I thought we were living out one of your kinky fantasies."

Layla's laughter pealed out across the land, and it warmed him from head to toe. "I'm sorry to disappoint, but most of my fantasies are very mundane."

"Tell me about them and I'll be the judge of that."

"Nice try."

"A man's always got to try."

She chuckled, casting a grin over her shoulder at him, and he felt his stupid heart skip a damn beat. She really was the cutest. He already loved her laugh, her sense of humor, her everything.

Jack needed to send Becca the biggest thank-you bouquet of flowers ever for dragging him into that stupid bachelor auction. He tightened his arm around Layla's waist and leaned in. "We're almost there. Just ahead."

She seemed to lean back against him, and it felt natural and right.

Was it possible to fall for a girl on a first date? Jack would have said no in the past, but Caleb had fallen for Amy the first time he saw her, and Hank was smitten with Becca for months before they went out. So maybe it was a Watson thing. Maybe they just fell hard and fell fast.

He was okay with that.

Jack halted Rocket and slid down the horse's side. Layla looked at him anxiously and gave a boneless slide into his arms, and then waddled forward gingerly, holding her ass. "My butt muscles are protesting."

"I'm happy to massage them for you if needed," he promised, rubbing Rocket's nose. "This is the spot. You like it?"

Most people would probably think the view wasn't much to see. They were at the top of a snowy ridge, but from this particular spot, the land dipped down and it seemed like it extended for miles up ahead, just rolling grasses and snow—and the ever-present mountains in the distance. He liked it because it was quiet here, and open. It let him think.

"It's beautiful," she admitted, hugging her arms to her chest. "I don't think I've ever been this far out of town. It looks like a Bob Ross painting out here."

He laughed. "Isn't that the guy with the weird hair?" He'd seen a few videos online.

"'Happy little accidents,'" she quoted. "I turn it on in the background sometimes when I'm working on something and need noise. I've never painted one, though. Have you?"

"Me? Nah. Definitely wouldn't be a happy little accident if I touched it. I'm not very artistic." He pulled the bundle he'd prepared for their date out of one of Rocket's saddle packs. Inside was a thin blanket, a thermos of hot cocoa, and a few cookies.

Layla turned to look at him as he began to spread out the blanket. "Are you serious? We're having a picnic?"

"Full cowboy experience, just like I promised," he said. "You should get your money's worth."

"What if I want my money's worth somewhere inside, near a heater?" She shivered in her coat. "You do realize it's February, don't you?"

He settled the blanket on the snow. "We won't be out here that long, fussypants. Come sit."

"Fussypants," she grumbled. "Really now." But Layla sat down on the blanket, pushed her glasses up her nose, and took the thermos cup he offered her. She made a little noise of appreciation at the hot chocolate, and then offered the cup to him as he sat down next to her. "Okay, so this isn't so bad."

He grinned at her reluctant praise. "Have to admit, sometimes I like coming out here to think."

"What does a guy like you think about?" she asked, taking the cocoa back from him.

He shrugged. "Might seem silly, but I think about having a ranch of my own someday."

Layla frowned at him, sipping the cocoa and then handing it back. "Why would that seem silly? I think if that's what you want to do, you should absolutely go for it."

He took a drink and then shrugged. Some of his self-effacing humor threatened to bubble up, but he held it back. "You don't think I'm too much of a clown to run a ranch?"

"Why would I think that? You're allowed to be a clown and still be good at your job." She leaned over, nudging him with her arm. "I happen to know a clown of an accountant who'd be more than happy to help you with your paperwork if you go that route."

He grinned. "You make it sound so simple."

"That's because it is simple. You just have to be stubborn enough to pursue it even when people tell you that you can't." She smiled up at him. "Look at me. I got my degree in a field my mother hated because it was something I liked. I started my own business even though she told me I'd fold in a month. And here I am." Layla shrugged. "It's not a huge business but I have enough to keep me busy and I love being in charge of my own life. So don't let anyone tell you that you can't. I'm going to tell you, as a clown accountant, that you can do it."

His smile grew wider with every word she said. He liked that about her—that Layla chose the positive aspects of life no matter what it threw at her. He wanted to point out that her mother was an absolutely wretched human being, but Layla knew that. Instead, he leaned in closer to her, watching her pink mouth as it settled on the rim of the cup again.

He wanted to kiss her.

She glanced up at him, and her gaze went to his mouth. Her lips parted, and for a moment, it felt like time stood still.

"Can this clown of a cowboy kiss you?" he murmured.

"This clown of an accountant will allow it," Layla breathed.

She didn't lean into him, but that was all right. Jack took the empty cup from her hands and set it down on the blanket, then touched a finger under her chin, tipping her face up. He leaned in, and he could smell the cocoa on her breath, and he'd have sworn it was the most erotic thing he'd ever scented, better than the most expensive of perfumes. Leaning down, he brushed his lips over hers.

She quivered underneath him, remaining perfectly still for a too-long moment, and then her mouth softened under his. His first impression was of sweetness, not just the cocoa but the feel of her against him, the way she was so soft and perfect. His nose bumped against her glasses, and she chuckled, pulling back long enough to take them off. "Sorry. It's been a while since I kissed anyone."

Good. He liked that, for some reason. That made her feel like his and his alone. He brushed his knuckles along her jaw again and brought her in for another kiss. He kept it soft and gentle, playful instead of intense. Lightly, he moved over her mouth, nipping and tasting as if he had all the time in the world to savor her. When her lips parted under his, a silent invitation for more, he brushed his tongue along the seam of her mouth.

She moaned against him, leaning in.

"God, you taste sweet," he murmured, cupping her face and pulling her closer for another round of kisses. He peppered her face with them, flirty, quick kisses, sometimes accompanied with a flick of his tongue, just enough to tease her into wanting more . . . he hoped. He wouldn't push. If Layla wanted more, she'd let him know.

And let him know, she did. When he pulled away again, she flung her arms around his neck and launched herself against him, bearing him backward onto the blanket. Her mouth was hot on his, and frantic. This time, it was her tongue that pushed into his mouth, and Layla took the lead on the kiss. Letting her kiss him was different, he decided, and he liked it. She was aggressive and hungry, her mouth wild on his own, her tongue flicking against his. She wanted this just as much as he did, and he groaned with the realization. They could flirt and banter circles around each other, but a kiss showed passion, and Layla was so passionate it made his chest ache.

Damn, he wanted this woman.

He lifted his head as she moaned and pressed one final, tiny kiss on her swollen mouth. "We should stop."

"Why?" There was a hint of a whine in her voice, and damn if that didn't make him hard as a rock.

"Because if we don't, I'm gonna be all over you and I don't want your prettiest parts getting frostbite out here in the snow."

"Shows how much you know," Layla commented as she rolled off his chest. "All of my parts are pretty."

God, she was perfect.

CHAPTER FOURTEEN

The cowboy date ended far too soon, to his thinking. Jack had wanted to stay out for a while longer, but the wind was biting, and Layla had started to shiver. She wasn't used to being out in this all day long, didn't wear the layers he did, and so he reluctantly packed their things up and helped her back onto the horse, and then they rode back to the barn.

Oscar was thrilled to see them return, tiny tail wagging back and forth as he looked from Jack to Layla and back to Jack again.

"I hope he wasn't any trouble," Layla said to Uncle Ennis.

"Not at all. I thought the two of you would be gone longer, to be honest." Ennis gave Jack a curious look. "My nephew losing his charm?"

His girl gave the most indelicate snort. "It's too cold out, even for someone as charming as him."

"So you admit I'm charming?" Jack couldn't help but butt in.

She ignored that, turning toward him.

"Are we still on for this weekend?" Layla asked even as she scooped up the dog and scratched his fat sides. "Because now that I've seen what it's like on horseback, you really don't have time to haul Oscar around with you."

He didn't point out that Uncle Ennis would be more than happy to keep the dog with him in the vet clinic on the ranch. Oscar looked mighty comfy tucked against Layla's chest, and for the first time, he was jealous of a dog. "You want him until the weekend, then?"

She gave him a teasing look. "I figure this way you have to go out with me again."

"As if you could stop me."

Her cheeks pinked and she smiled. "Like I said, I do want to visit Cora tomorrow."

"If you're sure you don't mind taking him?" When she shook her head, he pretended to reluctantly agree. "In that case, I'll let our son go with you on one condition."

Layla glanced over at his uncle, her face turning redder. "Do I want to know?"

Uncle Ennis made a face, throwing his hands in the air. "I'm hearing far too much." He nodded at Layla. "Nice to meet you, young lady, and I didn't get a chance to pull together that paperwork just yet, but I'll send it over with Jack this weekend."

Her mouth twitched with amusement. "I look forward to it." They watched silently as the elderly veterinarian left, and then Layla shot him a look. "Well? What's your condition?" Her gaze went to his mouth and he realized she was thinking of kisses.

Damn, he liked her idea better than his. "A goodbye kiss and I also want pictures at least once a day."

"Of me or the dog?"

"Yes," he agreed solemnly, and she burst into laughter again.

"Just one kiss?"

"For now." He'd take all her kisses soon enough, but for now, he'd be content with just one. Jack pulled her close until she bumped up against his chest and the dog was sandwiched between them.

"Watch your hands," she murmured, her gaze going soft and sultry as she looked up at him.

"Just a kiss," he promised her, and gave her a light, teasing one.

For now.

CHAPTER FIFTEEN

Jack thought about their date all night. A few things stayed in his head long after Layla had said goodbye and driven off with Oscar. He thought about her even after she texted a good-night picture of her and the dog in matching sleep shirts. He thought about the way her mouth had felt against his, the intoxicating taste of cocoa and Layla that was going to haunt him for the rest of his days. He thought about how good she'd felt in front of him on the horse; even though she'd been nervous and scared, she'd done real well. He thought about her sunny laughter. The constant stream of jokes and how she poked back at him. He loved all of that.

And he kept thinking about . . . the way she viewed him. To her, he wasn't the jokester youngest brother, good for nothing but chasing skirts. Layla hadn't seen a problem with him buying a ranch. She hadn't doubted him for a second. If he wanted a ranch, she thought he should buy a ranch. There was no doubt in her mind that he could do it.

It was that simple confidence in him that he hadn't realized he'd needed. He'd been sitting on the real estate agent's email for days now. She'd said she was ready to look at property whenever he was . . . but he hadn't been sure if he was ready or not.

Layla made it sound so simple. She was confident he could do it . . . and that was what he'd needed to nudge him forward. He pulled out his phone and sent an email back to the Realtor before he backed out.

Can we look tomorrow? I'm free in the afternoon.

The Realtor immediately emailed back, thrilled, and they set up a time and place to meet. Jack felt a rush of excitement course through him, and he wanted to tell someone.

Immediately, he flipped over to Layla's number. She'd texted the bedtime picture twenty minutes ago, so he didn't want to wake her up . . . but maybe she was still up.

JACK: You up?

LAYLA: Will you judge me if I say I spent the last 20 minutes scrolling through funny dog videos online?

JACK: Not as long as you send me the best ones.

JACK: I'm gonna go look at land tomorrow. For a potential ranch.

JACK: Kinda nervous.

JACK: You want to go with?

LAYLA: I wish I could but I'm busy tomorrow visiting Cora. I don't want to disappoint her! ☹

JACK: I forgot. No big deal. I just . . . I'm excited. Wanted to share it with someone.

LAYLA: I bet you'll find just what you're looking for. This is great, Jack! I'm so proud of you. And if you need an accountant to look anything over for you, I'm happy to help.

JACK: I really appreciate the confidence. Didn't know I was so nervous about this. Guess I keep expecting someone to tell me I shouldn't do it.

LAYLA: If they do, then that's all the more reason to get it done.

She sent the devil emoji, and he laughed. That sounded like Layla—stubborn and ornery . . . and fun.

JACK: Night. Thanks for listening.

LAYLA: Keep me posted. I want details!!

JACK: Will do.

CHAPTER SIXTEEN

The moment he saw the property, he knew.

Jack stared at his surroundings. He couldn't believe a piece of land this gorgeous—and reasonably close to town—was for sale. Snow covered everything, of course, but what he could see was rolling and pastoral and stretched all the way to a nearby stream. The water wound through the valley, bordered by hills, and the natural greenery was abundant, even in winter. It was perfect. It was everything he'd ever wanted. He envisioned piecing it off into different pastures, a horse corral over there, a large barn, and the house at the top of one of the hills. Beautiful, and exactly what he was looking for.

Jack pretended to consider it, though. He scratched his chin and walked around the stream several times, but his heart was racing.

"Well?" his Realtor, Anna, asked. "What do you think?"

"Kinda flat." Jack kicked a bit of mud off of his boot. "Kinda muddy, too." Really, neither of those was a problem. He just needed to make it seem as if he wasn't too eager.

"I thought so, too. I asked if it was in a floodplain and the owner assured me that it isn't. The stream's just high right now." Anna ruffled through a few printouts. "I asked her to send over plat information and a survey, but it doesn't look like I have it yet."

"I definitely want to see that," Jack agreed, but in his mind, he was already placing buildings. He was home.

He couldn't wait to tell Layla.

You look good, Miss Cora," Layla told the other woman as she spotted her. The Pine Grove assisted-living facility had some depressing residents, and she'd been a little worried that her visit might cause problems. The people at the front desk were extremely nice, though, and thrilled to see Oscar. Layla signed into the guest registry before she was led down a hall and into a chaotic-looking private room.

Cora was a woman after Layla's own heart. Not the endless Elvis Presley pictures and motifs that covered every surface, but that Cora was clearly unafraid to be her own person. She wore bright pink lipstick, a neon purple blouse, and a baby pink skirt with glittery sneakers. An equally pink bow was in Cora's fluffy white hair, and she had rings on every finger.

"I was wondering if you were going to show up with my dog," Cora said. She sat in an easy chair that had a bright chartreuse knitted shawl across the back, her walker nearby. The room looked a bit like Lisa Frank had vomited everywhere, but it was cheery.

"Don't get up," Layla said. "I'll bring him to you. He likes to be held all the time."

"Of course he does. Who wouldn't?" Cora held her arms

out for the dog, and Layla carefully placed him inside, mindful of the hand situation. Oscar settled in against Cora's narrow body as if he'd always belonged to her, his tail whipping happily as he licked her hand. Cora's face creased into a bright smile. "I'm glad to see you both. It's been a hell of a week."

Layla giggled. "Do tell."

It was really a lovely visit. Layla had never been close to her own grandparents, because her mother had no relationship with her parents and her father lived overseas. Visiting Cora was like having a grandmother, she supposed, as Cora went on and on about gossip at Pine Grove. Or so she'd thought . . . because the gossip quickly got dirty.

"I told Dottie to quit sleeping around because she was going to give everyone chlamydia, but no." Cora rolled her eyes, patting Oscar. "Next thing you know, Hubert and Frank both have it."

Layla cleared her throat politely. "I'm sure she didn't give it to them—"

"I'm sure she did. Ever since her husband died, Dottie thinks she's queen bee around here. If she was smart, she'd keep her legs shut. There's no good dick to be found around here." Cora leaned in. "Speaking of, how is your handsome young man?"

The look in Cora's eyes was far too sharp. "Um, great?" Layla rocked in the rocking chair across from Cora nervously, playing with the hem of her T-shirt. "I saw him yesterday, you know. For our official date."

"The one you paid for?"

Layla grimaced. "Yep. Everyone in town has been giving me shit for it, too."

"Nosy bastards."

That made Layla laugh. "Indeed. I guess I can't blame them, though. Jack is the hottest guy I've seen around here and I did pay quite a bit for him."

"Doesn't give them the right to stick their noses in your business."

Oh, she liked Cora a lot. "I thought so, too. But we had a lovely date."

"How lovely?" The sly look was back in Cora's eyes.

"Not quite *that* lovely. We kissed. That was all."

Cora snorted. "Sounds boring. You've got to bring me better gossip, honey. It's sad when Dottie gets around more than you, and she's eighty-three."

Layla's lips twitched, and it was an effort not to burst into laughter. "Well, we have another date this weekend."

Cora nodded. "Good. Lock that shit down before he gets away from you. Men that pretty don't stay single for long."

"That's kind of what I'm worried about." Layla bit her lip, wishing she had her crochet or some cross-stitch to occupy her hands. Maybe she'd bring some next time. She could work while Cora held Oscar. The dog himself seemed to be loving the attention—Cora scratched his fat flanks constantly and he was cradled perfectly in her arms, his head tucked into the crook of her elbow as he slept. "I'm a little nervous about the date," Layla confessed.

"Nervous? Why?"

"He's out of my league." She tucked a lock of hair back behind her ear. "Jack's gorgeous. Flirty *and* gorgeous. It's a lethal combination, you know? I really think he could get anyone, and me, well . . ." Layla gestured at her outfit—jeans and a T-shirt, her hair tucked into a bun. "I'm very . . . average." That was the nicest way she could think to put it.

"Bullshit." Cora shook her head. "You've got sparkle. That makes up for a lot."

"Sparkle?"

Cora nodded. "Guys like him can get any girl they want, you're absolutely right. And he's probably had a ton of pretty girls in his past."

"This isn't making me feel much better—"

"But you have sparkle. You're smart. And witty. And you've got a smile that lights up your whole face. You're happy. It shows." She nodded sagely. "Sparkle wins out over a pair of big boobs any day."

"I need to cross-stitch that onto a pillow," Layla joked.

"See? Sparkle." Cora winked. "Looks fade. Tits sag. Sparkle stays."

"I think I love you, Cora."

"Good. That means you'll come back." The older woman sighed and hugged the dog against her chest. "This place gets really dull sometimes. I like having visitors."

Layla's heart squeezed. She wanted to ask where Cora's family was, where her grandkids were. Maybe they visited and Cora was just being dramatic. Maybe she didn't have anyone. It didn't matter. "Can I come back on Tuesday? I promise to bring Oscar."

Cora's smile was sweet. "I'd like that. How are you at cooking?"

"Cooking?"

"Yeah, I could go for some cupcakes."

Layla sputtered. "Is this a shakedown for a treat-delivery service?"

"Maybe." Cora lifted her chin defensively. "You take your pleasures where you can find them."

"Now you sound like Dottie," Layla pointed out, and Cora barked with laughter. Her phone pinged; it was a text from Jack.

JACK: You should see this place. It's everything I wanted.

JACK: And the price is just right.

She beamed down at her phone. She could practically imagine his excitement, and she wanted to share it with him.

"That your man?" Cora asked.

"It is." Layla blushed. Her man. If anyone else asked, Layla would have denied it. But there was something about Cora's blunt nature—or maybe it was her obvious loneliness—that made Layla want to confide in her. "Sometimes he texts me just to get pictures of Oscar throughout the day. I think he misses him."

"Right. He misses the dog." Cora winked exaggeratedly. "Do you send him nudes?"

"What? No!" She mock-frowned. "I've got sparkle, re-member?"

"Sparkle only gets you so far, girlfriend."

And Layla collapsed into the rocker with laughter.

J ack watched his phone, waiting for Layla to text back. She'd said she was busy, but he needed to hear from her. Needed someone else to be excited for him.

Finally, the text came through.

> LAYLA: That's amazing! I'm so excited for you.
> You'll tell me all about it on Saturday? Bring details
> and we'll do some online investigating. And bring
> your financials so I can work up a P&L for you.

> LAYLA: So proud of you!

Jack grinned at his phone. That was what he'd needed to hear. And a moment later, when he got a picture of Cora, Layla, and Oscar all making funny faces, he burst into laughter.

Today, he decided, was a great day.

> JACK: I want to come on the next visit to Cora. Tell
> her I said hello and that she looks beautiful.

LAYLA: She says she knows and her calendar is free. ☺

His own calendar was filling up, and for the first time since leaving Alaska, he was looking forward to what Painted Barrel had to offer.

CHAPTER SEVENTEEN

All things considered, Layla was having a pretty good week. Sure, there were a few ugly spots—her mother had sent her a couple of snotty texts, implying that Layla was ungrateful and worthless, but not to worry, Janet had things covered. She was going to sell her land and make a fortune and then Layla would be sorry for being so mean to her mother.

Layla just rolled her eyes.

Then, of course, there were the nosy townspeople. Since the auction had picked up steam in the gossip mill, everyone seemed to want to talk to Layla about Jack, or speculate about if they were going to get married.

Considering they'd only had two quasi-dates, Layla wasn't about to chime in on that one. She let them say what they wanted, but sometimes it was hard to ignore.

Other than that, it was a good week. She got a few projects off her desk, the weather was nice, she'd had a date with Jack and seen Cora, and her phone was filled with funny texts from her friends . . . and from Jack. Actually, she and Jack had started texting all day long. At first it had just been a cowboy meme she'd sent to him. Then a picture of Oscar, lying meekly next to her enormous, cranky cat Sterling and letting the feline tongue-bathe his ears. By the end of the week, it had morphed into constantly checking in with each other, flirty little pings and sharing links that were interesting, and photos. Lots of photos.

So, yeah, it was a good week.

They'd texted all night Friday night, until late. He'd asked her what she was doing, and she'd mentioned amendments for a client. He'd asked what movie she had going in the background—proof that he knew her far too well already—and then had turned on the same movie and they'd texted each other throughout.

It was fun. He made even the mundane fun.

And now it was Saturday and she couldn't wait for their date.

Well, "couldn't wait" was a bit of a misstatement. She was excited . . . and also downright terrified. Because this was going to be an official date. This was dinner, and wine, and a session at a nearby Sip & Paint that Layla had always wanted to try. She'd offered to organize the date when he asked her where she wanted to go, and so he was going to show up at her place at five and they'd head out.

That afternoon, Layla tried on every single piece of clothing she owned. She prided herself on being low-key and casual, but today she wanted to be fun and flirty, and she wanted Jack to find her sexy. The last few times he'd seen her, she was wearing jeans and a T-shirt. Tonight, she'd wear a dress and maybe some heels.

Layla loved casual wear . . . except when it came to shoes and purses. With those, the more pricey the better, and she pulled out a pair of stiletto Louboutins she'd gotten secondhand from Amy and hugged them close. God, she loved pretty shoes. They were utter crap to walk in, but they made her feel sexy. She tried on dress after dress, searching for just the right look, and eventually settled on a high-neck long-sleeve dress that she'd bought online a few years ago and had never had the chance to wear. It was fairly plain, a muted olive green that was probably all wrong for winter, but she didn't care. She'd bought the dress because the hem was embroidered with flowers, and between each flower and the next was a filthy, delicately embroidered French cuss word. She could wear this with her black Louboutins, though, and still feel somewhat stylish and sexy. Layla pulled her hair up in a neat bun, added some dangling earrings, and worked for nearly an hour on getting decent-looking wings to her eyeliner.

When it was close to go time, she took Oscar for a quick walk in the backyard and then tucked him back inside his bed. He didn't like to be left alone, but she'd given him calming treats and put on a ThunderShirt, which helped settle him. He'd been snuggling with Sterling lately, and she hoped that between all those things, he wouldn't panic. Just to be on the safe side, she tucked one of her sleep shirts in the bed with him so he could have her smell.

Her phone rang. She checked the screen and inwardly winced when she saw it was Janet. Her mother really had terrible timing. Layla clicked over as she slicked on some lipstick. "Make it snappy, Mom, I have plans."

"Hello to you, too, dear, and I know you're lying." Janet sounded miffed. "You never have Saturday night plans unless it's work."

"Well, I have a date, thank you very much." God, how petty was she that she had to fling that into her mother's face? Layla had told herself time and time again she had nothing to prove to Janet, and then she felt the need to point out things like that.

"Did you pay for this one, too?" Janet cooed.

Layla gritted her teeth. And that was what happened when you gave Janet information. She used it against you. "No. Jack and I are having a real date now. There's no exchange of money, thank you."

"Oh, a date? I'm so excited for you, honey. Make sure you have some liquid courage, Layla-belle. It'll help you loosen up." Her mom's tone had changed from sniping to sweet in an instant, and Layla wasn't sure how to handle it.

She was nervous, though. Her skin tingled with anxiety and she wanted nothing more than to grab her crochet stuff and hook a few rows just to get some of the nerves out. "Are you telling me to get drunk?"

"I absolutely am. I love you, Layla-belle, but you know how you get."

Her stomach churned. When Layla got nervous, she got loud, and a bit obnoxious, and chatty. The more she tried to stop, the worse it got, too. "It's fine, Mom."

"All I'm saying is that you don't want to act like a virgin around a man like that or you'll definitely lose him." She tittered. "I might have to show up just to scoop him up if you do."

Okay, she was definitely going to have a drink or three the moment they got to the restaurant. The words "act like a virgin" made her feel like an utter loser, just as they were intended. "Did you need something, Mom? I'm about to head out the door."

"I just wanted to see if you were interested in having lunch this week. Or maybe this weekend? I can tell you all about my investments and you can tell me what you think!" Her mother's tone took on a chirpy note, as if she were doing Layla a favor.

"Oh gosh, I'm real busy, Mom. Let me take a look at my schedule and get back to you—"

"You know I have a buyer for my land?"

"The floodplain?"

"It's not a floodplain. The paperwork was wrong." Janet huffed. "We're disputing it right now, no thanks to you. It'll sell and then I can go yachting in Mykonos with Adrian."

Yachting? Mykonos? Adrian? She knew her mom was dropping tidbits because she wanted to steer the conversation, but Layla didn't have time. "Maybe next weekend?"

"Let me know. Love you, Layla-belle. Remember, liquid courage!"

Oh, like she was going to forget now?

The doorbell rang, five minutes early, and Layla's heart leapt in her throat.

"Coming," she croaked, and winced at how unnatural that sounded. She tottered toward the door in her shoes—okay, they were a bit higher, heel-wise, than she'd anticipated, but she'd get used to them—and opened the door.

Jack stood on her porch with a single flower and a grin, and he took her breath away.

This was quite possibly the first time she'd seen him without his cowboy hat on. She knew from his sideburns and beard scruff that he was dark-haired, but she had no idea that his hair was so damn thick and had just a hint of curl to it, making it wave roguishly over his brow. He wore dark jeans and a big silver belt buckle, and cowboy boots, and his shirt was a somber button-up in deep gray that fit him far better than any shirt had a right to. She was willing to bet the man didn't have an ounce of fat, and the thought was both thrilling and a little alarming, because Layla loved a damn doughnut, and her pudgy stomach showed it.

He held the flower out to her, a single red rose. "Cliché, I know, but sometimes a good cliché is worth it." His gaze roamed over her, and the look in his eyes was appreciative as he noted her dress and bare legs. "You look stunning."

A million pithy, sarcastic jokes sprang to mind and then quickly died. "Thanks," she croaked, and hated that she sounded like a dying frog every time she opened her mouth. "Do you . . . want to come in?"

"Is Oscar going to want to chaperone if I do?"

"Good point." She grabbed her jacket and purse and glanced into the living room. Already, Sterling was crawling into the dog bed next to Oscar, licking the sleepy dachshund's head. "I think we're good." She stepped outside and gave Jack a bright smile. "Who's driving?"

"I'm happy to drive if you'll tell me where we're going." He gave her an easy grin. "Or is it top secret?"

"Not a secret. Dinner and then we're heading over to the Sip & Paint."

"The what?"

"It's a place where you drink wine and paint a picture. I got the idea after you mentioned Bob Ross the other day, and it's something I've wanted to do for a while. Is . . . that okay?"

He shrugged. "I'm game as long as I'm with you."

Layla beamed at him with relief. "Awesome, shall we get going?"

He tilted his head at her, and he looked so boyish that her heart stopped. "We forgetting something?"

She furrowed her brows. "Oscar? Because I don't think they'll let us bring him in—"

His hand went to her waist and he pulled her in against him. Jack smiled down at her, his nose brushing against hers before he leaned in and gave her the lightest of kisses. "Hello," he whispered. "Missed you."

Oh god, this man was going to make her melt into a puddle. "Missed you, too." She curled her fingers against his shirt. "Is . . . this how we're going to greet each other from now on?"

"I think it has merit, don't you?"

"I don't know," she teased back. "I didn't get any tongue—"

Layla didn't even get the words out before Jack's mouth

was on hers again, and this time, his tongue swept into her mouth and conquered her with dizzying strokes. By the time he pulled away, she was breathless and wobbly-kneed, and his mouth was smeared with her nude lipstick. She'd never seen anything sexier.

"That's how I should greet you every time," he told her.

"I like your idea better than mine," Layla managed. Okay, if this was a sign of how the date would go, it was off to a great start. She was a little nervous, she realized as she reached up to brush some of the smears of her lipstick off Jack's mouth, but a glass of wine or two would help with that.

He grinned down at her, swiping the back of his hand over his lips and wiping away the rest of her lipstick, and that nervousness doubled in her belly. Why was she so anxious?

Oh right, because he was sexy and gorgeous and kissed her like her virginity belonged to him. Tonight could be her night.

The butterflies in her stomach seemed to triple in size.

Jack wondered if it was a bad sign that his cute, sexy date was downing wine like it was going out of style. Layla seemed to be in a good mood. She'd chatted happily as they'd drove a few towns away to grab dinner at a casual restaurant, and she'd ordered a glass of wine. He'd kept to water, since he was driving, and figured she was just enjoying herself. Nothing wrong with a nice glass of wine.

But then she'd ordered another.

By the time they finished dinner, his date was decidedly tipsy. The tip of her nose was pink, and her cheeks were flushed, and she just kept smiling at him as if he'd hung the moon.

It was cute . . . but it was also a little odd. After she'd downed her third glass of wine before dessert, Jack had begun to wonder if something was wrong. Did she normally drink herself into oblivion on dates? Or did she just not go on many dates?

He suspected it was the latter, given that her mother had made the virginity cracks, and Layla herself had never confirmed or denied it.

"You okay?" Jack asked as she downed another glass of red. The waiter set dessert in front of them—a wedge of cheesecake covered in strawberry slices and topped with whipped cream—and placed two spoons on the table.

Layla beamed at him, her expression sweet. "I'm having a wonderful time, actually."

"You drunk?"

She shook her head, so slowly and sternly that it told him, yes, she absolutely was drunk. Layla leaned in, as if confiding a secret. "I'm just having a little wine to loosen up."

"Ah." His mouth twitched. "Because I'm so scary and intimidating?"

"Very," she told him solemnly. "You're too pretty." Layla grabbed a spoon and sliced off a bite of the cheesecake, nibbling on it.

"So you'd feel better if I was uglier?"

"Oh, *so* much better," Layla agreed. "Then I wouldn't feel so overwhelmed."

"Overwhelmed?" He was honestly surprised. "Because of me?"

She nodded solemnly. "I like you. And I'm afraid I'm not your type."

"Who said that, your mother?" Not his type, was whoever said that crazy? He liked how refreshingly fun she was, how positive. He liked her beaming smile and the way her glasses slid down her nose, the way she always looked slightly disheveled. She was absolutely his type.

Layla bit her lip and reached for her wine again, only to realize too late that it was empty. "Maybe."

He wanted to throttle that woman.

He'd never before felt like hating anyone's mother, but damn if Layla's mother wasn't a real piece of work. "Whatever she told you, she's wrong," he reassured her.

"You should try one of these strawberries," Layla told him, drunkenly pushing one under his nose. "They're really good."

"Are you trying to change the subject?"

"Yes? Strawberry?"

He chuckled and took it from her fingertips, letting his lips graze her fingers.

"Oh," Layla breathed, and put her fingertips to her mouth. Damn if he didn't get hard right then and there.

"Does this mean I get to take a turn and feed you?" he asked, sliding his chair closer to hers. He picked up another slice of strawberry and held it out to her, and she licked his fingertips in a way that was entirely not restaurant appropriate, her gaze locked on him.

Yeah, he definitely had a problem in the front of his pants now. He couldn't stop staring at her full, kissable mouth, though, and he hated that she was drunk.

Drunk was off-limits, far as he was concerned. He wanted more from Layla than just a cheap hookup, and he'd be damned if he let their first official date turn into one. So he scooted his chair back a safe distance, flagged down the waiter, and got the check. He noticed Layla wasn't eating much of the cheesecake after that last bit, and he glanced over at her. "You want to take that home?"

She squinted at him. "I . . . think so? My stomach's a little . . . not good."

Ah hell. "Do you need to make a pit stop to the bathroom?"

She shook her head, pursing her lips. "I'm okay."

He wasn't so sure about that. Luckily, the waiter seemed to realize the problem and cashed them out quickly. Jack left him a hefty tip as a thank-you, grabbed the box of cheesecake, and then put a hand at the small of Layla's back. "Come on, baby girl. Let's get you home."

"Home?" Layla said, a little too loudly as they walked out to the parking lot. "We can't go home. We have a painting date! Painting and wine."

"I think you've had enough wine for tonight."

"I'm not drunk, cowboy," Layla declared. "And we are absolutely going painting. I already paid a deposit to hold our seats. So come on."

She marched three steps ahead of him—and immediately tumbled off the curb of the sidewalk.

CHAPTER EIGHTEEN

Jack let out a yelp of surprise as Layla went down, legs sprawling. His heart pounded in his chest, sheer terror ripping through him as she lay on the asphalt, her legs sprawled in those ridiculous (but sexy) shoes and her dress almost riding indecently high under her coat. "Layla! Are you okay?"

She gave a drunken giggle. "Look out for that last step. It's a doozy."

Jack groaned, running a hand down his face. "Jesus, you scared the hell out of me." He leaned over, offering her a hand. "Come on." He'd tossed the cheesecake away the moment he'd seen her go down, and the sad black container sat on the sidewalk alone. He'd have to scoop it up, right after he scooped up his girl.

Layla took his hand, but the moment she tried to put weight on her foot, she hissed and collapsed again. "Ow."

He squatted next to her. "Where's it hurt?" His fingers moved over her legs, skating over her ankles.

"Well, my pride is absolutely brutalized," she began lightly. "But . . . my ankle."

"I've got you." Jack ran his fingers up and down her ankle, but nothing seemed to be swollen. "Does it hurt when I touch it?"

She shook her head.

"Probably not broken, but that doesn't mean you should walk on it." He slid an arm behind her back and braced himself. "Hold on."

"What are you doing . . ." Her voice trailed off as he hauled her into the air. Layla's arms went around his neck and she clung to him. "Oh. You're carrying me."

"I'm carrying you," he agreed. She sounded a bit more sober than she had in the restaurant, but he imagined that the pain was a hell of a wake-up call.

"My shoe," she murmured. Sure enough, one of her feet was bare, the toenails painted a whimsical purple that seemed very Layla.

"I'll go back for it. Let's get you settled first."

She just sighed and clung to him.

Jack managed to get her into the passenger seat of his truck without too much trouble, and by the time he got her buckled in, he saw that the waiter had come out after them and retrieved Layla's shoe and dessert. He handed them over to Jack with a sympathetic look, and Jack tipped him again for the help. Once he was settled back in his truck, he looked over at his date. Her eyes were closed and her mouth was settled into an unhappy line. "You okay?"

"Just hurting," she whispered, and then licked her lips. "Wine's not sitting so well, either."

"You're a lightweight, I take it?"

"Oh yeah."

"I'll try and drive slow." Something told him it wasn't going to help.

*   *   *

Layla threw up twice on the drive home. She'd thought it was a short drive out to the restaurant, but the return trip seemed to take such a long time that she knew she wasn't going to make it. She'd break out into a clammy sweat, then make an awful noise in her throat, and Jack would immediately pull the truck over so she could have a good puke. The sour taste of wine and vomit stuck in her throat, making matters worse, and her ankle throbbed with pain.

Tonight had been a train wreck.

She wanted to apologize to Jack. To tell him that she knew she'd messed up. That she'd guzzled so much wine because she'd been nervous and her mother had made her feel like a messy virgin, and then she'd gotten drunk. Puking all over the place and spraining her ankle weren't helping the situation, either. It was like fate was determined to make her realize just how wrong she was for Jack by throwing a spanner into the works every time they got together. If she wasn't locking herself in the bathroom, she was getting drunk and making a fool of herself.

Now she'd ruined her chances with the hottest guy she'd ever met, a hot guy who'd seemed into her, and she'd messed it all up because she didn't want to "act like a virgin."

"We're here," Jack told her as he parked the truck. "Wait there and I'll help you inside."

Like she was moving? Layla pressed her sweaty face to the window, feeling overheated and sick. She was going to puke again. She just knew it. She kept her eyes closed and wanted to just hide until he left. Maybe he'd get the idea and just abandon her at the curb in front of her house. That seemed about what she deserved.

"Come on," Jack murmured, and then he was carrying

her to the house. The swaying made a fresh sweat break out on her face and she concentrated on not throwing up all over him. At some point, she realized she was on the couch, and she wondered how he'd gotten the front door open. Then again, she had no idea where her keys were, and she didn't care. Everything was spinning, and her ankle was killing her.

A cool, wet cloth was placed on her forehead.

Oh. That felt so good that she moaned.

"Better?" Jack's voice was soft.

"You're still here?"

"What, you think I'd leave you?" He moved to her feet, pulled her shoes off—at some point she'd put them both back on again—and then pulled a knitted afghan over her legs. "What can I get you?"

"I could really, really use some dignity right about now."

He chuckled. "Fresh out of spare dignity, but maybe some crackers?"

"Ice pack for my ankle, maybe." Everything else could wait.

"Be right back."

She must have fallen asleep, because the next thing Layla knew, all the lights were off and she was in her bed, Jack tucking the blankets around her, Oscar snuggled against her front. She drifted back to sleep again . . . and woke up when she rolled over and bumped into a big, strong body.

Oh. Jack was in bed with her.

Layla sat up, squinted at the alarm clock. It was pitch-black outside, and the glaringly red alarm clock read three forty-five in the morning. Ugh. Jack was asleep next to her, atop the blankets and fully dressed except for his boots. She rubbed her face, feeling like hell.

"You okay?" He touched her arm briefly. "Want some aspirin?"

She nodded, he brought her some and a glass of water, and she lay back down. Through her foggy mind, she vaguely realized that Oscar was now tucked between the two of them on the bed, and for a moment, she was jealous of a silly dog because he got to cuddle against Jack's front and she didn't.

Jack probably would never want to cuddle with her again after tonight, though, and with a disgusted sigh at herself, Layla went back to sleep.

Layla woke up the next morning to Oscar licking her face, the sound of dishes downstairs, and an utterly egregious hangover. She groaned and pulled a pillow back over her head, but Oscar wiggled under and kept licking her face. Her mouth tasted awful. Her head felt awful, and Jack was apparently still around despite last night's disastrous date.

Everything was awful.

After a moment of self-pity, Layla pulled herself from bed—and nearly fell flat on her ass again as a wave of pain raced up her leg. Right. She'd screwed up her ankle. Ugh. She leaned on furniture and hobbled to the bathroom, keeping weight off her bad leg. Once there, she brushed her teeth, took some aspirin, washed her grimy-feeling face, and then hobbled right back to bed.

Maybe if she ignored Jack, he'd quietly leave and spare her the humiliation of last night.

Then she heard heavy boots coming up the stairs, and a cheerful whistling, and she knew she wasn't going to be spared.

There was a gentle knock at the door, and then Jack poked his head in. "Layla? You awake?"

"Oh yeah." She gave him a falsely bright smile and squinted at her blurry surroundings. Her glasses were on the nightstand but she'd left them off, and for some reason it made her feel vulnerable. "So this is terribly awkward."

"Is it? Why?" He moved into the room with a plate of toast and a cup of coffee, all casual gorgeousness. His clothes were slightly rumpled from sleeping in them, and his hair was messy, his jaw shadowed, but he still looked unfairly beautiful. Meanwhile, she felt like death warmed over.

"Made you toast and coffee," he said, sitting on the edge of the bed and setting the plate down on the nightstand.

"Thank you." She quietly took the mug and sipped it, because she wasn't sure what else to say to him. When they were both silent, Layla sighed.

"So why is this awkward?"

"Well, let me think. I got shit-faced on our date, twisted my ankle, and then puked all the way home. As dates go, it definitely wasn't in my top five. Pretty sure it wasn't in yours, either."

He just chuckled.

"You didn't have to stay, you know. I swear I'm fine."

Jack gave her a puzzled look. "You weren't feeling well. Didn't think it was right to just abandon you. Lemme see your ankle."

Before she could move, he was pushing the blankets aside and revealing her legs. Her dress had hiked up all the way to her hips, and Layla's panties were visible, much to her chagrin. If he saw them, he didn't say anything, but she was acutely aware of just how vulnerable—and half naked—she was as he carefully examined her ankle.

"Still not swollen," he murmured. "A little bruised. It might be a good idea to wrap it up and stay off it for a few days." He glanced up at her, all concern. "Do you want to go to the doctor? I can take you."

"No, it's fine. I shouldn't have worn high heels . . . or drank so much . . . or left my house." She gave him a rueful smile. "It's all good."

He settled back, but she noticed he kept a hand on her leg. "Well, I thought you looked beautiful. And I was glad you left your house."

Layla bit her lip. "I'm so sorry."

"Why are you sorry?"

"Because I ruined our date." She arched a brow at him. "Don't tell me you had tons of fun taking care of a sick drunk."

"It wasn't how I'd anticipated spending my night, but I didn't think it was all bad." His beautiful mouth twitched with amusement.

"Just mostly bad?"

"Just mostly," he agreed, teasing. His thumb stroked over her ankle. "So will you tell me what she said?"

For a moment, Layla had no idea what he was talking about. "What who said?"

"Your mother called you right before our date, didn't she?"

Oh damn. Had she babbled about that when drunk? Layla swallowed hard. Lie and feign ignorance? Or fess up and sound childish? Even though it made her seem silly, she decided to go with the truth. "You know, she said the usual mother stuff."

"Oh, I can imagine." His tone was dry. "Let me guess, tore you down before our date to make you nervous, right?"

Layla shook a teasing finger at him. "Have you been talking to my therapist?"

Jack just gave her an understanding look. "The next date we go out on, you're not allowed to talk to her ahead of time."

Layla picked at the hem of her dress, nodding, and it took a moment for his words to sink in. "Wait, you want to go out again?"

"Why wouldn't I?"

"Oh, I don't know. Every time we get together it ends in

disaster? That might be a good reason why we should give up."

"That's bullshit," Jack murmured, his thumb caressing circles on her leg. "I happen to think we've had more positive than negative on our dates."

Mmm, she wasn't sure she believed that, but it was getting hard to think with his fingers distracting her. "Clearly you're a glutton for punishment, but I'm game if you are."

He grinned, and, god, he was just the most beautiful man. "Are you free today?"

"Well, I think my marathon plans have been canceled." She wiggled her toes. "Probably gonna spend the day farting around with paperwork and watching Netflix."

"Would you like company? Farting around's my personal favorite."

She smiled back at him, feeling shy. How was he so incredibly sweet? Here she was, a hungover wreck, and he was making her feel so much better. "Thank you."

"For what?"

"For not making me feel like a disaster."

"Oh, you're a disaster. It's just one I can live with."

Layla laughed and flopped back on the bed. "Great."

To her surprise, he got up and moved to the other side of the bed, then lay down next to her. He reached over and pulled her against him, and the next thing Layla knew, her head was cradled against his shoulder. His arm was around her back, and she was snuggled against him . . . and it was heavenly. She pressed her cheek to his chest, listening to his heart beat. Had she ever snuggled with a guy before? She didn't think she had, and it was such a lovely experience. Clearly she'd been missing out. "Thank you again," Layla murmured.

"You really need to quit thanking me." His voice sounded deep and timbrey through his chest, and it fascinated her.

"Most guys wouldn't be quite so understanding after a date like that."

He just snorted, his hand on her back drawing enticing little circles. "You keep making me out to be some kind of saint, and that's not the case at all. Was I disappointed that things went south? Sure. But most of the date was real enjoyable."

"Except for the part where you held my hair back while I puked, right?"

"Well, see, that part wasn't great, but it meant I got to wake up next to you this morning, and we get to have some time together now, so I'd say all in all it's a win for me."

She smiled, tracing a finger over his chest. "You gonna try and steal a kiss?"

"I think you misunderstand me."

Layla froze. Oh god, had she totally misinterpreted their banter as light flirting? "I'm sorry—"

"Stealing a kiss implies that I'm going to be sneaky about it," he continued blithely on. "And I absolutely plan on kissing you."

Layla groaned and buried her face against his shirt. "I don't know if I find that sweet or if I want to deck you."

"You can want both," he teased. "I get that a lot."

"I bet you do."

Layla flicked at one of the buttons on his shirt. She knew she should eat the toast and coffee he brought for her, get up and dress, check her email, a dozen things sprang to mind . . . but she was reluctant to leave the bed, especially when he was so deliciously comfortable and warm. "I am disappointed we didn't get to paint."

He patted her back. "I'll ask my niece Libby if I can borrow her watercolors."

She giggled, an action that made her head ache. "What?"

"Sharing is caring and all that." His hand strayed up and

down her side, as if he was stroking her through the fabric of her dress. "How are you feeling right now?"

"Right now right now? Lazy and warm."

"Hangover not too bad?"

"It sucks, but it'll get better. Why?" She opened an eye to peer at him.

"Was just thinking about how much I wanted to kiss you, that's all."

The breath caught in Layla's throat. She lifted her head to look him in the eye. This close, she could see long, dark lashes, laugh lines at the corners of his eyes as if he was in a perpetual state of smiling, and the most perfect mouth God ever put on a human being. A dark lock of hair curled over his forehead, making him look boyish and younger than he was, and she reached up to brush it back. "How do you know I don't have the most beastly morning breath ever?"

"I can smell your toothpaste." He grinned and then grabbed her, rolling them both over on the bed until she was pinned underneath him. "Were you hoping I'd come and wake up Sleeping Beauty with a morning kiss?"

"No, it was more like Sleeping Beauty woke up and her mouth tasted like something died, so she had to fix it."

He laughed, then leaned in and lightly kissed her mouth. "Tastes pretty good to me."

"Are you sure?" she breathed, pulse quickening. "Maybe you should taste again."

"Excellent idea."

Jack's mouth brushed over hers again. He tasted like coffee and sugar, sweet and bitter at the same time. His jaw was bristly from not shaving, but she liked the texture of it, just as much as she liked the soft feel of his lips on hers. His tongue swept into her mouth, and then Layla was lost to everything but Jack and his mouth, Jack and his kiss, Jack and his incredible tongue that dragged against hers in ways that made her ache deep between her thighs.

She'd never kissed anyone like this before. Okay, she'd kissed a fair amount of men in the past, on dates that turned sour and during relationships that didn't quite pan out. Most of the men she'd been with had seemed to be terrible kissers, never quite hitting her just right. They would either jackhammer their tongues into her mouth or use teeth or something that ended up making her want to never kiss them again. With Jack, it was different. The way he kissed her made her toes curl and her body sing. It was like his tongue stroked against hers in just the right way, as if he were born with the knowledge of how to touch her. It was unfair that a man should be this incredible all in one package . . . either that or she was the luckiest girl in the world to have him with her right now.

CHAPTER NINETEEN

Jack gazed down at her, his handsome face momentarily serious. "Been waiting all week to touch you, you know."

"Have you?" His words made her ache. She touched his cheek lightly, fascinated by the planes of his face.

He nodded, then leaned in and dipped over her for a light kiss. "Been thinking about what it'd be like to have you under me, to feel your body against mine. Been having all kinds of dirty thoughts about you, really."

"Stuff for your spank bank?" It made her breathless.

He gave a short nod, leaning in and nipping at her jaw. "Like right now, with your dress all hiked up around your waist," he murmured, putting a hand on her hip. "Gonna be thinking about that a lot."

Layla moaned. Her lips parted and she tried to follow his mouth, hungry for another kiss, but he moved to her neck, and, oh god, that was really, really good. He nipped her there, then sucked so hard she knew she'd have a mark . . . and she didn't care. The way his mouth felt there sent quivers deep through her belly. "You know what else I like?"

"Mmm?"

"I like that you wear your hair up." He reached up for the ponytail holder that had somehow made it through the night, though only half of her hair remained in it. "Because then I get to imagine me freeing it." He groaned, burying his face in her hair. "Get to imagine it falling all over the both of us while I kiss you."

"Do you think about kissing me a lot?" she asked, breathless.

"All the damn time." Jack's mouth was on her throat again. "When I wake up, I think about kissing you. When you text me, I think about your mouth. When you laugh, I want to put my mouth all over your damn body. I'm utterly crazy about you, Layla." He moved up to her mouth again and gave her another searing kiss that made her toes curl. "Let me make you come, baby. That'll take care of your hangover."

She sucked in a breath, startled at his bold words . . . and utterly thrilled.

Okay, and nervous. She'd danced around the whole virginity topic for a while, but what if he figured out that it was true? What if she was a terrible lay and he didn't want anything to do with her after this? What if—

Jack lifted a hand, stroking her hair away from her face. "You got quiet, Layla—"

To Layla's side, there was a fierce snarl, and then Oscar attacked Jack's hand.

"What the fu—" Jack jerked backward, and Oscar barked, yipping and angry and high-pitched.

"Hands," Layla breathed, still dazed.

Jack stared at the dog, then flopped onto his back and laughed. Oscar chased after him, growling, trying to get at Jack's hand.

"Right. Sorry, buddy. I forgot about hands." He rolled off the bed and onto his feet, and then pressed a kiss to Layla's head, where she still lay sprawled and boneless in the bed. "Forgot you were still here. Maybe you and I should go for a walk to cool down, right, buddy?" He scooped up the dog and grinned at Layla. "Eat your toast and when you're feeling better, maybe we'll watch something."

"Sure," she said weakly.

He turned and left, and then she was alone in her bedroom. Alone, and really turned on. Damn it. He'd offered to make her come and she didn't say "yes, please."

The dog had cockblocked her and now the moment was gone, and she wasn't entirely sure she was brave enough to ask for him to come back.

Jack figured he was pushing Layla too hard. She'd been warm and passionate and so sweet while they'd kissed, but when he'd asked to do more, she'd frozen underneath him. Layla had gone silent, which hadn't exactly filled him with confidence, and he figured he was moving too quick. He needed to go slower with her, to take his time. She was worth waiting for, even if he wanted her so badly that she invaded his thoughts every hour of the day.

The distraction with Oscar had been teeth-grittingly bad timing, but in a way, it had also been good. He didn't want to push her into something she wasn't ready for yet.

He was just going to have to freaking wait, no matter how badly he wanted her. It was just damn hard, when she woke up with her hair falling out of the messy bun, her eyes dazed, and her dress crumpled around her hips. He'd wanted to jump right on her then and there, and it had taken everything he had to keep it light and flirty.

After Oscar was good and walked, he fed the dog—one

of the rare times the dachshund didn't mind being set down—and went back upstairs to Layla. She was dressed in pajama pants and a T-shirt, and her hair was pulled back up in a clip, probably as a silent gesture to tell him to slow the fuck down. She was worth taking his time.

So he talked about nothing in particular as he helped her down the stairs and settled her on the couch with her foot propped up. She seemed uncomfortable with Jack's fussing, which of course just made him want to do it more. He got her a drink, her laptop, and a blanket, and the remote for the television, and set Oscar down next to her. Immediately, her cat pushed his way over and dropped into her lap, and Layla sputtered with amusement. "How am I supposed to get anything done like this?"

"Be glad I don't do the same," he teased, though secretly he was envious of the pile-on in her lap. He wanted to be there with his head on her thighs . . . or between them.

But Layla just blushed and opened her laptop, reaching around her pets, and started typing.

He wondered if she was trying to get rid of him. Jack glanced over, but Layla was impossible to read. She had an awkward look on her face, but she wore that look often around him. She was focused on her laptop, but maybe that was shyness.

Jack had never dated many shy girls in the past. His type were the ones that got in your face and flaunted what they had. Layla wasn't like that, and while he liked that about her, it was also a mite bit frustrating trying to figure her out. Was she mad he'd offered to give her an orgasm? He hadn't asked for one in return . . . he'd just wanted to taste her. To watch her face as she lost herself in pleasure.

Jack glanced over at her, then turned on the television. "You want to watch anything in particular?"

"Just whatever," she said, typing. Her cheeks were pink,

though. Shyness, then. He thought for a moment, turned the TV back off, then moved to the ottoman where she had her feet propped up and lifted her legs.

Layla frowned at him as she shifted uncomfortably, and the big gray cat on her lap gave him a look that promised death. "What are you doing?" she asked.

"I'm gonna rub your feet and talk to you, if that's all right."

Her cheeks turned even pinker, which was adorable. "Oh, you don't have to—"

"I know I don't have to. But your ankle hurts and I feel responsible, so I figure I'm gonna try and make it better. And as a bonus, I get to talk to my favorite woman in town."

Her smile quirked and some of her sharp humor returned. "So you have favorite women in other towns?"

"Shhh. That's a secret between me and thirty other cities."

She snorted and shifted her lap again. The cat growled and moved over two feet, then curled up around Oscar and began to wash his fur with his tongue.

Jack took her feet in his hands and adjusted his long legs on the ottoman. And began to rub. She closed her laptop, biting her lip. "Something tells me I'm not going to get much done right now."

"No?" Not that he was sad about that.

"Nope. When Sterling wants attention, he pushes things off my desk and makes a nuisance of himself. I suspect this is the human equivalent."

He threw his head back and laughed, because she wasn't wrong. "Maybe I just feel I'm too pretty to be ignored?"

Layla rolled her eyes. "Too vain, you mean."

"I can be both." He moved his fingers gently over her bad ankle. "Does this hurt?" When she shook her head, he kneaded a little harder. "You probably just tweaked a muscle. Not really sure why you wore such tall shoes in February."

"Because Louboutins don't come in flats. Or if they do, that's just sad." She shrugged and managed a small smile. "I have a thing for shoes, and I never get the occasion to wear them. I thought it might be fun."

"You can wear them for me," he said solemnly.

She smiled.

"But you have to promise not to leave the house."

Layla's brows drew together. "So where am I supposed to wear them? In the kitchen?"

Or the bedroom, he thought, but just grinned. "You can wear 'em after I'm done with your foot rub if you like, as long as you keep your feet propped up."

She snorted, her hand going to her hip. "So I'm supposed to just sit here and look pretty"—her eyes widened as he began to rub the sole of her foot—"ooh."

"Good stuff?"

He loved the sexy way her lips parted, as if she was losing track of everything around her. "Oh yeah."

"Can I ask you something?" He continued to rub, fascinated by the way her eyes closed and she seemed to go boneless against him.

"Sure."

Might as well go for broke. "If I'm too pushy, would you tell me? If I made you uncomfortable?"

She opened her eyes and gave him a soft look. "Of course. You don't make me uncomfortable, Jack. I just . . ." She spread her hands. "Feel a little out of my depth. Not in a bad way—"

"In a virgin way?" he guessed. Might as well get it all out in the open.

She nodded. "Yeah. I'm not a virgin because I've been pining away over someone or because I was hurt in the past. I just . . . really want to trust and like someone before I get intimate with them, and it's hard for me to trust sometimes."

"Because of your mother," he guessed.

"Not just my mother, but my father, too. Instead of trying to raise his daughter, he bailed out and moved halfway around the world. Last I heard, he's in Spain visiting distant relatives. I haven't had someone stable that I can depend on in my life. I guess in a way I'm looking for that before I can really let myself go."

It explained a lot, really. Both of her parents were flakes, so Layla was responsible. She ran a business, she handled money, and she was in a line of work where she was trusted to handle finances for a great many customers. She still had a quirky, fun streak, but it had been tempered by past experiences.

His poor, lonely Layla. He rubbed her toes. "I understand."

"I just worry that I'm not the kind of girl you're going to stick with, you know?" She bit her lip. "You're fun and flirty and I'm an accountant that crochets in her spare time."

He shook his head, kneading the arch of her foot. "You're reading me wrong, baby. I'm not looking for someone to party all night with. I'm looking for someone I can talk to that doesn't bore me to tears. How many times do I have to tell you that I like you before it sinks in?"

"At least twice more," she teased.

"We're going to have to come up with a set of rules for our next date," he grumbled as his fingers moved over her foot. "One, no talking to Layla's mom in advance. Two, remind Layla at least twice that she's sexy and fun. Three . . ." He paused. "What do you want three to be?"

"Foot massages," she said dreamily, wiggling her toes in his grasp. "You're really good at that."

"Three," he agreed. "Foot massages before every date. Oh, and four—fuck-me pumps remain in the bedroom."

"They were not fuck-me pumps!"

"They absolutely were, because they made me want to fuck the hell out of you."

She giggled, but the blush was back in her cheeks. "Well, maybe I need some rules for you, too."

"All right, then. Lay 'em on me."

Layla tapped her lower lip with a finger, thinking. "No belt buckles bigger than a plate, for starters."

"There goes half my damn wardrobe," he joked.

She snickered, her lips curling into a smile. "And you should always greet me with a kiss."

His fingers stilled on her feet. Jack glanced up at her, and her eyes were soft and aroused, and damn if his cock didn't jump to life in his jeans. "You like it when I kiss you?"

"Too much," she admitted.

"No such thing." He set her feet down carefully and slid over to the couch, pushing aside the dog and the angry cat, who glared at him as if he was committing a grave sin. He didn't care; they could move. He was going to sit next to his girl. Jack wedged his way onto the couch, then pulled Layla's legs across his lap. "We could make a different rule about kissing," he suggested, sliding a hand up and down her pajama-clad leg.

"I'm open to amendments." Her voice was breathless.

"Maybe we use kisses as currency," he began.

"Now you're speaking an accountant's language." Layla chuckled.

"If I want to ask you something, I have to offer up kisses in return. Just like if you want to ask me something, you need to kiss me to purchase it."

"Tough, but fair," she teased. "Is it just for questions, then?"

"Well, I think a nice foot rub is at least worth two kisses."

She pretended to consider it for a moment. "I think that's

fair. So would you like to collect your kisses now or at the end of this date?"

"Are we on a date? I thought we were just hanging out." He slid his hand to the small of her back and tugged her forward, until she was practically in his lap and close enough to kiss. Her arms went around his neck, and her gaze slid to his mouth.

"So I owe you two kisses," she breathed, her look entranced as she stared at his mouth.

He glanced up at that clip in her hair and wanted to take it back down again . . . then paused. "I want to ask you something first."

"Then you'll owe me a kiss."

"We can cancel each other out, I guess." He nodded, gesturing at the clip. "Did you pull it up because you wanted me to slow down? You won't hurt my feelings if the answer's yes. I just need to know."

Her cheeks flamed bright red and she bit her lip. "No," she said softly. "I put it up so you could take it down again, because you said you liked to."

And she gave him a look of such yearning that Jack groaned low in his throat.

"I'm still owed that kiss, aren't I?" he asked huskily. "Come here, sweetheart."

CHAPTER TWENTY

Jack's mouth was sweet and flirty on hers, his kiss playful and nipping, with just the occasional flick of tongue. He didn't devour her with his mouth like he had before. He was keeping it light and airy, and she knew the message behind it—no strings attached. She could end this at any time. It was just flirting. Just fun.

Problem was, it made Layla hungry for more. She'd made a big speech about holding him at arm's length, and now that his mouth was on her again, she wanted nothing more than to shuck that thought. She wanted him to touch her. She wanted him to give her more than just a peppering of kisses. She wanted that wild hunger she'd felt before.

So when the kiss broke and Jack smiled down at her and rubbed his nose against hers, she didn't climb off his lap. Layla wrapped her arms tighter around him and leaned in, nipping at his lower lip. His jaw really was bristly and tearing at her skin, but she didn't care. It just added to the wicked sensations. "Are we doing more bargaining?"

Jack arched an eyebrow at her. "Did you have something in mind?"

"Well . . ." She studied his mouth, so full and soft and perfect for kissing. "I know what the price is for a kiss . . . what's the going price for you to touch me?"

Jack stiffened for a moment, and then his eyes flared with heat. "Baby, are you sure that's what you want? I'm not trying to pressure you—"

"I know," Layla interrupted. She plucked at one of the buttons on his wrinkled shirt. "I just . . . I like it when you kiss me. And I like your hands on my back, and on my ankle." She felt vulnerable as she spoke, and oddly enough . . . powerful, too. Confessing what she liked was both terrifying and exhilarating, and Jack was looking at her with such a hungry, possessive gaze that it made her all kinds of turned on. Her pulse felt as if it was throbbing directly between her thighs, and if she squeezed her legs together, she could feel just how wet she was. "I don't want to stop," she told him softly. "So what's the currency?"

He groaned, burying his hand in her hair and pulling her close for another kiss. This one was different than the others, deeper, hotter, wetter. It made her toes curl with need. It made her pulse race. It made her breathless and aroused and she pushed at the collar of his shirt until she could slip her hand inside and touch warm skin. Maybe if he didn't want to touch her, she could touch him—

His mouth broke from hers, and Layla let out a whimper of protest. "Kiss," Jack breathed, even as he leaned in to kiss along her jaw toward her ear. "I get to kiss you. And I get to pick where."

Layla moaned, her imagination running wild at the thought. "Are we sure that's fair—"

"Fuck fair," he growled.

"Okay," she agreed, breathless. Fair was going out the window. "Where—"

"I'll show you." Then his mouth was on her ear, and his tongue traced the shell of it before he took her earlobe in his mouth and gently sucked. Layla clung to him, a whimper escaping her throat. His mouth on her ear turned something she rarely thought of—an ear, of all things—into an utterly sensual and highly ticklish body part. Her dangling earrings from last night were gone; he must have taken them off her when she was drunk. Her ears were bare and when he nipped at her skin, it sent shivers racing through her and made her clench in all kinds of pleasant places. Oh god, yeah, she was liking ears.

But then he moved to her neck, bristly jaw scraping against her skin, and she sucked in a breath, holding him against her as he mouthed her neck and sucked on her skin. Okay, necks were also highly sensual, it turned out. Then again, maybe it was just Jack that made even the most boring of body parts into highly erotic nerve bundles.

"I don't wanna go too fast for you, Layla," he murmured against her neck, then dragged his tongue along the cords. "You tell me if I go too fast."

Her fingers were knotted in the front of his shirt, and she clung to him as if he was the only thing keeping her together. As if the moment he let go of her, she'd crumble into a thousand needy pieces.

He lifted his head and gazed at her, long and hard, and it made Layla feel breathless. "What is it?"

Jack kissed her again, softly. "Wait here."

Like she was going to go anywhere with her bad ankle? But she didn't protest when he slid her off his lap and got to his feet. The front of his jeans was tented as he stood, and it sent a little thrill of excitement to see the effect she was having on him.

"Much as I like snuggling with you on the couch," Jack drawled as he moved to the other side. "It's a bit crowded." He picked up Oscar, who was settled with Sterling on the far end of the sofa, and gently moved the dog to his bed in the corner. Before he could reach for the cat, Sterling hopped up and followed after him, tail flicking with irritation. Jack grinned over at her. "I think your cat doesn't like me."

"That's okay. Half the time I don't think he likes me, either."

His gaze grew hot, his eyes seemingly so dark in his handsome face. "Impossible."

That simple word stole the breath from her lungs. The look he gave her was so intense she was practically squirming, and when he moved back to the couch, where she sat, she threw herself at him, her mouth seeking his. Their lips met again, tongues teasing, and when Layla moaned, his hand went down her hip and held tightly to her there.

"You wanna guess where I'm going to kiss you?"

"Is it someplace good?"

He chuckled, kissing her upper lip. "I think so. I hope you think so, too." Jack brushed his mouth over hers again. "You tell me if anything is too much for you and I'll stop."

She was starting to think "too much" wasn't a thing that would happen with Jack. Every touch he gave her was more exciting than the last, and she wanted nothing more than for him to peel her shirt off and touch her.

"Lie down with me on the couch here, baby," he murmured. "So I can touch all of you."

Like she had to be told twice? Layla shimmied down until she was lying flat, then elevated her bad foot on the arm of the couch as he lay next to her. His hand moved to her belly again, and he kissed her one more time.

"Gonna kiss these pretty breasts of yours, unless you tell me no," he told her between nips of her bottom lip.

Oh god, that sounded amazing. "Why would I tell you no?" She was practically squirming against him at the thought.

"Because I don't want to rush you—"

"Rush me," she blurted. "Please rush me."

He grinned down at her and kissed the tip of her nose. "God, you're cute." His hand stroked lower, lingering at the waist of her pants. "I kiss your pretty tits, and that means I touch you, right? That was the deal we had?"

Layla had thought that by touching he meant her breasts, but when his hand skimmed over the juncture between her thighs, she realized she hadn't been clear enough. And oh . . . now she wanted that, too. Lord, but he was making her greedy. She sucked in a breath and nodded.

She liked his idea far better than hers.

"Part your legs for me, Layla," he murmured as his finger rubbed between her legs, moving perfectly over her slit despite the layers of clothing. Suddenly she was panting and needy, all from that small touch, and she'd never wanted anything as much as she wanted this man.

"Jack," she breathed. "Oh god, please, Jack—"

"I've got you," he promised. "And I'll make it so good for you, sweetheart." He kissed her one more time, soft and lingering, and then began to work his way down her neck again. All the while, he stroked her folds through her pajamas, making her hips arch up against his touch. She was so wet she could feel her clothing sticking to her, but he murmured against her neck how sexy that was, and Layla lost herself to his touch.

She was panting and needy, a whine escaping her when his hand lifted to pull her shirt up. She needed his hand back between her thighs, so she grabbed the hem of her top and jerked it over her head like a shameless wild woman. She couldn't pull her bra off without tugging the entire thing over her head, but he caressed her skin and then tugged one strap down her arm, pulling the cup down until her breast spilled free of its confines, and a new quiver went through her when Jack groaned.

"Fuck, that's pretty," he whispered, leaning in to kiss her. His hand went between her legs again, and she practically screamed with joy as it did.

He nuzzled at her breast, rubbing his cheek and jaw against her skin before running his mouth over the tip, and Layla slid her hands to his shoulders.

"Just as pretty and soft as the rest of you," he murmured against her skin, and as she watched, he flicked his tongue over her nipple.

Layla moaned.

"Gonna kiss you here," he promised, taking her nipple in his mouth and lightly scoring it with his teeth in a way that felt shocking and utterly arousing, and her hips jerked of their own volition. "I know," he promised her. "I've got you."

"Jack," she breathed. "I need—"

"I know." He dipped his hand into her sleep pants, tugging them downward, and then rolled them and her panties down to her thighs in one smooth motion. Then his hand went back between her legs and he cupped her mound. The breath hissed between his teeth. "You're so wet. Look at how wet you are, baby." He dragged his fingers through her folds, and she could hear it just as much as she could see it, and it was the most obscene and erotic thing she'd ever experienced.

Then his mouth was on her breast again, kissing and licking and sucking on the sensitive tip even as he pushed a finger into her. Layla whimpered at the invasion—even though she was wet, it felt tight and hot, and she knew it was because his fingers were so big. He stroked it into her, murmuring against her skin, and then she felt his thumb brush against her clit.

Everything inside her tightened as he began to rub it back and forth with the pad of his thumb. Her whimpers took on a new degree of urgency, and Jack sucked on her nipple and murmured filthy things to her while he worked her pussy with his hand, driving into her with a finger and teasing her clit at the same time.

It was too much for her to last long. Layla began to pant, drawing in one short breath after another as everything quickened, and when he sucked hard on her nipple and pushed his thumb against her clit at the same time, she practically came off the couch.

"That's it," he encouraged in his sexy, deep voice. "You come for me, baby. You come all over my hand and let me feel all of it."

He jiggled his thumb over her clit, not stopping the tight, quick motion, and a tiny shriek erupted from her as she dug her fingers into his shoulders, an orgasm ripping through her harder than she'd ever experienced in her life. She'd made herself come plenty of times, but this was on a completely different level, and it cascaded through her so hard that stars danced behind her eyes, and her body was making obscene noises as Jack fingered her and she didn't even care. Everything tightened and unraveled in slow motion, until she finally settled back into herself, breathless and lost in Jack's arms. A slow, dazed moan escaped her as he moved back over Layla to kiss her mouth again.

"Was that too much?" he asked softly, stroking her folds one more time.

"It was perfect," she whispered, and it was.

She'd never felt so beautiful, or needed. Sure, Layla was currently lying with her pants around her thighs and a boob out of her bra, but she couldn't find it in herself to care. And when Jack slid down next to her and held her close, wrapping his arms around her, she felt so damn good that she wondered what she'd ever worried about. Being with Jack had felt natural and right. Like she'd waited all her life for someone to touch her in a way that made her want to forget all her worries—and she'd found it.

Layla sighed happily, snuggling up against his chest.

"Not nervous any longer, I take it?" he murmured into her ear.

"Nope." She smiled lazily. "Give me a few to catch my breath and we'll take care of you."

Jack chuckled and brushed his thumb over her nipple again, as if unable to resist the temptation of it. "It's not quid pro quo. I'm fine."

She looked over at him in surprise. "I can feel something very distinct against my leg that calls you a liar."

He grinned down at her. "Busted. But I didn't do that because I wanted my cock sucked. I did that because I wanted to touch you, and I plan on doing it again." He kissed the tip of her nose. "And again." And then he grimaced. "But for now, I should probably head out to the ranch and make sure my brothers have things covered."

"Oh, you have to go?" The thought was depressing. She wanted him to stay. She wanted to curl up with him all day long and just laze on the couch and watch reruns of *Law & Order*. She wanted to hog absolutely all of his attention.

But of course he had things to do. Just . . . did he have to bring it up now? When she was all vulnerable and needy? "You can't stay for a little longer?"

He hesitated and then kissed her. "Of course I can. Just let me text Caleb and Hank."

Jack squeezed in next to her on the couch, and even though it was a tight fit, she didn't care. He pillowed his head on her breasts as he texted, and she wrapped her arms around him and tried not to read over his shoulder, even though it looked like one of his brothers was sending over strings of gobbledygook.

"Hank's terrible at texting," Jack murmured, grinning over at her. "Too much callus on his big fat fingers and he just sends a mess."

"You going to call him?"

"Nah. He can guess where I'm at. My truck's been parked in front of your house all night."

Layla inwardly cringed. She lived smack-dab in the middle of town, across the street from one of the local shops. Her neighbor ran the dry cleaner and loved to gossip. Of course everyone would notice. They would piece together that she'd bought Jack at the auction and they were sleeping together a whole week later.

She was now a fast, desperate accountant. Layla groaned and put a hand to her forehead. "I guess it's too late to do damage control."

Jack glanced up at her, his hair messy against her skin. "Damage control? You should be proud to be dating me, Layla Schmidt."

"Dating you isn't the part that's damaging," she said, poking his nose. "It's the part where everyone thinks I'm a cheap slut for buying you and then having you stay overnight to screw my slutty self into oblivion."

"Hey now. I'll have you know that slut is my girlfriend."

Layla snort-giggled. "Thanks."

"If it makes you feel any better, I'm sure there are some that thought you were a slut the moment you bought me." He pulled her hand to his mouth and kissed her fingertips. "It's a small town. You learn to ignore the idiots."

Easy for him to say: he didn't work with them or do their taxes. But . . . Jack made her happy, and the damage was done, so she was going to do her best to ignore all of it.

CHAPTER TWENTY-ONE

They snuggled on her couch for a good hour before Jack had to get up and leave, and he made sure to wrap her ankle tightly for her before he left, insisting that she call him if she needed anything. They kissed at the door for a solid ten minutes before he got into his truck and left, and she knew the look of regretful longing he shot in her direction was echoed on her face. Layla wanted him to stay all night. Tomorrow night, too. Heck, every night. But Jack's job at the ranch didn't make that sort of thing possible. He had responsibilities.

And responsibility was a thing she absolutely understood.

The week managed to go by quickly, somehow. Her ankle sucked for a few days, but it felt better by the end of the week and she no longer limped everywhere. Work was busy—she had a client that had filed his W-2s for his employees twice in the same year (how the heck did that mistake not get caught?) and so Layla had to go back and amend his tax returns, quarterlies, and W-2s filed, along with letters to the employees explaining the mistakes. It was messy and time-consuming, but nothing she hadn't fixed before. In a way, she was glad for the project, because it kept her from having to converse with her nosy office mates.

The secretary sniffed every time she saw Layla, apparently deciding to treat her like the whore of Babylon. The other guys in the office smirked and asked how her weekend went so often that she knew they knew. And everywhere she went, people made little comments. When she got coffee at the bakery, Megan made a crack about the bathroom and asked if she was still seeing "the hot guy." At yoga, well, no one gave her too much grief because she was flanked by Amy and Becca, but she still felt painfully obvious.

"Ignore them," Becca had said staunchly after class. "They'll eventually find something new to talk about, and there are worse things for them to gossip about than whether or not you bought yourself a boyfriend."

Layla wasn't sure if she agreed with that assessment, but she said nothing. It had been all over town for the longest time about how Becca had been left at the altar by her first fiancé. It had been a nightmare for Becca, but she'd gotten through it. Layla supposed she would, too.

She just hated the smirks and the whispers.

Even her mother was in on it. She texted Layla all week, at first crowing about how she'd gotten a bid on her land that was three times what she'd paid for it and that Janet Schmidt was about to be rich. Then her texts had changed in tone when Layla didn't respond, becoming sweeter and more interested in Layla. How had her date gone? Was she still seeing that nice young man? Why didn't she ever tell her mother what was going on? Janet texted her daily, until Layla was ready to scream.

It was like the world had sensed that Layla had a vulnerable spot and was doing its best to poke her with a stick in said spot.

Layla didn't like being vulnerable. She hated it, actually. It made her feel out of control and ever so slightly angry, like she was when she was a child. She cross-stitched a few four-letter words onto a pink pillow, took a bubble bath while listening to calming music, and tried to ignore it all.

The bright spot was Jack.

When Jack was around, everything was ten times better. Layla knew she was absolutely head over heels for the man, but she didn't care. Jack was just so . . . perfect. He was funny and sweet and charming, and he had an easygoing outlook on life. If she was working late, he'd bring her dinner. If her ankle was hurting, he'd swing by to pick up the dog—and kiss her for a good half hour. He ended up coming by most nights to see her, and when they weren't together on the couch, making out like teenagers, they just enjoyed spending time in each other's presence. Jack liked sports, so Layla watched the games with him, her crochet in her hands and her legs in his lap. Layla was a fan of board games, so they'd pull one of hers out and give it a go, and both of them were as bad at losing as they were at winning. They streamed movies and made dinner.

It was everything Layla had ever wanted. Jack was perfect for her. He was just so easy to be with, so fun that she couldn't imagine not being with him.

And Layla wanted to give him everything.

They'd seen each other so many times over the last week and had so many intense kissing sessions that Layla started getting aroused the moment Jack showed up. Just being around him made her start squirming, and it didn't take long for her panties to get damp. Jack was determined to go slow, which was sweet . . . and was making her a little crazy. They kissed. They petted. They sent each other dirty texts. They fooled around for hours on the couch. She loved his hands on her breasts and the way he touched them. She loved his hand between her thighs even more, and he'd made her come on his hand several more times . . . but he didn't want her to reciprocate.

He'd wait, he said.

Layla was beginning to feel like a pump that had been primed a few too many times, though. One more kiss, and she'd just start gushing everywhere, though the mental image made her grimace.

She wanted to have sex with Jack. She wanted everything.

And so when he asked her to come over on Saturday because he had something to show her, Layla decided she'd have a little something to show him, too. She'd wear her sexiest lingerie (that she'd had overnighted to her) and let him know exactly what she had in mind.

After all, everyone was already talking about them. Why not give them something to discuss?

Jack was nervous.

It was a week of big moves for him. He'd let his uncle know that he was looking to buy a ranch, and if he did, he wouldn't be available to help around Swinging C much at all. To his surprise, Uncle Ennis had not only been supportive, but also offered to help Jack get on his feet with a few calves from the herd and some extra equipment. His brothers had been equally supportive.

He'd talked to his Realtor and put in a bid on the land, and it was accepted. It was a hell of a lot of money, but with bank loans and a down payment, he could make it work.

And of course, there was Layla.

Layla, with her eager kisses and even more eager hands. She was the one for him. It didn't take the entire week for him to know that. He'd realized it when he'd showed up at her place, ready to play a board game with her, and she'd had football on instead, his favorite beer in the fridge, and hot wings in the air fryer. She didn't mind watching the game with him because he rubbed her feet and she poked one of her projects with a needle, or cuddled Oscar and watched it with him. There was no drama over what one of them had wanted to do, no compromise . . . because they liked the same things. And if they didn't, they found ways to enjoy the other person's presence regardless.

He'd looked over at her and realized just how easy it was to be with her, how much he looked forward to her smile.

He was gonna marry that girl, Jack decided.

Of course, it was too soon to push that sort of thing. Too soon for a lot of stuff, no matter how eager his Layla was. Jack was determined to go slow, to make the timing right. So he went home every night and took a lot of cold showers. He made sure Layla came, but took nothing for himself. He wanted to make a hundred percent sure she was comfortable before he pushed anything on her.

And this weekend, he was going to show her his property. His pride and joy. His future ranch.

He picked up dirty clothes off the floor of his small cabin, his mind already set on the future. He hoped she liked his land. He hoped she didn't think it was a mistake, or that he was jumping into something foolish. Jack was so lost in thought as he straightened up that the buzzing of his phone with her text came as a complete surprise.

LAYLA: I'm here. Where do I go?

Right. She'd been to the ranch once before, but not to see his place. He quickly texted back.

JACK: I'll come get you.

With one final shove of laundry under the bed, he smoothed a hand over the blankets and then jogged up to the front of the house. Layla was waiting there in dark stockings and heels, her knee-length coat covering everything else. She shivered as she waited by her car, the dog tucked under her arm.

"Look at me, the worst boyfriend ever," Jack joked. "Making you stand out in the cold."

"It's okay," she promised him with a smile as she handed off Oscar. "I didn't realize it'd be so chilly out."

He eyed her nearly bare legs and completely ranch-inappropriate heels. Uh-oh. He hoped she wasn't expecting to go out on the town. He'd told her that he'd wanted to take her somewhere special, and it looked like she'd interpreted it as a fancy dinner. Shit. Maybe he could change plans on her, see if they could get a reservation somewhere. Not that she didn't look fantastic in heels—boy, did she—but he'd wanted her to walk around the land with him, talk about his plans with her, show her what he saw when he looked at the flat, empty fields.

"So you don't live in the main house?" Layla asked, clutching her oversize purse against her chest as they walked the gravel path back to his cabin.

"No. I can if I want to—Uncle Ennis would be happy to have company—but I like having a cabin. It makes me feel less like I'm living under my dad's roof again."

Layla chuckled, and he glanced over at her. She seemed a little . . . anxious tonight? Was she nervous about something? He hoped not. He'd been waiting to see her all day . . . He hoped she wasn't upset that he wasn't dressed up. He was wearing jeans, boots, and an old T-shirt. Nothing fancy like her shoes.

"So you live in a cabin behind the main house?" She held her coat tight against her frame, her steps quick to keep up with him. "Do all of your brothers?"

He pointed at the row of small cabins. "Some of them are just used as storage right now. Caleb lives in that one there, but he spends a lot more time with Amy than here now. And before Hank married Becca, he lived in the big house with Uncle Ennis because he had his daughter, Libby, and needed more space."

"So this one's yours?" Layla took a few steps forward and put her hand on the door to his cabin. "And you're the only one out here?"

Again, that nervous note entered her voice. "Well, yeah. Caleb spends the weekend attached at the hip with Amy. You know how they are. And it's a little quiet, but I don't mind it." Funny how he actually had minded in the beginning. He'd been unhappy when Hank moved into the main house, even though it was best for Libby. And with Caleb dating Amy, he'd been feeling a mite abandoned by his brothers. He wanted them to be happy, but it was difficult when it made him feel miserable and forgotten.

But he hadn't been feeling either one lately. In fact, his thoughts had been so consumed with Layla and spending time with her that . . . he got it. He understood. It had nothing to do with Jack at all and everything to do with falling head over heels for a pretty smile and laughing eyes.

She put a delicate finger on the door, grinning at him. "Can we go inside or are we just going to stand on your porch?"

"Sorry. I was just distracted." When she arched an eyebrow at him, he chuckled. "You know you're distracting. And please, go on in."

Layla's smile grew wider, and she opened the door, peeking inside before stepping through. Jack juggled Oscar under his arm, following his girlfriend into his place, and he hoped it wasn't too messy. He wasn't much of a housekeeper, so the bed wasn't made all that neat, and there was probably a fair amount of dust on the shelves, but it was all right by his standards. He watched her face as he set Oscar on the corner of the bed, wondering what she thought.

"Well?" When she remained silent, he couldn't resist. "Too small? Too messy? You're horrified and thinking up intricate ways to break off our relationship?"

She snorted and shook her head, walking around his place slowly. Her heels thumped on the wooden floors. "I was just thinking, actually, that it doesn't look like you."

"It doesn't?" He glanced around. Sure, the rugs were some ugly pattern that his uncle had decorated with, and he didn't fill his room with books like Caleb did. The art on the walls was the same pictures that had come with the room. He'd bought the TV and DVD player, though, and his laptop sat on the nightstand.

"No. It actually looks more like a hotel room than the room of a guy under thirty." She shrugged. "I don't see a lot of . . . junk. No video games, no concert T-shirts thrown over furniture, no nothing." She turned and gave him a curious look. "Are you sure you're not some sort of android? A cowboy android pretending to be human?"

He put his hands out. "Beep, boop, you figured me out." When she laughed, he shook his head. "Nah, I just . . . I dunno. This is where I'm staying, but it's not really home to me. Plus, I grew up in a one-bedroom cabin out in the middle of nowhere, Alaska. There wasn't a lot of room for clutter."

Layla nodded, looking around thoughtfully. "No video games?"

Jack pulled out his phone. "I play a mean *Candy Crush*." She turned to face him, and he noticed she still kept her coat clutched to her chest. Was she cold? "Do you want me to turn up the heat?"

"It's fine." She studied him for a moment, then moved to touch one of his cowboy hats hung on pegs near the door.

"So is that why you took up ranching? Because you liked animals and being in the wild? Or did you always want to be a cowboy?"

"I actually loved Alaska and didn't want to move down here." He was fascinated with the way her fingertips traced along the edge of his hat. Who would have thought a brim could be so damned erotic? "But Uncle Ennis needed help for a while, and we needed the money to repair some equipment, so it seemed like a good idea. The plan was to go back, but then Hank met Becca and Caleb met Amy and so here we are." He shrugged. "My dad was a rancher until he moved to Alaska, and every calving season, he'd send us boys to go work the ranch with Uncle Ennis for a few months to help out. We'd be back before the first snow hit in the fall, and so it was just natural for us to show up and help out. I just didn't realize it'd be permanent this time."

And it didn't bother him like it used to. Not when he was looking at a gorgeous reason to stay.

"And your parents? Are they still in Alaska?" She glanced over at him.

"Dead. Dad died about seven years ago, Mom when I was real young."

Layla's expression turned sympathetic. "Oh, Jack, I'm so sorry."

"It's all right. He was happy right up until the end." Jack shrugged and moved toward her. "You wanna give me your coat?"

"I'm good." She slid away from him, walking to the other side of the room. "I could tell you about my parents, but the less said about them, the better. My mother's an awful person and my dad moved away when I was little because he couldn't stand to be around her and didn't care enough about me to ask for partial custody." Her smile was light despite the painful words. "I actually became an accountant because it was something I knew I was good at—

I'd been balancing my mother's checkbook for her ever since I was ten. Also, I knew she'd hate for me to have such a stodgy career, so that made it *extremely* appealing."

"I'll bet." He moved toward her again and noticed she skirted wide, crossing the room, and it was almost like she was avoiding him. "Is . . . everything okay?"

Layla turned a wide-eyed gaze to him. "Why wouldn't it be?"

"You seem a little . . . on edge."

Her smile was a little overbright. "It's totally fine. I'm just distracted, thinking about our date today."

Jack ran a hand through his hair. "Yeah, about that. I didn't realize you were gonna dress up, baby. I mentioned someplace special, but . . . I don't think you're going to think it's that kind of special and I hope you're not disappointed. Now I feel bad that you got all pretty for just a car ride."

Her eyes widened, and she put a hand to the neck of her tightly buttoned coat. "Oh. The shoes? I'm not wearing them for our date. I don't care where we go . . . or if we go anywhere at all." She fidgeted with her coat for a moment longer and then gave him a tremulous smile. "I just . . . wanted to do this."

And she opened the neck of her coat and let go of the belt at her waist. He realized the coat wasn't buttoned all the way up after all, that it was held closed by a sash, and when she let it free, the entire coat fell open.

Layla was wearing nothing but lingerie underneath her coat.

His jaw dropped. Jack stared at Layla, fascinated that she was bold enough to do this . . . and loving that she did this for *him*. She wore black and red lingerie, the bra with two bright red hearts over the nipples and black mesh for the cups. The panties were similar, heart-shaped and with bright red cutouts through the black mesh. She wore black garters that kept her stockings up and they were patterned with little red hearts. When she turned around, her underwear looked like a heart-shaped package, a present just for him with a bow right over her backside.

"Well, well," Jack murmured. "Is it my birthday already?"

She finished twirling and gave him a look that was half sass, half shy. "It's my way of saying Happy Valentine's Day."

"Valentine's Day was earlier this month," he pointed out. "You won me at an auction."

"I did," she agreed, and sauntered toward him. "But we really didn't get a chance to celebrate, and I thought we should."

"I like the way you're thinking," he murmured, and put his hands on her hips. "What did you have in mind?"

"His and hers orgasms?" she said lightly, putting her arms around his neck. She bit her lip and looked up at him. "I thought maybe we'd go a little further today, because I was thinking about it and I really want to put my mouth on you."

CHAPTER TWENTY-TWO

He was in heaven. His girlfriend had come to his place in lingerie and demanded to blow him? Surely there was nothing better than this. Ever. "I think that sounds like an amazing idea, but only if I get to reciprocate."

Layla's cheeks pinked. "I'd like that."

He leaned in and gave her a feather-light kiss. "You don't know how long I've been wanting to get my mouth on you, baby."

She let out a shuddering little sigh. "Oh?"

Jack nodded. He'd been going exquisitely slowly with Layla, mindful of how skittish she was. He wanted to let her set a pace she'd be comfortable with, and so all of their encounters had been heavy on the kissing, and he'd made her come with his hand, but they hadn't gone further than that.

Obviously that was too slow of a pace for his greedy, perfect girl. God, he loved this woman. Even as he thought it, he pushed the thought back out of his head. It was infatuation, he told himself. It was far too soon for love, no matter how right she might feel in his arms.

Maybe if he told himself that often enough, he might even believe it. Because he could see Layla with him ten years from now, or fifty. He'd still find her adorable and sexy and smart even when they'd gone gray together.

Definitely too early to declare something like that, he figured. So he kissed her enthusiastically, loving the way her mouth went soft under his, like his kiss was the best thing she'd ever had. Like nothing existed outside of their locked mouths. He loved the way she felt in his arms as much as he loved her enthusiastic reactions. Every time he gave her pleasure, she made him feel like he was a damn king.

Her tongue brushed against his, and Jack groaned. A king with a hell of a lot of patience, he decided. A king who had spent the last week with night after night of blue balls and cold showers.

A king who would happily do so for another week or ten if it was what his queen needed.

But Layla was an impatient sort, which was adorably cute given that most of the things she chose to work on were detail oriented. She'd sit for six hours and cross-stitch, but when it came to him, she was possessive and grabby and impatient . . . and, god, he loved that.

"I get to go first," Jack murmured between kisses.

"Like hell you do. I'm the one in the panties here." She slid out of his arms with a little wiggle. "If I take them off, then you don't have anything good to look at when I'm kneeling in front of you."

Jack groaned and raked a hand down his face. He wanted to point out that her naked ass would make him just as happy, but she was so clearly thrilled with the lingerie—and so brave for showing up in nothing but a coat—that how could he possibly refuse? "You drive a hard bargain."

"Oh please. I do not." Layla gave him a cheeky look and

grabbed his hands, dragging him toward the bed. "You might want to put our son in the bathroom, though. I think he's too young for what's about to happen."

He'd forgotten all about the dog. Jack looked over at Oscar, and the small tail wagged happily. "Right. Give me two minutes to get him situated."

"You have two minutes on the clock," Layla agreed, and sauntered away with an exaggerated sway of her hips that made her rounded ass look like a gift-wrapped peach. God, that underwear was sexy. With the stockings and heels, she was a walking dream.

Jack had never moved so damn fast in his life. He scooped up Oscar and his low-sided laundry basket, made a nest for the dog in the bathroom, and then stuffed Oscar's favorite hollow toy with peanut butter as an offering. Then he washed his hands, shut the door, and looked over at Layla.

His girl was on the bed, still wearing her heels and lingerie, stretched out on her side in a pose that was probably supposed to be sexy but looked far too tense. She squinted up at him, and he realized she'd taken off her glasses.

"Can I make a weird request?" he asked, sidling back over to her.

"Of course."

"Can you put your glasses back on?"

She tilted her head, looking up at him in surprise. "Really? I thought I might look sexier without them on."

"Really. I think you're always sexy but I love the way you look in your glasses. Plus, don't you want to get a good look at the goods?" He winked at her, teasing.

Layla rolled her eyes at him, but she was smiling. "I'm not that blind without them."

"Can I help it if I think you're cute in glasses?" Jack sat down on the edge of the bed, watching her as she reached across to his nightstand, her breasts straining against the festive bra.

"Those aren't my eyes," she teased as she put them on and caught him staring.

"I know. But I just like looking at all of you." He grabbed her leg and tugged her toward him on the bed, noticing that her hair was up in another loose bun, held together with a pencil that was just begging to be pulled free. She knew just how to work him. "You sure I can't go first?"

Her breath caught in her throat, and then Layla chuckled. "Something tells me if I let you go first, I'm not going to get my turn."

"Oh, I'd absolutely let you have your turn." If she wanted to suck on his cock, he was extremely willing and enthusiastic.

She pretended to consider, then shook her head as she crawled across the bed to him. "Ladies first."

"I like how confident you are," he murmured. "It's gorgeous."

"I'm hiding my terror well," Layla admitted, moving to kneel on the bed. She reached for his T-shirt and tugged on it. "I felt incredibly silly all the way here, but then I saw the look on your face when I took my coat off, and I got my second wind."

"You're stunning," Jack promised her. "Absolutely fucking stunning."

"Ooh, an F-word. That's how you know it's serious," she whispered, pulling his shirt over his head. He lifted his arms to help, and when she tossed it aside, she stared down at his chest and sighed. "It's a good thing you weren't shirtless at the auction. I might have tossed them my entire wallet at the sight of this."

He was glad that she liked what she saw. "Not too flabby?"

"Flabby?" She squinted up at him in that adorable way of hers. "Jack, I swear you have an eight-pack. You look like you could give Aquaman a run for his money in the sexy department." Her hands went flat on his pectorals and then she smoothed them all the way down his chest. "There's not an inch of fat anywhere." Her voice turned soft, reverent.

And damn if that wasn't making him hard as a rock. His cock ached in his jeans, but he held still as Layla ran her hands up and down his chest, exploring him with curious fingertips. She outlined his abdomen with her fingers, then touched the swirls of hair dotting his chest and down to his navel.

"You even have a happy trail," she said with fascination, touching the line of hair that disappeared under his belt. "I've been wondering for days now."

"Were you thinking about my cock a lot, then?"

Layla bit her lip again. "Far, far too much."

He groaned, flexing his hands so he'd resist the urge to just grab her and kiss the hell out of her. "Where do you want me?"

Her tongue swiped over her pink lips, fascinating him. God, he was obsessed with her mouth. "I think standing up? Can we do that?"

"We can do anything you want, baby." He loved that she smiled back at him. That she looked so eager and aroused all at once. "You just tell me where you want me."

"Stand up," she repeated, and steered him toward the foot of the bed. He stood there, watching as she sat on the edge of the bed and slid her legs between his. "Can I strip the rest of you?"

"I would love it if you did."

Layla took in a deep breath and peeked up at him as her fingers went to his belt. "I feel like I'm going to unwrap the naughtiest Christmas present ever."

"I don't think this present has ever wanted to be unwrapped more."

She chuckled, her hands undoing his belt. "I just hope this isn't one of those Christmases where you really want a PlayStation and instead you get underpants."

"I don't think you'll be disappointed." Sure, it was arrogant to say, but he'd never had complaints in the past.

"So confident." Her lips curved. "That makes me feel good about my present." Her hand boldly slipped down the front of his jeans, feeling him, and her eyes widened. "Okay, that's a bigger . . . bow . . . on my present than I expected."

He just grinned. "Told ya."

The urge to grab her hand and pump into it was overwhelming, but Jack forced himself to remain still, to let her explore him as she wanted. If she was a virgin, the last thing he wanted to do was paw at her and make her feel like she wasn't in control of the situation. So as her fingers explored him through the front of his jeans, tracing his outline, he tried to think about other things. Things like the upcoming calving season. Saddles that needed repair. The cost of horses if he bought breeding stock, pedigreed cutters who'd—

Jack sucked in when her hand delved lower, cupping his sac. The touch of her was just enough to be teasing through the denim, but it also wasn't nearly enough to satisfy. When she gave him a delighted smile, he couldn't resist adding, "I'd feel a hell of a lot better out of my clothes, just so you know."

"That's the plan." Layla moved her hands back to his belt, pulling it free of the loops and tossing it onto the floor. She undid the buttons on his fly and then wiggled the waistband of his pants lower. She hummed a little at the sight of his plain black boxers. "Step out of your boots for me?"

"Gladly." He took a step backward and pulled his boots off, tossing them aside, and then went ahead and removed his pants, leaving only his boxers on. He noticed her cheeks pinked up as his pants came off, so he left the boxers for her. She could leave them on for as long as she was comfortable, that way. Jack put his hands out, doing a slow twirl. "How am I doing?"

She giggled. "No complaints here." Layla sat down on the edge of the bed again and put her hands on his hips, pulling him toward her. "Please be serious," she told him in a mock-stern voice. "This is a very delicate situation."

"Of course. My apologies." He gave her a little nod, playing along with her game. "What can I do to help?"

"Just stand still," she told him and tugged his boxers down to his thighs. Layla sucked in a breath the moment his cock hit the air, and she blinked for a moment, then glanced up at him. "Porn really does not prepare you for this sort of moment."

"We can stop—"

"No," she breathed, letting his boxers drop to the ground with a swish. "No, I don't want to stop."

Good, because he didn't either. The intense way she was looking at him was making him harder than a rock. Precum dotted the head of his cock and had started dribbling down his shaft, evidence that she was making him utterly crazy with need. He watched her as she licked her lips, a thoughtful expression on her face, and lifted her hands. She didn't put them on him, though. They fluttered in the air for a moment, as if she was considering the situation, and then she put her hands on his thighs, rubbing up and down as she pulled him a little closer.

"You're going to find this hard to believe," she whispered, "but this is the first time I've done this. Super-ultra-virgin in the house."

"Never wanted to before?" he asked, voice husky with arousal. Damn, he liked that he was her first. It didn't matter, not really . . . but he still liked it.

She shook her head. "I wanted to make sure what I felt

for someone was really a thing. I didn't want to have sex just to have sex, you know? So I waited. And waited. And . . ." She blew out a nervous breath. "Here I am, far too old to be this anxious about blowing you."

"Don't be anxious. You're gorgeous." He reached out and caressed her jaw, and she leaned into his palm. "If it makes you feel any better, I've been dreaming of this moment since I met you, and right now is exceeding all my expectations."

Layla preened a little at that. Her hands stroked up and down his thighs again, sending bolts of aroused need racing through him. "Brace yourself for impact, then."

The chuckle bubbling in his throat died when she curled her hands around his length and bent down to take him into her mouth.

CHAPTER TWENTY-THREE

He tasted . . . salty. Like skin, of course, Layla thought, but it was also a different, curious sort of taste. Not quite bitter, not quite musky. Just . . . Jack-tasting.

She decided that she liked his taste, almost as much as she liked the way he felt. Layla had read all kinds of books and watched far too much online porn, but experiencing was something different entirely. She'd heard the euphemisms, like "velvet monster" and "silk over steel," when it came to a man's cock and, well, they were pretty accurate. He was incredibly soft, warm skin sheathing a rock-hard, thick length that made her quiver deep inside. She slid her fingers up and down his shaft even as she ran her tongue over the tip of him, and wondered if he'd let her just touch him for hours.

Really, a penis should not feel so darn fascinating if men wanted it sucked on. It should be boring and uneventful so she could focus on her task. Instead, she found herself sighing and lifting her head, running her lips along the tip so she could enjoy the heat of him, letting her fingertips trace over the vein on the underside of his shaft. Soft, but hard. Incredibly hot. Incredibly firm. Big. Real big.

Layla hummed approval to herself.

"Is there . . . any particular touch you like?" she asked, looking up at Jack. His body had gone rigid as she explored him, and when she looked up, she'd expected to see tension in his face. Instead, he had the look on his face like he did when they kissed and he made her come—heavy-lidded, almost sleepy, and utterly aroused, his pupils dark and huge in his gorgeous eyes.

Oh.

She pressed her thighs tightly together.

"All of it," he rasped. "I like all of it."

She bit back a smile, because he sounded like he was on the verge of losing control, and she liked being the one to do that to him. She hadn't been too sure about showing up at his place in flirty panties and a bra—and nothing else— but his reaction was really gratifying and he looked at her as if she was gorgeous, not as if she was crazy.

Layla was enjoying herself.

She slid forward onto her knees, on the floor of his cabin. "If you won't tell me specifics, I'm going to have to learn for myself." She kept her tone teasing and flirty, and when he groaned low in his throat, it took everything she had not to smile, because smiling stretched her mouth too tight and she'd just end up using teeth on him.

She was not a professional at this sort of thing, but she absolutely knew teeth were bad.

Using her tongue and hands, she explored him. She licked him from head to base, pressing kisses along his shaft. She followed the vein on his length. She curled her fingers around him and tried to measure just how big he was. She licked swirls around the head of his cock and then used the tip of her tongue to try to discover any secret spots she hadn't yet figured out. He seemed to like it when she breathed hot, light kisses along the shaft, and he *really* liked it when she licked the underside of his cock head. She wanted more of a reaction from him, though, so she took the head of him into her mouth and sucked gently.

Jack's hips jerked and he swore above her.

Layla immediately sat back, releasing him. "Did I do something wrong?"

He groaned, his head falling back. "No," he panted. His hand went to her hair and he pulled her forward again. "More. More of that."

Ooh. She could do that. Eager, Layla curled her fingers around the base of him again, guiding his cock to her mouth once more. She sucked on the head of him, using the flat of her tongue to tease and coax. When his breath hitched, she knew she was on to something, and her movements grew more enthusiastic, her tongue more ardent. She sucked him in deeper and found that it was difficult to continue as she was. He was simply too big for her to take more of him and continue with the suction. This . . . was a problem she hadn't anticipated. So she experimented a little, taking him as deep as she could and using her hands and tongue to make up for what she lacked.

"Layla," he panted, his hand going to her hair again. "You feel amazing."

Thrilled, Layla worked him with enthusiasm, loving that she was giving this to him. After so many orgasms where she'd come with just his hand between her legs, it felt powerful and heady to be able to make him come, too. She bobbed her head on his length, pumping the base of him with her hands, and when he began to nudge his hips into motion, she made a sound of encouragement in her throat. She liked that. She liked it even more when his hips shuttled against her mouth, pushing in with small, quick motions. She could feel Jack's hand in her hair, feel his excitement, and the taste of him was on her tongue. She leaned in to him, her hands gripping his ass tightly—lord, he had a fantastically firm ass—and let him use her mouth. Each thrust pushed against her glasses, but she didn't care. He'd taken over the control, and that was all right with her. Her body was pulsing with need, and she loved that he was on the edge.

"Where do you want me to come?" he asked, teeth gritted.

Oh. She hadn't thought about it. Layla just sucked on him harder, her hands gripping him tighter as he thrust into her mouth again. She made a humming sound in her throat that she hoped he realized was encouragement, and in the next moment, when his hand tightened in her hair and he pushed deep, her mouth flooded with his taste.

It was . . . a lot. Her mouth filled with him, and the hot, sticky wash of his release seemed to be everywhere. He pulled out of her mouth and it leaked down her face, and Layla jumped to her feet and raced to the bathroom.

Okay, maybe she wasn't ready to swallow that much just yet.

Coughing and sputtering, Layla cupped her hand under the water and drank, rinsing the taste of him out of her mouth and washing her chin. Oscar stared up at her from his basket, and she could have sworn the dog was giving her a judging look.

"You all right?" Jack touched her back, standing behind her.

She straightened, blushing, and wiped her face with a towel again. "That was just . . . a little more than I expected. Sorry."

He gave her a sexy grin that made her flutter all over. "Never apologize. You were perfect." Jack leaned in and kissed her.

Layla slid her arms around his neck, loving the feel of his bare skin against hers. He was damp with sweat, his skin flushed, and she loved that his disheveled, sated expression was because of her. "You might not want to kiss me after what I just did."

"Like I care?" He kissed her again, as if just to prove that he didn't. "You did it for me."

"Not just for you," she pointed out. "I liked doing it." Her hands slid down his sides and then she grabbed his ass, unable to resist. "I liked touching you. I liked all of it, Jack."

"Then I am the luckiest man alive." He kissed her again. "Smoking-hot girlfriend who loves touching her boyfriend."

"I think your standards are a little lax," she joked. "Not sure about the smoking-hot part, and I'm pretty sure most women love touching their boyfriends."

"You let me be the judge," he told her, and kissed her again, his tongue flicking over hers enticingly. "Come on and hop on the bed for me."

For a moment, she was confused. "Shouldn't we get going? I brought a dress in my purse—"

His brows drew together. "Not until you get your turn, baby."

Oh, right. While she was aroused, she also was starting to feel awfully shy. She'd worn the lingerie and blown him because she wanted to. She didn't want him to feel as if he needed to reciprocate out of obligation. "You don't have to."

Jack snorted and picked her up. "I don't have to do anything. I want to, and that's the difference, Layla." He set her down gently on the bed. "You think I haven't been dying to get my mouth on your pretty little pussy?"

Her breath caught. "Have you?"

"Fuck yes." The look he gave her was intense. "You think I'm content to just use my hand when my mouth could be between your thighs? Baby, you've got me all wrong." He leaned over her on the bed. "Give me a kiss, and I'll get Oscar settled again."

She kissed him, just as requested, and remained on the edge of the bed, nervous and a little jittery. She still had the taste of him in her mouth, the feel of his cock fresh in her memory as she'd touched him. Layla shifted her weight on the bed and, yup, her panties were damp. She took off her smudged glasses and reached up for the pencil that held her bun of hair. Oh. At some point it had come free, and she hadn't even realized. She'd been too wrapped up in Jack.

The bathroom door shut, and she looked up at Jack. He was still as naked as could be, and to her surprise, his cock was at half mast. For some reason, she'd imagined it deflating like a balloon after he came, but that was dumb, wasn't it? She liked the look of him naked, though. God, he was beautiful, and just as she'd suspected, there was zero fat anywhere on him. How on earth did he end up with a girl like her?

"I can practically see the wheels turning in your mind," Jack drawled as he approached the bed. "Stop panicking. I said you were gorgeous, and you are. You want me to show you how gorgeous?"

"Yes, please?" As nervous as she was, Layla was not about to turn down oral sex. She was nervous, but she was absolutely not crazy.

"Sit back on the bed for me, baby." He gave her a confident smile, his gaze roaming over her again. "Let me enjoy looking at you."

She wiggled backward a little, her heels catching on the edge of the bed as she scooted back. She thought for a moment and lifted one foot in the air. "Should I take the shoes off?"

"Hell no. Those are sexy as hell, and I want them on your legs when you have them over my ears."

"Have what over your ears?" she stammered.

"Your legs."

The visual made her weak. Hot need pulsed through her core. "Right. Of course." Man, she felt like a virgin.

She lay back on the bed and stared up at the ceiling, wondering if it was possible to feel any more awkward. She'd felt sexy and in charge when she was the one giving pleasure, but now that it was her turn, she just felt . . . weird. Not that she didn't want it, of course. She did. It was just . . . she had been the only one to ever touch that area before Jack, and now he was going to put his face down there, and her nerves were eating her alive.

"You're tense," he pointed out unnecessarily as he rubbed his hands up and down her legs. "You okay?"

"Just nervous."

"Why?" He chuckled. "It's me. I've had my fingers all over this pretty pussy. I've made you come all over my hand a half a dozen times this week. What about this is weird?"

"It's weird because your face is involved."

"Did your face have any complaints about my dick?"

"Of course not."

"Exactly. So mine has zero complaints about your pussy. Well one, actually."

She tensed. "What?"

He leaned in and pressed a kiss to the inside of her thigh, sending ticklish sensations all through her body. "That it's taken so long for me to get here."

Layla let out a deep breath. "Don't do that to me, Jack. Not funny."

"I wasn't being funny." He kissed the inside of her thigh again. "I meant every word of it. You think you're the only one that fantasized about this? About going down on the other?" He nibbled inward, moving closer to her center, and her body shivered in response. "I've been thinking about putting my mouth on you ever since I saw your face last fall."

That made her sit up a little. She propped up on her elbows, startled. "You what?"

"Yup." He grinned at her from between her thighs and hooked her legs over his shoulders. "You were wearing your glasses and had your hair pulled up and you were wearing a sweater with hot dogs on it. It was the most random thing I'd ever seen, and you were the cutest. You gave me this look that practically dared me to say anything about your sweater, pushed those glasses up your nose, and then looked right through me." Jack grinned and leaned forward, pressing a kiss right to the crotch of her panties. "I went home and jerked off to you that night."

The breath shuddered from her lungs. "You did?"

"Oh, hell yeah," he murmured, and then he licked up and down her covered slit. It shouldn't have felt nearly as obscene as it did, but, oh god, did it ever. She wanted to writhe against his mouth, even as she wanted to grab his face and press it there again . . . or make him take her panties off and do it to her bare skin. "Like I told you before, you're all over my spank bank."

"Aren't you supposed to jerk off to . . . celebrities?" she asked, her voice stuttering as he lapped at her again. Oh dear god, he was such a tease, and it was such a turn-on, too. The next time he licked her, she whimpered and lifted her hips, trying to follow along with his tongue.

"Eh. Celebrities are boring. I like thinking about you." His mouth landed at the apex of her folds, and he pressed there, watching her reactions. "I like thinking about the expressions you make when you come. When my mouth is on you. That's what turns me on."

She moaned, half wanting to flop back down on her back again, and partially wanting to watch his mouth on her like an utter pervert.

Her breath caught.

"Can I take these off now or do you need a few more minutes to get used to the idea?" Jack pressed a kiss right over her clit, his gaze meeting hers, and Layla felt as if she was going to melt right into the mattress.

She swallowed and nodded. "You can take them off."

"Not that they're not pretty," he told her, a smile curving his gorgeous mouth. "But I prefer what's underneath." He put his hand on the waist of her panties and tugged them down her legs, easing her thighs back off his shoulders so he could remove her underpants. They caught on the heels of her shoes, because of course they did. Layla always seemed to be awkward when it came to sexy moments, but Jack didn't laugh or tease her. He just worked the fabric off her shoe while she flushed with the awkwardness of it, and then he tossed them across the room, where they landed atop his nightstand.

"If you meant for those to be in the laundry basket, you missed," she joked, though it came out far more wooden and unnatural than she'd wanted.

"No, I wanted them right there." Jack winked at her before hooking her legs back over his shoulders again and rubbing the stubble of his jaw along the inside of her thigh. "I'm keeping them."

"What?"

"To jerk off with later. Gonna imagine peeling them off you again and come with them wrapped around my dick." He gave her a wicked smile and tugged her hips down, pulling her toward him on the bed. "Quit scooting away."

Was she scooting away? "Sorry."

"Are you still nervous?"

Layla gave a choking laugh. "Of course."

"Why?" He seemed genuinely puzzled at this.

"Because you're you, and I've never done this, and what if—"

He shook his head, rolling his eyes at her excuses, and before she could finish her sentence, his mouth was on her folds, his fingers pushing them apart even as he licked her.

The words died in her throat. A squeak might have choked out of her, but mostly, she was just shocked. It felt . . . different than she'd thought it would. She hadn't fallen into a puddle of bliss at the touch of his tongue, and porn (and books) had made that seem like the case.

"You still nervous?" he asked, kissing her again, his mouth hot and wet right over her clit.

Layla swallowed. "Not . . . not as much."

"Good." He gave her pussy another lazy lick of his tongue, and she shivered, watching the obscene sight. His mouth looked so pink and wet against her, and when he made contact, her body made *noises*. Sloppy, wet noises.

She didn't know how she felt about that.

"You want me to stop?" he asked between kisses.

Layla shook her head, mute, as his tongue pressed against her clit again. It really was the filthiest thing to watch, him tonguing her pussy, and she couldn't stop staring.

As she watched, his tongue circled around her clit, and Layla shivered. That felt . . . there were no words. And when he put his entire mouth against her and sucked gently on her clit, she gasped. Okay, now that she was getting past her initial trepidation, she was liking this. Her hands slid to his hair, because she was desperate to touch him, to anchor herself somehow. He made a low sound of approval in his throat and didn't lift his head from her folds, too focused on the task at hand. He felt good, she decided. His tongue was teasing and stroking in all the right ways, and she was wet enough that the glide of his mouth against her clit had a delicious feeling to it. With a little sigh, she relaxed, her head falling back on the mattress.

She didn't stay relaxed for long.

It snuck up on her, she decided. One minute she was

lazily enjoying his mouth on her and the next, her hips were lifting when he sucked on her flesh. The pleasure had ramped up, and instead of being something to distractedly enjoy, it had turned into the utter focus of her body. When he rubbed a finger against the opening to her core, she whimpered. God, when did his tongue start feeling so damn good? She lifted her head to look down at him and their eyes met, and she shuddered, moaning as he continued to flick a steady pattern against her with the tip of his tongue. Oh god. Okay, yeah, she got it now. She understood why everyone went crazy for oral sex.

He was absolutely ruining her for other orgasms.

And when Jack pushed into her with his finger, the dual sensations of his mouth on her and the pressure inside her made her buck. "Jack," she panted, an aching whine in her voice. "Oh god, Jack."

"I've got you," he breathed against her pussy, and thrust his finger into her again with a slow, steady motion. He dragged it back and forth, pausing to tease at the entrance of her core, where she was the most sensitive.

She whimpered again when he added a second finger, stretching her, and his thrusting began to take on a faster pace. The noises Layla was making were downright embarrassing, but she didn't care, didn't care that she was making those little whiny grunts with every pump of his fingers into her, all the while his mouth made lascivious noises on her pussy and licked her in ways that felt like they should be against the law.

Then, he . . . did something. His finger moved inside her, touching a different spot, and it was like gasoline being poured onto a fire. Layla gasped and practically came off the bed, crying out. Her fingers curled tighter in his hair, and when he tried to lift his head, she moaned and pushed him right back down. She ignored his chuckle of amusement, because she was so damn close, and when he kept rubbing and licking, her hips quaked and she moved along with him until the orgasm swept over her a moment later, shattering in its intensity. The noise she made when she came was utterly ridiculous—it might have been his name mixed with a cussword—and her pussy clenched so hard and so often that her entire body felt as if it was shaking. Jack lifted his head and began kissing the inside of her thigh instead, his fingers sliding away from her body, and he held her as the orgasm raced through her, until she could breathe again and the stars swimming in her vision disappeared.

"Holy . . ." Layla breathed, staring up at the ceiling again. She felt boneless and hollowed out and . . . god, so damn good.

Jack chuckled again, kissing the inside of her thigh. "That's my girl." He moved up onto the bed, lying down beside her, and put his arms around her waist. He kissed her shoulder, watching her face. "How was that?"

"I . . . have no words."

"You liked?" He sounded pleased.

Layla made a noise in her throat. "I liked, yeah."

"Not shy anymore?" When she shook her head, he pressed another kiss to her shoulder. "So you wouldn't object if I did that again? Repeatedly?"

She looked at him as if he was crazy. "Object? Never. I think you've ruined me for everything else."

He grinned, looking rather satisfied with himself. "You say that, but maybe someday we'll do it all, hmm? Reserve judgment until then."

Layla was feeling good—and, okay, pretty frisky after that intense orgasm—and she turned on her side, facing him. She hooked a leg around his and shrugged. "We could always do it right now."

Jack smiled at her and then leaned in and gave her the most chaste kiss ever—a peck on the nose. "Maybe after I show you my something special?"

Right. He'd wanted her to come over for a reason. "Is it here?"

"No, we have to drive somewhere. But it's not far, I promise."

She wanted to pout and crawl back under the covers . . . or basically just twine herself around him until he gave in and wanted to have sex, but one look at Jack and she gave up on that idea. He looked excited and nervous about something, like a kid on Christmas morning who was half afraid that Santa had brought him nothing but coal. Whatever this was he wanted to show her, it meant a lot to him.

So she leaned forward and gave him a kiss. "I brought a dress. Let me change."

CHAPTER TWENTY-FOUR

Layla was not doing well with the whole dating thing. After this afternoon? She was pretty much ready to devote herself entirely to Jack, his hands, and his mouth. The rest of Jack could come along, too, she thought with a dopey smile as she watched him drive. Maybe it was endorphins that were racing through her, but Layla felt incredibly good. Like she could conquer the world with Jack at her side.

He glanced over at her as he turned onto the highway. "You keep looking over at me."

"Sorry." She wasn't all that sorry, though. He was nice to look at. Really, really nice.

"It's my fault for being so damn cute, right?"

"I'm not going to answer that and inflate your already tremendous ego," Layla teased. She turned away from him—which was harder than it should have been—and peered out the front window of the truck. "Please tell me this isn't another February picnic?"

"Nope. Something totally different."

Layla squinted at the countryside they drove past. While she wasn't exactly the world's biggest adventurer, she was familiar enough with the area to know that there wasn't a whole heck of a lot down this particular road. And when he exited and turned down a side road that she was extremely familiar with, a wry smile of disgust curved her mouth.

Oh yeah, she knew this area all too well. This was where her mom had bought her dud property, the one that was nothing but a big mud puddle. "I hope you realize there's nothing out here but hills and a stream," Layla teased, glancing over at him.

Jack looked even more excited, which was mystifying. "You'll see."

As they pulled closer and closer to her mom's land, Layla started to get more and more uncomfortable. She didn't even like being around here. It was a reminder that her mom was a horrible person who used people and didn't care who she stepped on . . . and even so, Layla still wanted her approval for some stupid reason. Janet tried to drag her daughter into her schemes, and Layla fought back. It was kind of their thing, the only connection they really shared— the only thing they had in common sometimes.

Which was sad, but there it was.

As they pulled up to Janet's land, Layla felt sick. Her stomach plummeted as she saw the FOR SALE sign with JS PROPERTIES LLC on it. That was Janet's shell company, the one she was constantly trying to find ways to get around tax laws. The one based out of a PO box at some shady strip mall in Nebraska. The one that Janet planned on dissolving the moment she sold her land and got her money.

Layla swallowed hard.

Jack pulled the truck up and parked it. "This is what I wanted to show you."

Was this some kind of wacky intervention, then? Was he

wanting to show it to her to point out how terrible a person her mother was? Layla knew. Oh, she knew all too well. But what did he expect her to do about it? "O-okay?"

A brief look of disappointment flickered across Jack's face. He reached for her hand. "I'm showing it to you because it's important to me."

His hand felt warm in her clammy one. "This is?"

He nodded proudly, and the look as he scanned the land spreading out in front of them was fierce with joy. "I'm buying all this. I'm going to start my own ranch, and I wanted you to be the first to know. Well, other than the real estate agent." He chuckled and squeezed her hand. "Come on out. I want you to get a good look at everything."

Oh.

Oh god.

This was much worse than an intervention.

Her mom was going to sucker Jack for every dollar he had.

This was an utter nightmare.

Wooden, Layla got out of the truck and took a few wobbling steps forward. Immediately, her heels—her stupid heels—stuck into the muddy ground.

"It's just a little wet," Jack reassured her. "The property's close to a creek, but it's not going to be a problem. I went over all the documentation."

Oh god. The documentation her mother had cooked that she'd wanted Layla to sign off on.

"In a way, the stream's good," Jack said, moving to her side of the truck. "Fresh running water for the animals at all times. Come on, I want to show you where I'm going to put the house . . ." He took her hand and paused when she didn't follow along with him. "You all right, baby?"

"No," she whispered, feeling like the biggest fraud ever.

"You look kind of green." Jack moved back to her and slid his arms around her waist. "Do you need to sit down?"

His concern made her want to cry. Why was he so amazing and here she was lying to him? Layla couldn't let him buy this land. It was a money pit, an absolute disaster, and her mother was the worst for even trying to pull this. She had to get out of here, and if it meant faking sickness, she'd absolutely do it. "I think I need to go home, Jack."

Disappointment flashed across his face. "Of course."

"I'm sorry. I'm sorry to ruin your afternoon," she babbled, and she felt like the worst person in the world. Jack had wanted to show off the land because he was proud of it, proud of the decision he was making to strike out on his own . . . and he had no idea it was such a disaster.

And she didn't know if she could tell him.

Layla had to fix this somehow without Jack knowing just how involved she was.

CHAPTER TWENTY-FIVE

Jack was silent on the trip back to the ranch. She knew he was confused by her actions, by the way she'd been fine—and frisky!—all damn afternoon, only to freak out the moment they went out to the land. Then she'd clammed up on him and made him turn the truck around. She wished half a dozen times on the drive back that she'd taken her own car, because the awkward silence between them was killing her.

She let out a breath of relief the moment he parked next to her car.

"You sure you're okay?" Jack asked her again, a frown on his face.

"I just . . . need to go home for a bit. Take some medicine—"

"I can take care of you," he offered, reaching out to brush a lock of hair off her forehead. "I've got some stomach stuff and if you need something, I can go to the pharmacy. I wouldn't mind having you stay."

"No," she blurted. "I need to go."

"Layla." He took her hand in his. Held it tight. "Are you freaking out about something between . . . you and me? About what happened between us today?"

Oh god, of course he'd think that. "No, Jack, I swear I'm not. I just . . ."

"Need to go. I get it." But she could tell by his expression that he didn't. He sighed and moved away, and she felt like the world's biggest jerk as she moved to her car, tossing her purse into the passenger seat.

"Will you keep Oscar?" she asked, pulling out her keys.

He gave her an odd look. "Of course."

Layla nodded and then impulsively moved back over to him and kissed him. "We're good," she promised him with a fierce note in her voice. "I swear to you that we're good."

He gave her a curious look. "You want to talk about it? Whatever's bothering you?"

"I can't."

"Ah." His smile faded but he gave her a nod. "Okay. Call me, I guess, when you feel better."

Layla knew in that moment that he suspected she wasn't sick. She wondered if she could puke on command. Right now she kind of felt like vomiting . . . but nothing came up. Figured. She managed a smile for him and got into her car, buckled in, slowly pulled out of the driveway, and headed back down to the main road.

Instead of turning toward Painted Barrel, she headed onto the highway.

Her mother was getting a visit.

Layla parked in front of her mother's apartment complex and sucked in a deep breath. She hated confrontation—especially with Janet, who always managed to turn it around on her—but she needed answers. No matter how ugly things got, Layla had to fix this. Jack couldn't buy that land. He'd be dead in the water before he ever got his house built. The first big rain of the spring, combined with the melting snows, and he'd be sitting right on a lake. He'd lose his savings and everything, and she absolutely was not going to let her mother do that to him. So she got out of the car, steeled herself, and then marched up the stairs to Janet Schmidt's apartment.

She knocked.

Waited.

Tapped her foot.

Finally, there was a bit of rustling inside and the door opened. Janet had a glass of wine in her hand and was wearing a pretty day dress that looked as if it cost a fortune. She had on high heels, her hair was pulled up artfully in a clip, and classical music played in the background. Even when "relaxing" at home, Janet liked to live as if she were entertaining, which meant she had to look her best.

"Hi, Mom," Layla said loudly. "What the fuck?"

"Layla-belle, what are you doing here? I have a date tonight." Janet gestured that Layla should come inside. "You can stay, but not for too long. I do have to point out it's terribly selfish of you to come by without warning, though, honey—"

"Spare me, Mom." Layla stormed inside and immediately went to her mother's desk. "Where are your papers?"

"What papers? Do you want a glass of wine? I just opened up the loveliest Chianti—"

"The papers for the sale of the land." Layla picked through a stack of folders. "I want to look at them."

"I don't know what you're talking about—"

"Bullshit you don't." She pulled open a file drawer and started flipping through. Her mother was terrible at filing anything, and bills were just stacked right and left, crammed into every possible space. "Don't play games, Mom. If you want me out of here before the latest boyfriend shows up, you'll let me look at your paperwork and I'll get out of your hair."

"Did I tell you my new boyfriend is rich? He's also younger than me by five years." Janet took a sip of wine. "We're going to the Bahamas together soon. He told me he'd take care of everything."

"Super." Layla flipped past a stack of overdue bills, unsurprised to see a bunch of notices in pink proclaiming PAST DUE. It wasn't that Janet didn't have the money to pay for things—it just wasn't a priority for her. She spent her money on her primary concern—and that was Janet. "I'm serious, Mom, where is it?"

"Where is what?" Janet asked sweetly.

Layla turned to look at her mother, wanting to scream. "You know what! Where is the damn paperwork for the sale of the land in Painted Barrel? The floodplain?"

Janet rolled her eyes and shrugged her shoulders, acting innocent. "It's not a floodplain."

Okay, Layla was definitely going to start screaming if this continued. She turned and faced Janet entirely, scowling. "Then show me the details where you got it changed. Show me the surveys. Show me the FEMA documentation that changes the floodplain designation."

Janet rolled her eyes. "You're being so dramatic, Laylabelle. Did you really come over here all this way just to harass me? Don't you have better things to do on the weekend?" She shook her head. "If only you'd go out with some of the nice men I take so much time trying to set you up with."

"Mom." Layla got to her feet. "I'm about to knock that wineglass out of your hand if you don't quit being obtuse and just show me the paperwork. I know you're selling the land, because my boyfriend is the buyer. And I know he wouldn't buy a bunch of ranch land in a floodplain, so stop playing games and just show me the contracts, okay?"

Her eyes widened. "You and that rancher are dating? Isn't he the one you paid for at the auction?" Janet bit her lip. "Oh, Layla, honey, he probably thinks you have a lot of money after you spent so much on him. I'm worried that he's using you."

Layla glared at Janet and moved to the kitchen counter, where her mom tended to keep the day's mail and important documents before tossing them out of sight into whatever drawer was nearest. When that didn't provide the paperwork, Layla began pulling out drawers in the kitchen. Sure enough, there was a blue folder emblazoned with a real estate logo on it. Layla pulled it out, glared at Janet, and began to flip through the paperwork. Her heart pounded as she saw Jack's signature all over it. The amount he was paying for the land was staggering—three times what her mother had paid. The bank loan was for an amount that made her faint.

And he'd put down a deposit of thirty grand of his own money.

Thirty grand. The sheer amount of money was horrifying. She knew he didn't make a lot as a cowboy, so he must have saved up for years and years to come up with that kind of down payment. He'd cleaned out every penny he owned to buy the land.

The land that was a floodplain that most certainly flooded all the time, regularly.

Layla felt sick. This had to stop. And when she pulled out an elevation map, nothing showed a floodplain at all. "I don't understand. You and I both know this is wrong. Jack wouldn't sign off if he knew the land wasn't usable."

"Well, maybe he should have checked."

Layla glared at her mother. "You're the one providing the documents and stating that they're correct. If anyone's in the wrong, you are. He shouldn't have to triple-check everything you send over to make sure you're not lying. You're not supposed to be lying!"

"You're yelling, Layla-belle." Janet winced. "I don't like it when you get so upset over nothing."

"Nothing? We both know this is wrong, and now you're going to saddle my boyfriend with your problem!"

"Well, he can always back out. He has thirty days from signing."

"And lose his deposit! I saw how much money that was!"

Janet smiled and took another sip of her wine.

God. Layla knew her mother was a piece of work, but she'd never thought of her as explicitly evil. But this? What she was doing right now? This was straight-up awful. Either Jack got saddled with terrible land that he couldn't use, or he lost his deposit. "Once he finds out what you did, he'll sue you, Mom."

"He'll have to sue my LLC," Janet said sweetly.

Which meant she'd just declare bankruptcy and skate away from her debt, like she always did. Somehow, Janet always managed to come out ahead despite leaving a mountain of unpaid debt behind her. It was unreal. It made Layla want to scream.

She shook her head and picked up another document. "I don't know how you got this to go through."

"I have a friend that helped me. We got the elevation corrected and it was all updated through FEMA." Janet's tone was defensive and overly sweet, as it always was when she was lying. "Everything is on paper, as it should be."

She had the elevation "corrected"? That seemed . . . wrong. "You found someone to fudge your documents? What kind of crooked idiot went along with your plans?"

Janet giggled. "You did, Layla-belle."

"Excuse me?"

Janet took another sip of her wine. "I knew you were

busy with that cowboy and I knew you'd want to help your mother if you weren't being so *very* stubborn about things, so I went to your office and borrowed your notary stamp."

"You what?"

"Oh, come on," Janet said, irritated. "This isn't like the time I borrowed your social security number and got all those credit cards. This is just a teensy-weensy document that corrects a few things that makes my land worth money again." She smiled ever so charmingly at Layla. "If your boyfriend doesn't agree, he's more than capable of reselling the land for himself."

Layla gaped. She couldn't believe what she was hearing. Her stomach churning, she flicked through the paperwork, looking for a notary seal. Sure enough, there was hers on some letterhead, stating that she assessed that what Janet Schmidt claimed was accurate. Right next to her seal was her signature.

Her own mother had forged her signature.

Layla sat back in her chair, stunned. Was Jack going to think she was playing him if this went through? Dear god, this just got worse and worse. "How could you do that, Mom?"

"What do you mean?"

"I mean, you've forged my stamp—"

"I didn't! It was your stamp!"

"You took it! The whole point of a notary is so the document is witnessed before someone that's trusted with the law. And you just crapped all over that so you can shove your problems onto someone else!"

Big, fat tears pooled in Janet's eyes. "I really don't know why you're screaming—"

"You do know!" Layla yelled. "You absolutely know!"

"It's a harmless crime—"

"You're hoodwinking my boyfriend! You're going to

take his money and sell him garbage, Mom. How can you think I'm okay with this?"

Janet sniffed, looking woebegone. "What do you expect me to do?"

"Cancel the contract. Give him his money back. Fix these records. Take my name off them." Layla shoved the paperwork across the counter at her mother. "Keep the land. Or sell it for a loss. I don't care."

"Layla," her mother whispered. "I need the money."

"Not from Jack, you don't."

More tears flowed from Janet's eyes. "So you'd rather your mother end up on the street than your boyfriend get some land that he wanted? What's the harm?" She shook her head. "Why are you being so unfair? He can use the land . . . most of the time. Just tell him to get flood insurance and it'll all work out." Her gaze brightened. "He could get the insurance company to give him a fat payout. This is a win-win, Layla—"

"No," Layla said flatly. "He's not going to defraud an insurance company and neither are you. We're not doing this. You are going to give him his deposit back."

"So I can be the one that suffers in this? No, Layla. It's not my fault he didn't do his due diligence." Janet shook her head and went to pour herself another glass of wine. "Your cowboy may be pretty, but that doesn't mean I have to pay the price if he's not going to question things."

Layla gritted her teeth. Why would Jack question legal documentation submitted on the land? Of course he'd assume it was legit. Any rational human being would . . . but Janet wasn't rational, and therein was the problem. "If you don't tell him about the floodplain and give him his money back, I will."

Janet just shook her head. "And how do you think that's going to look? You knew all along that I was going to sell it, but it's a problem now because you know him? That makes you look like a terrible person, Layla." She tsked. "So self-ish. You're only upset because it's your boyfriend that's in-volved. You wouldn't care if I sold it to anyone else."

That wasn't true. She'd just never thought that her mom would go through with it.

Or . . . had she? And had she just been too wrapped up with Jack to think about it very much? Guilt washed through her. Was this her fault?

"I know," Janet said brightly. "Why don't you go and kiss your boyfriend and tell him that everything is fine. And just emphasize the flood insurance. It'll all turn out for the best, Layla-belle, wait and see." Her mother paused and then added, "You're good at that part."

Layla just shook her head. "Why are you doing this to me, Mom?"

"You think everything is about you, you selfish girl." Janet's mouth flattened. "Really. I don't know where you get that from."

Layla just laughed hysterically. It was either that, or cry.

CHAPTER TWENTY-SIX

Jack worried he'd somehow messed things up with Layla. He'd wanted to take his time with her, to romance her properly, but then she'd showed up at his place in that cute little get-up and "slow" had sped up a few notches. Even after he'd made her come, he thought things were okay with them. It was only after they got in the car that she acted strange and her face lost all its color. He'd driven her back to her car and she'd retreated as quickly as she could.

Logic told Jack that it really wasn't him . . . except what else could it be? He didn't know. Sometimes the most obvious answer was the right one, which was depressing.

Now he had a new problem—did he call Layla and try to talk to her? Or did he let her have space so she could figure things out? He had no damn idea. In the past, if a girl had retreated from him, he'd let her go. No big deal. Relationships had always been about having fun and nothing more. He'd never been serious about anyone.

But it was different with Layla. Everything was different. The thought of letting her walk away gutted him, left him hollow. He wanted to fix this, even if he didn't exactly know what he was fixing. He just knew that she'd been unhappy and panicked and he wanted to make it better.

Jack decided against calling her, determined to let her have her space, no matter how difficult it was for him. He worked in the barn all afternoon, Oscar set up nearby on a square bale of hay. He tried not to dwell on Layla's reaction and thought about his land instead. How many rooms would he build in his house? If it was meant to be a long-term sort of thing, it needed to be big enough for a family . . .

Which made him think about Layla again.

He groaned, ducking his head as he grabbed a pitchfork, and attacked the fresh straw with vigor. Maybe he'd just try to think about football instead. But then he thought about sitting on Layla's couch with her, her legs across his lap as she worked on her crochet and asked him about the game.

He couldn't lose her. It didn't matter that they were still early in their relationship. She was his. He was hers. It felt natural and right to be with her. He'd never met a girl he'd wanted to share his every thought with before Layla, and it was killing him that he couldn't figure her out.

Jack cleaned stalls and oiled saddles until it was late, and when he was done, he ached with exhaustion . . . but his head wasn't clear. He kept circling back to that afternoon. Layla on her knees in front of him. Him with his mouth on her. She'd smiled so sweetly when they were done, and her kisses had seemed sincere . . . but everything after that mystified him.

There'd be no solving it tonight, it seemed. He scooped up his sleeping dog and headed toward his cabin, but the moment he walked in the door, it felt like a mistake. His cabin smelled like sex, and Layla's panties were tossed atop his nightstand. Jack set Oscar down in his bed, took a shower, and then checked his phone.

No messages.

Okay, he could play this casual and go to sleep, or he could text her like the besotted fool he was.

Really, besotted seemed the only way to go.

JACK: Just checking in on you. You left pretty
quickly earlier. I hope you're feeling better.

He had a million things he wanted to ask her. *Are you all right? Did I move too fast? Did I do something wrong and scare you?* But Jack kept it safe; she'd said she felt sick, so he'd make sure she was okay, nothing more.

To his relief, her answer came almost right away. Three dots popped up on his phone and he watched, holding his breath, waiting for her response.

LAYLA: I'm okay. Thanks for asking.

LAYLA: Sorry to bail on you earlier. It was just . . .
a lot.

LAYLA: My stomach, that is.

It was just as he'd suspected, then. He'd moved too fast and she'd panicked and retreated. Jack sighed heavily. Okay. If that was the case, he could deal with that. He'd just have to move slower. Nothing but kisses and hand-holding until she was ready for more, until she made the first move—

Except she'd made the first move earlier today, hadn't she? Damn, but his brain was scrambled over this.

JACK: Glad you're feeling better. If you need me to
bring you medicine, let me know. And if you want
me to leave you alone, you let me know that, too.
I'm here for you, either way.

This time, the three dots popped up and then disappeared, and he stared at the phone for so long that he began to suspect that she'd bailed out of the conversation. That she didn't want to talk after all.

Just when he was about to drop the phone on the nightstand and go to sleep—ha, yeah, right, as if he could sleep right now—a new text from her popped up.

LAYLA: Thanks, Jack. I'm sorry if I'm being weird. I just need to clear my head of some stuff.

LAYLA: But I'd like to talk. Not tomorrow . . . but Monday. Do you want to meet up?

JACK: This sounds like a breakup speech.

LAYLA: It's not, I promise, but it's important. I won't be able to relax until we talk.

JACK: You don't want to meet tomorrow? I can come to you.

LAYLA: No, not tomorrow. I need time to think.

LAYLA: Night. I'll text you.

Jack stared down at his phone. What the hell was that all about? She said it wasn't a breakup speech, but in his experience, that was precisely what it sounded like. He'd given plenty of them in the past, most of them involving the phrases "it's not you, it's me" or "need time to think."

Hell. He wasn't ready for this to be over. Even if he lived to be a hundred, he wasn't sure if he'd ever be ready for this to be over between them. He wanted to grow old with Layla at his side. He wanted to wake up to Layla's smile, to watch her push her glasses up her nose in that cute way she did. He wanted more than weekends and casual dates with her.

He was ready for forever.

But it seemed like he might be the only one.

CHAPTER TWENTY-SEVEN

Layla spent all day sitting on her couch, stress-eating ice cream and trying to figure out a way to defuse the ticking time bomb her mother had dropped into her lap. This was what Layla did. She was a fixer, a problem solver. She could do this. She had a notepad in hand, her cat curled up atop the couch, and she brainstormed ways to fix the mess of her mother's land. But by the time night hit, Layla was bloated, out of ice cream, and despairing.

Every way this could go, it was bad.

She had to tell Jack about the land. As much as it made her want to run away, screaming, he'd never trust her again if she didn't. So Layla was going to tell him tomorrow.

If Jack backed out of the sale after learning the truth, he'd lose his hefty deposit. It would take him years to save up again.

If Jack went ahead and bought the land, he couldn't build there. It'd either be worthless to him, or he could try to sue her mom for misleading him. If he sued her, Janet would just fold her company and declare bankruptcy, and Jack would be out court fees and still be stuck with the land.

Or he could skip the suing and report her mother to the authorities. If that was the case, Layla would be investigated, too, because her stamp was all over the paperwork. Janet was a convincing liar, and Layla wasn't sure that her mom wouldn't try to play ignorant and somehow pin it on her by accident.

At least, Layla hoped it would be by accident.

Any way she looked at it, though, the situation was awful. Someone was going to lose in every scenario, and if it wasn't Jack . . . it was Layla.

She didn't know what to do. And the person she wanted to ask most? The person she wanted to lean on? Was Jack. But she wasn't entirely sure he'd be on her side for this.

After all, her mother was right—Layla had known about her plans and still hadn't stopped her. That made her complicit, didn't it? And now Jack would probably hate her.

Driving up to Jack's house that Monday was the hardest thing she'd ever done. She hadn't slept a wink all night, and now she was surviving purely on coffee and adrenaline. Her stomach was too knotted for her to eat, and she'd canceled her client meetings that day. She was in no mood to work, not when her personal life was crashing down around her. She'd texted Jack that morning and agreed to meet at his place, since he was working and couldn't abandon things as easily as she could.

The day was beautiful, at least. The snow was pristine and fresh, but the skies were blue and clear. It was a perfect early-March day . . . sort of. If the world wasn't falling down around her ears, she would have enjoyed the weather. As it was . . . Layla swallowed hard. She finally got out of her car and approached Jack's cabin. She knocked, her stomach fluttering.

"Not there."

Layla turned in surprise. "W-what?"

The man standing on the porch next door was Jack's brother. Caleb, she was pretty sure. He had a similar face to Jack, but in her eyes, he was less handsome. He seemed far more serious, his expression solemn, and he had a basket of what looked like laundry under his arm. Right. Amy had mentioned that Caleb pretty much only went home to do laundry.

"Hi," Layla breathed. "I—"

Caleb pointed at the barn, cutting her off. Right. Caleb wasn't much of a talker. How he'd ever hooked up with her friend Amy, she had no idea.

Not that it was important right now.

"Thanks," she said meekly and headed for the barn. Inside, she could hear the sound of voices, a deep, gruff one, and Jack's smoother tone answering in a distracted sort of manner. She couldn't make out what they were saying, but the gruff one sounded irritated. Stuffing her hands in her pockets, Layla headed for the barn and knocked on the big, open wooden doors there, feeling like an idiot. "Hello?"

"Come in," Jack called.

She stepped inside, smiling a little overly brightly at the two men. Jack was there, his coat zipped up to his neck, and he had a pitchfork and a mess of hay around his boots. One of his brothers—Hank, she assumed by the full, bushy beard—was glaring at Jack. He looked over at Layla, nodded, and then shook his head. "Tell Caleb I'm doing a fence run."

"Appreciate it," Jack called to his brother.

Hank just glared at him from over his shoulder.

Layla bit her lip, waiting until the scary-looking older brother was gone, and then she took a few more steps toward Jack. "Am I . . . causing a problem?"

"Nope." Jack gave her a slow, dreamy grin that made her heart flip in her chest. "It was my turn to go out and check the fences in the more distant pastures, but I told Hank I needed to talk to you. He's going instead, and he's not thrilled because he was going to have lunch with Becca today."

"Oh." Layla winced. "I'm sorry."

"Don't be. He can suck it up."

So now two of the Watson brothers were going to hate her. Wonderful. "I . . . can we talk?"

The grin slid off his face. "Of course."

"Should we go someplace private? To your cabin, maybe?" She glanced at the horse stalls nearby. No one else seemed to be around, but the barn felt very open and exposed. In a weird way, at least she could hide in Jack's cabin.

"I guess?" He rubbed his jaw and put the pitchfork aside. "All this subterfuge is killing me, though, Layla. Can't you just spit it out?"

"It's not that easy."

He grunted, his mouth flattening, and for a moment, he looked just like his stern older brothers. Then his zipped-up coat shifted, and Oscar poked his head out of the collar.

Layla smiled despite herself. "You're carrying Oscar?"

"In a baby sling," he admitted. "You know how he loves attention, and it kept my hands free so I could work."

Oh, she did, and a baby sling was a great idea. She felt guilty that she'd left the dog with him, because of course it was going to hamper his work. Just another card to add to the guilty pile. Ugh.

CHAPTER TWENTY-EIGHT

They headed to his cabin in utter silence. Layla's pulse pounded in her ears. It felt like walking to her doom. How could she possibly expect Jack to understand when she didn't even understand it herself? How could her mother do such a thing? How could her mother screw a perfect stranger over like this? Or Jack? Her mother knew she was dating Jack, didn't she? Surely she'd recognized his name on the paperwork . . . and yet she'd said nothing at all.

Because no one mattered to Janet except for Janet.

It always came back to Layla to fix Janet's messes, too. The moment she got into something over her head, she'd call Layla up, cry, and swear it would all be different, and Layla would fix things for her as much as she could. She'd let Janet borrow money more times than she could count. She'd paid Janet's taxes. She'd shown up at the water department to argue that Janet's water should be turned back on. She was always there to bail her mother out because they were family.

And look what it had done for her.

Jack opened the door to his cabin and unzipped his coat, releasing Oscar. The dog wiggled on the bed, rolling happily, his tail flicking with excitement at the sight of Layla. She couldn't stand it. With a sigh, she sat on the edge of the bed and put her arms out, and he jumped into them.

"Didn't even flinch at your hands," Jack said proudly. "He's getting used to us."

Layla tried to smile. She pulled Oscar close and kissed his floppy ear, wanting to cry. "I suppose if he can be brave, I can be, too."

"That sounds . . . dire." Jack's voice was no longer laughing. When she looked over at him, his expression was shuttered. Serious. "You're worrying me. You want to tell me what's going on?"

"No. Not really." Layla managed a weak smile. "I don't want to talk about it at all, but I really don't have a choice."

He thumped down on the bed next to her, all big, solid presence. "Can you just spit it out already? It's been making me crazy for days. Tell me what I did wrong. Tell me how I can fix it, because I like you. Whatever I somehow fucked up, tell me so I know what's not on the table when it comes to me and you."

She stared at him. "It . . . it's not you, Jack," Layla stammered. "You're perfect."

"Then what the hell is it?"

She swallowed hard. Forced herself to spit out the words. "You can't buy your land."

There was a long moment of silence. Jack paused. Squinted at her, as if not entirely sure he'd heard her correctly. Then he said simply, "Huh?"

"The land," Layla repeated. "The land you bid on. I can't let you buy it."

And even though it was hard, Layla spilled out every single awful detail.

CHAPTER TWENTY-NINE

Jack rubbed his jaw, trying to process everything Layla had told him. She'd spoken so rapidly, her words tumbling over one another, that for a few brief moments, he'd thought she was making it all up. But the serious expression on her face, the way her eyes shimmered as if she were holding back tears, it all told him that she believed every word of what she told him.

"I thought the land seemed awfully low-lying," Jack began. "So we triple-checked the surveys. It's not in a flood region."

"It is," Layla insisted. "The paperwork has been completely fudged. JS Properties is the owner, right? JS is my mom—Janet Schmidt. She bought up that land years ago in one of her get-rich-quick schemes, only she didn't bother to look at the paperwork herself. She was going to subdivide it and sell it off to someone to make money, except it's in a floodplain. Not a hundred-year floodplain, where you *might* get flooded. This land literally turns into a lake every spring. In about a month or so, you'll see just what I mean." Her expression was downright miserable. "Mom knew that no one was going to buy it like that, so she got some shady friend of hers to help her forge some paperwork and sell it to get it off her hands. When you took me there Saturday, I panicked . . . I knew she had a buyer, but I didn't know it was you."

He could feel his brows furrowing as he tried to decipher everything, to let the enormity of the problem sink in. He tried to envision the lovely property he was buying, the creek overflowing with runoff and rain. If Layla was right, it would turn into a small lake and he wouldn't be able to use it. A little mud, sure. But land that constantly flooded? Repairing fences would eat his profits away and he'd have to constantly watch his animals closely to make sure nothing got mired in mud or broke a leg. A floodplain wasn't the worst . . . but it wasn't good. He shook his head. "I don't understand. That property's been for sale for months now."

"I know," Layla said miserably.

"You knew about this?" He stared at her. "You knew she was forging paperwork and you were fine with it until you found out it was me?"

"No, of course I'm not fine with it!" Layla held the dog in her arms tighter, as if she could draw strength from Oscar's warmth. "I just . . . didn't think she'd go through with it. I was busy, and my mom always has schemes and . . ." She shook her head.

He got to his feet and pulled out the documents he kept in a folder on his desk, because he'd looked at them a dozen times in the last few days, mentally planning the future. "Your stamp's right on the paperwork, Layla. You signed off on everything." He'd noticed that when he signed off on the initial contracts, because seeing it there had made him proud of her. It also made him feel better about his purchase. Layla was always so thorough and detailed when it came to her work. Anything she signed off on was safe.

Layla bit her lip. "My mother went to my office and borrowed my notary stamp. That's not my signature; that's hers."

"What?! That's illegal!"

"I know! I just . . . didn't think she'd do it." She looked miserable.

"This is your mother we're talking about, Layla. You've told me a dozen times that she's a narcissist. That she only thinks about herself. Of course she'd do it." He gave her an incredulous look. "She's stepping all over you. Did you call the cops when you found out she stole your stamp?"

"No." She stiffened. "She's my mother, Jack."

"She's breaking the law and she's forging documents. Do you know how much I put down as a deposit on this land?" He felt sick. Years of saving . . . and he was going to lose all of it if he bailed now. And she was defending her mother? The mother who admittedly did terrible things and made Layla fix her problems? "She's a terrible mother."

"She's still my mother."

He tossed the paperwork down on the bed. "I'm getting a lawyer involved. I'm going to demand my money back. Once they find out the contract's not legit, she can't hold me to it."

"Jack, you can't get a lawyer involved! My mom will go to prison for forging documents." She looked utterly distressed. Layla carefully set Oscar down on the bed and got to her feet. "Is my mom being incredibly dumb about this? Yes. But someone probably filled her ears with all kinds of money-making schemes and she's just listening to them. It's not her—"

"It is her," he said firmly. "You may not see her as a problem, but all I know is she's the one who bid against her own daughter at an auction, announced to the world that she was a virgin just to humiliate her in front of everyone, and is now a woman who makes up bogus documents to sell land she knows isn't worth a dime. And now I'm on the hook for thousands of dollars, Layla. What do you want me to do here?"

"I don't know," Layla whispered. She hugged her chest, arms crossed. "My name is on those documents. My seal is. I could lose my notary and that'll screw my business, Jack. If this gets out, it could ruin me, too. It's a small town. People talk. They'll think I'm as crooked as her."

Jack raked a hand through his hair. "So you're just going to let her get away with this?"

"I don't know." Tears spilled from her eyes. "I honestly don't know what to do. I've always done my best to fix her problems in the past, but I don't know how to fix this one."

"You shouldn't have to fix her problems. She's an adult. Let her realize the consequences of being an adult. Let her realize she can't walk all over everyone."

"She's my mother," Layla said brokenly. "She's the only family I have."

You have me, he wanted to say.

She ducked her head and began to pace, stress radiating out of her. "I've tried and tried to think of a way to pull this all apart, but my mother won't give your money back even if you back out."

"Then I'll sue her."

"You think she has any money for you to take?" Layla shook her head.

He snapped his fingers. "Better yet, I'll let everyone know what she did. That she stole your stamp and forged your name. I know she's your mother, but she broke the law. Maybe she should go to jail."

"And if I asked you not to do it?" Layla whispered, looking up at him with sad eyes.

Jack shook his head. He had no answer for that. He

wanted to help Layla, he really did, but if it meant letting her crooked mother get away with his money . . . just the thought made him both furious and disgusted. "I don't know how I feel about that, baby."

"I could pay you back the money," Layla began. "It'd take a while, but . . ."

He shook his head. "Once again, you're bailing out your mother. I don't want you to suffer over her choices. When are you going to let her learn from her own mistakes?"

Layla's lip trembled. "Give me twenty-four hours to figure out a solution."

"So you're picking her side?" Jack narrowed his eyes at her. "Really? You'll let her fuck me over just because she's your mother?"

"That's not it. That's not it at all." Layla sniffed hard, swiped at her cheeks, and headed for the door to his cabin. "Just . . . twenty-four hours, all right?" She raced out before he could stop her, and Jack was torn. Part of him wanted to go after her . . . if only to shake some sense into her.

How was it someone as awful as Janet had such control over sweet, enthusiastic, eager-to-please Layla? He looked down at the documents scattered on his bed next to Oscar. One of the pages was for barn plans, another for a building layout for a home. His future home.

Jack crumpled it up and tossed it in the trash.

Even though she hadn't been to therapy in a few months, Layla texted her therapist and asked if she could come by for a session. She needed to clear her head, and her therapist always had good, unbiased advice. If nothing else, Layla could use her as a springboard for ideas.

She'd wanted to reach out to Becca and Amy, her closest friends, but they were both involved with Jack's brothers. They'd take Jack's side.

And . . . Jack's side was the right side. Layla knew that, but even so, how could she turn her back on her mother like that? It was one thing to refuse to help her. It was another to assist with a lawsuit against her and contact the police. She knew her mother was selfish and crappy, but getting law enforcement involved felt like a step she wouldn't be able to walk back from.

If she lost her mother, who did she have left for family? No one at all. Her father had been out of the picture for so long that sometimes Layla forgot he existed at all.

Either way, Layla was going to lose someone.

So . . . therapy.

Her psychologist was able to squeeze her in that afternoon, and Layla showed up, a nervous, twitchy wreck, and gushed it all out. She told her therapist everything and waited expectantly for advice.

But her therapist only clasped her hands and gazed at Layla. "You know what I'm going to say."

Layla cringed. In a way, she did. She knew what the right answer was . . . but it was so hard. "I just . . . I guess I wanted to hear it from another person."

The therapist gestured at Layla. "Look at it this way. This is a pivotal moment in your relationships. It's not about who's right or who's wrong. Both are asking you to take a strong stand on their behalf. The question is, who do you want to stand with?"

"I want Jack," Layla whispered, toying with the hem of her sweater. She hadn't thought to bring her crochet and her hands were fidgety. "I think I'm in love with Jack, but I don't think he'll want me after this."

"Ask yourself about the future, then," her therapist said calmly. "Play this out a year or two from now. Five years from now. Imagine your life going forward. I'm not here to judge. You have to do what's best for you. What will make you happy and satisfied? Where do you see yourself in five years based on today's decision? The answer might not be obvious, so I want you to go home and think about this."

Layla didn't need to go home to decide, though. She knew what her answer needed to be. Five years from now . . . she saw herself with Jack. Smiling with Jack. Laughing with Jack. Curled up on the couch with Jack. Enjoying life with Jack. If she sided with her mother despite everything . . . all she would have would be exactly what she had right now.

A relationship with someone who only used Layla for what she could do for her.

It was obvious. In a way, it had been obvious the entire time.

"It's just . . . it's hard," Layla said, twisting her hands. "It's really hard."

"Choosing to put yourself first is, sometimes." Her therapist smiled gently. "But you're not the one that set up these ultimatums. It's not up to you to fix the situation. It's not your situation. It's up to you to support, nothing more."

In that, her therapist was wrong. Layla could do more. She could do a lot more, and when she left the therapist's office, clearheaded and determined, she got to work.

CHAPTER THIRTY

It wasn't hard to flush her mother out of hiding.

Layla suspected that Janet would ignore her phone calls if Layla continued to act angry, so she opted to text her mother instead, and used a lure.

> LAYLA: Hey, Mom, a friend of mine gave me a few of these purses. I think they're expensive? If you want one, come pick it up.

She texted a photo of her Birkin bag (that she'd bought secondhand off of Amy for a ridiculously low amount of money last spring). Janet didn't know Layla had a thing for nice shoes and purses, but Layla absolutely knew her mother did. It was obvious bait, but she suspected Janet would be lured in anyhow.

Sure enough, she got a text back within an hour, a record for her mother.

JANET: When can I come by?

LAYLA: I'll be free tonight after seven.

JANET: You know that doesn't work for me.
Tonight's my book club. You know that! I'll be there
before five.

Normally, Layla would scramble to accommodate her
mother, feeling like she was the problem. She hadn't forgotten about her mother's book club. It was just passive-
aggressiveness on Layla's part to pick that particular time.

LAYLA: Sorry, I won't be here.

LAYLA: I'm visiting clients until seven.

It was a lie. Such a lie. And yet . . . Layla felt gleeful
saying it. What kind of awful person was she that lying to
her mother was such a thrill? It was just . . . she finally felt
like she was the one holding all the cards, and it was a
heady sensation. Riding high, Layla went ahead and texted
Jack, too.

LAYLA: Can I come over tonight?

LAYLA: It'll probably be late . . .

LAYLA: And you're probably angry at me.

JACK: I'm not and it's not. Come over whenever. We
need to talk.

She swallowed hard and sent back his wording.

LAYLA: That sounds like breakup-speak.

JACK: It's not. Just come over already.

LAYLA: I will. See you tonight.

She sent a half-dozen kiss emojis and felt like crying all at the same time. Whatever happened today, Jack was on her side. And because of that, she felt stronger, more resolute. She could do this.

Layla laid the paperwork she'd spent all night working on out on the kitchen table, poured herself a cup of coffee, and began to work on a new cross-stitch project to pass the time. Something with hearts and smiley faces and a few four-letter words suited her mood.

CHAPTER THIRTY-ONE

The doorbell rang at six thirty.

Of course it did; Layla had been expecting Janet to show up early. It was just another way Janet wanted control of the situation. No one else's schedule was important but her own. Layla considered pretending not to be home, and she stitched a few more times in her project, deliberately taking her time. Eventually, she got up and went to the front door. Before she opened it, she took a deep breath.

She could do this. Jack was on her side. He didn't even know what she was up to, and he supported her and still cared about her. That was enough for Layla.

With a steely look on her face, she opened the door.

Janet was dressed in a pair of tight designer jeans and a flowing silk blouse, a half dozen gold necklaces around her throat. Her hair was freshly highlighted with red streaks, her nails long and manicured, and Layla noticed new eyelash extensions, too. She gave Layla a knowing look. "I see you're home early."

"Something like that."

Her mother went inside Layla's place without asking, looking around. "I can't stay long. I just came to see those purses and to borrow some sugar, if you have some."

"I have sugar. But the purses were a lie." Layla marched over to the kitchen table and picked up the first stack of papers, holding them out to her mother. "This is for you."

Janet narrowed her eyes at Layla. "What's this?"

"This stack is a police report I'm filing against you."

"What?" Janet stared at her in horror.

"I'm going to file charges against you for breaking and entering my office, theft, and forgery." Layla's stomach clenched miserably, but she ignored it. She had to get this out, or she'd never be able to do it. "I wanted to let you know in advance before I did it. It's a misdemeanor to forge my signature, of course, but if you're found guilty it means fines and up to a year in prison."

Janet narrowed her eyes at her daughter. "This isn't funny, Layla-belle. You made me drive all the way over here for this? I don't appreciate it at all."

"I'm not being funny, Mom. I'm dead serious." Layla gestured at the paperwork. "I spent all afternoon filling that out. I haven't filed it officially yet, but I'm going to the moment you leave. I've also had the locks changed at my office and I've left instructions with the receptionist that if she sees you, she's to call the cops."

Janet said nothing. She gave Layla a withering look, her mouth tight, and flipped through the paperwork. After a long, tense moment, she threw it back down on the table. "Why would you do this to me, Layla? Your own mother?"

"Because I'm tired of trying to fix your messes for you. I'm not going to let you forge my signature on documentation I know is faked. I've also contacted the documentation department at FEMA to let them know that your elevation 'correction' request was fraudulent. I'm sure they'll be looking into it as well."

Big, fat tears glimmered in Janet's eyes. "You're really trying to get me sent to jail, Layla? Why? Haven't I been a good mother to you? Sure, I've messed up now and then, but don't you feel like this is an extreme step . . . ?"

"You mean extreme like how you stole my notary seal and forged my signature?" Layla threw back. "Don't act like the victim here, Mom. We all know it's not you."

Janet crossed her arms and tilted her head, gazing at Layla. "You haven't filed this yet. You're not going to. You wouldn't do that to me. You're just trying to scare me."

"I absolutely would and I absolutely am," Layla agreed. "I won't file it on one condition, though." She paused for a moment. "Actually, it's a few conditions, but they're all tied together."

"Is this about that boyfriend of yours? Is he filling your head with ideas? He's trying to get my land for free—"

"This is absolutely about him, and he doesn't want your land, Mom. No one does." Layla calmly reached over and picked up the next stack of paperwork on the table that she'd prepared. "This is a document where you'll back out of the sale of the property and agree to give Jack his deposit back. Your Realtor will need to sign this, too, but I'm sure you can work it out with him." She picked up another piece of paper. "And these documents will dissolve your JS Properties corporation, since we all know it's a joke. I've already filled them out for you as your accountant. All you need to do is sign on the noted spots." Layla picked up the next stack. "And this paperwork states that you're going to donate that land to the local fire department, since it's of no use to anyone."

Janet's mouth hung open. She took the paperwork as Layla handed it to her, saying nothing. When the last piece was presented, she lifted her gaze to Layla. "You're trying to ruin me."

"I'm not. I'm doing the right thing. I'm not going to let you screw Jack out of his money, or anyone else. I'm sorry you spent so much on that land, but that doesn't mean you get to pass the buck to someone else. It's your problem. These are solutions for you. Legal solutions."

Her mother set the paperwork down on the table. Janet shook her head. "I'm not doing this. That money is already spent. My new boyfriend—"

Layla raised a hand into the air. "Don't tell me. I don't want to know anything about him, because the less I know about him and his unscrupulous suggestions, the better. I'd hate to have to leave an anonymous tip with the authorities."

This time, her mother made an outraged sound in her throat. "You wouldn't!"

"Try me."

Janet recoiled at Layla's deadly tone. "This isn't like you, Layla-belle. What kind of notions has that boyfriend been filling your head with?" She shook her head and pushed the paperwork away from her. "I'm not doing any of this."

"Yes, you are."

"Why would I?"

"Because it's either that or I file my police report against you and ask them to come and dust for fingerprints at my office. I think we both know what they'll find." Layla pulled out the next document, the one that hurt her to fill out but was also absolutely necessary. "And I'm also going to file a restraining order against you if you don't go along with this."

Janet made a wounded sound. Her eyes filled with tears again, and Layla felt like the most awful daughter in the world. "You wouldn't."

"I would. I'm sorry, Mom, but you've left me no choice." Layla nudged the documents toward her. "If I can't trust you not to destroy my career or those that I love, I'm going to have to protect myself from you. It hurts me, but I have to do it."

"I don't think it hurts you at all," Janet cried out, snatching up the stacks of paper. "I think you're heartless and you're forcing your mother into a corner. You want me to be broke forever, don't you?"

"No, Mom. You know I don't." Layla's eyes got misty, but she dug her fingernails into her palms until the urge to cry passed. "You know I love you. I've tried to help you so many times, but all you've shown me is that I can't trust you. I'm sorry, but it has to be like this. Give Jack his money back. Get rid of the land. I'll help you do both—legally. If not, you and I are done."

Janet clutched the paperwork to her chest. "You ungrateful, awful child. When I think of all the things I've done for you, it breaks my heart." She shook her head. "I may never speak to you again after this."

"I know. I've thought about that a lot," Layla said calmly. "But this is the decision I've made, and it's one I'm going to have to live with. I'm sorry if it has consequences on our relationship, but I'm not budging. If you don't cancel the contract and give Jack his money back, I'm pressing charges."

"You'd really try to get me thrown in jail?" Janet sounded heartbroken, and even though Layla knew it was an act, it still hurt.

"If you go around forging my signature, yes, Mom. You've left me no choice."

They stood face-to-face, a silent standoff. After a long, tense moment, Janet sniffed and wiped her nose delicately with a tissue. "Well. I didn't expect to have my heart ripped out and stomped on by my daughter tonight. You've cornered me, it seems."

"I have," Layla said, oh so calm despite feeling like a million broken pieces inside. "You've cornered me, so I'm cornering you back."

"You'll have the documents back in the morning—"

Layla sensed victory, and she moved in for the kill. "Oh no," she said, and produced a pen. "You're going to sign off on them right now."

CHAPTER THIRTY-TWO

By the time her mother left, it was late and Layla was wiped.

Janet had cried. Of course she had—she believed herself the victim. Layla had been prepared to be hard-hearted to her mother's tears, but the reality was difficult. She didn't like to see anyone cry, much less her mother. It didn't help that Janet went on and on about how it was Layla's fault, and what a terrible daughter she was, and how this was the thanks she got after doing what she could to survive, and so on and so forth. Her mother was good at painting herself a victim, and no matter how many times Layla pointed out that Janet was the one breaking the law, it always somehow came back to things being Layla's fault. It was never Janet's fault.

It was . . . exhausting. Mentally and physically, Layla was wiped. All she wanted to do was curl up in a ball and hide for the next few days, until some of the hurting went away. She couldn't, though. Jack deserved to know what was going on, and she'd promised to come over, so she snuggled a cranky Sterling for a few minutes, scanned copies of the documents, then put on her shoes and got into the car.

When she started to drive, the enormity of the situation hit her.

She'd just destroyed her relationship with her only family. Granted, it wasn't that Janet was a good person. It wasn't that Janet was in the right. But now Layla was completely alone. Hot tears poured down her cheeks and made it hard to see, but she kept on driving. Maybe she'd get all the crying out before she got to Jack's. She'd feel sorry for herself for a little bit, and then get on with her life. Either Janet would understand and get over it, or she wouldn't, but Layla had made her decision. There was no going back now.

By the time she made it to the Swinging C Ranch and parked her car, she was mostly done with the crying. Flash drive clutched in hand, Layla headed for Jack's cabin. It was cold and dark outside, the chill February wind biting into her skin. She'd forgotten to wear something heavier than her sweatshirt, and now she regretted it. Oh well. She wasn't going to stay long. She was just going to give Jack the paperwork and let him make his decision about how he wanted to handle things—how he wanted to handle them— from here. If he didn't want to speak to her anymore, she would understand. It would hurt, and her heart would be broken, but she wouldn't blame him. Layla was determined not to pressure him.

Of course, all that determination withered the moment he opened the door. He stood there in an old, faded T-shirt and jeans, his hair rumpled and a five-o'clock shadow on his firm jaw. His eyes warmed at the sight of her and he looked so good and so incredibly appealing that her breath caught.

He looked like home.

All the tears Layla thought were done burst out of her again, and she began to cry even harder.

* * *

Jack was startled to see Layla show up at his doorstep so late at night. She'd mentioned she'd be coming by late, but he didn't realize how late until he'd dozed off watching a few late shows, Oscar tucked at his side in bed. He'd woken up to her knocking, and when she burst into tears, his heart clenched.

"Come here," he told her gruffly. He hated the sight of her tears.

He intended to just pull her inside the warm cabin, but the moment she stepped in and looked so lost and forlorn, he pulled her into his arms instead. Jack tucked Layla against his chest, shutting the door, and then wrapped her in a big hug.

She cried even harder, but clung to him.

"What's wrong?" he asked, rubbing her shoulders as she clung to him. "Layla, talk to me."

She took a deep, shuddering breath and tried to compose herself. "I got your money back," she managed to choke out after several moments.

Of all the things he'd expected to hear, that wasn't on the list. Jack went still. "What are you talking about?"

Layla pulled out of his grip and swiped at her face with the back of her hand, lifting her glasses to get rid of the wetness underneath. "I met with my mom. I cornered her. Told her I was going to press charges unless she terminated the contract on her end so you could get your money back." She fumbled in her pocket and produced a zip drive, offering it to him. "Here's copies for you. The Realtor still has to sign off on a lot of these, but a check should be coming back to you in the next few days. Your Realtor will probably call you about it tomorrow, too."

He took the drive, staring at it in shock. "You . . . how'd you manage this? I thought you said your mother was determined to go through with the sale." Jack had been kicking himself for days over everything. He'd seen the amendments to the surveys and had simply assumed it was all on the up-and-up. Layla's stamp had been all over them and so he hadn't questioned anything, and now he knew why. Since he'd seen her last, he'd been busy trying to figure out a way to make it work. What did one do with a floodplain? He'd read up on ranches in floodplains online, and the messages had been clear enough: it was a money pit. So he'd tried to think of other things he could do— terraforming the land, or having dirt dumped to build up a barrier. He hadn't come up with a single solution.

He'd also been worried that he'd have to press charges against Layla's mother, and how his girlfriend would take that. He was stuck, because he didn't want to mess things up with Layla. She was more important to him than any land, and if she'd asked him to let her mother get away with it, how could he say no? Then again, how could he say yes if it meant destroying his hopes of having his own place someday?

Jack had been very much stuck.

And Layla, being the fixer she was, had somehow salvaged the situation. He wanted to look at the documents, but right now the crying woman in front of him was a priority. He set the thumb drive down and pulled Layla into his arms again. "Come sit down and tell me everything."

He steered her toward the edge of the bed, and Oscar immediately crawled forward, tail wagging, and gazed up at Layla with sad eyes. She melted and picked the dog up, holding him tight and patting his belly. "You're the best boy, Oscar," she murmured. "I hope Dad's been taking good care of you."

"The best. Now spit out the details, Mom." He put a hand on her shoulder, rubbing her back again. "If you don't want to talk about it, I understand, but I'd really like to know."

She offered him a tremulous little smile. "No, I can talk about it. It's okay."

And she began to speak. Layla told him all about how she'd cornered her mother, prepared to file charges against her. How she'd drafted up documentation to donate the land, to get rid of her mother's company and undo all the damage the woman had caused. Jack was stunned . . . and in awe. Layla had stood up to her mother for him. She'd more or less forced Janet Schmidt to cave in and managed to get his money back and get him out of the land contract. She'd single-handedly salvaged the situation . . . at her own expense.

"You did that for me?" Jack asked, humbled.

She looked up at him, a confused expression on her face. "Of course I did it for you." She hesitated. "Well, not just for you. I didn't like that she was doing it in the first place. But when I realized what it meant if she got her way, I couldn't let it happen."

"Yes, but she's your mother."

"Yeah, well, I love you," Layla blurted, and then immediately clapped a hand over her mouth. Oscar, startled, began to snarl, and Layla quickly set him down on the bed and jumped to her feet. "I didn't say that."

Jack jumped to his feet, too. "You did say that."

"Oh god." She began to wring her hands and pace. "Jack, I'm so sorry. I—"

"Hey. Hey." He grabbed her hands before she could twist them again, forcing her to face him. "Why are you panicking?"

"Because only a crazy person starts declaring love after two weeks?"

"Does it matter if I say I love you, too?"

Layla paused. She blinked up at him. "You're not just saying that because I got your money back for you?"

Stung, Jack took a step back. "What? No. I knew it from our first date."

Her jaw dropped. "You what? The horseback-riding date?"

"Why not?" He grinned down at her. She really was so cute. He cupped her face and pressed a kiss to the tip of her nose. "You make me smile. You're funny. I think you're gorgeous. The moment I met you, I knew you were the one."

Layla gave him a skeptical look. "I'm allowed to be head over heels that quickly because I'm a big old virgin who's never been in a serious relationship. I'm not sure what your excuse is, Jack Watson."

He threw back his head and laughed, because even now, Layla was giving him shit. He loved it. "Maybe you're the first person I've ever wanted to be serious with." He reached up and pulled the pencil out of her bun, her hair falling down around her shoulders in glorious dark waves. "The first one that's made me think I want more than just having a good time." He ran his fingers through her hair, smiling at her serious expression. "When I saw the land, I couldn't wait to tell you about it. I couldn't wait to show you, because your opinion was the one that meant the most to me in the world."

Her expression fell, and Layla bit her lip. "And I was partially responsible for what a shit show that turned out to be. I should have said something the moment we drove up."

"You panicked. I get it. When you told me about the floodplain, I panicked, too. But now that I know what happened, I understand. You didn't really think your mother would do this, did you?"

Layla shook her head, her face pale. "She's always had schemes going on, some wackadoodle way to try and make a quick buck, but she's never been so willing to break the law. I guess she figured if it was paperwork, it was a harmless sort of crime." She bit her lip. "I want to say I can't believe she broke into my office and stole my stamp, but if I look back with a clearer head, this isn't the first time she's stepped all over me to get what she wants. So in a way, it's good that this came to a head. I just wish it hadn't happened in such a horrible situation." She touched Jack's chest, gazing up at him. "I'm so sorry about the land. I know you had big plans."

He lifted her hand to his mouth. "I did. But there'll be other pieces of land for sale. Something will come along. Maybe not right away, but I'm willing to wait." He pressed a kiss to the inside of her palm, loving the way her eyes lit up at the touch. "I happen to know a really great CPA and CPB who will help me look over the paperwork anytime I like."

"CPP," she corrected softly, smiling. "And day or night, your place or mine."

Damn, he liked how that somehow sounded incredibly dirty. "In a way, I'm glad that it was just the land. When you freaked out on me that day, I thought it was because of something I did. That I'd moved too fast and scared you off."

Her brows furrowed. "Something you did?"

"Yeah. Like maybe you weren't into oral sex or something."

Her face went crimson. "I can assure you that I had zero issues when it came to that. What, like I'm going to get mad that you made me orgasm so hard? If that's the biggest problem I have, I'm the luckiest woman in the world."

"Then we're agreed. You are absolutely the luckiest woman in the world."

Layla laughed, shaking her head at him. "And you're the most incorrigible man in the world."

"Big word. Someday I'll even ask what that means."

She giggled harder, the sound so bright and happy that it filled him with relief. He pulled her close, unable to keep his hands off of her. "I much prefer the sound of you laughing," he murmured softly. "Hate seeing you cry."

"It's been a hell of a week," Layla agreed. "But . . . you and me are okay?"

"You and me are more than okay." His hands slid to her waist and he leaned over her, moving in for a kiss. "Didn't I just tell you that I love you, Layla? And I'm pretty sure you said it, too."

"I'm a neurotic sort. You'll probably have to tell me at least a half a dozen times before it sinks in." Her gaze went to his mouth, her lips parting.

"I love you," he murmured before kissing her again. His lips moved over hers, whisper soft. "I love you. I love you. There. That'll give you a good head start."

"Thank you." She licked her lips, as if wanting to keep the taste of him fresh in her mind. "Where do we go from here?"

"Where would you like to go?" He wanted to kiss her again, but he'd let her decide how to proceed.

She gazed up at him, her hand playing on the front of his T-shirt. "Can I . . . stay the night?"

That . . . was unexpected. "You mean—"

Layla immediately flushed. "I know this sounds very schoolgirlish of me, but I don't know if I mean *that*. I just . . . I missed you the last few days and it's been lonely. I was wondering if we could just be together. Maybe throw some kissing in there."

He pulled her close and immediately kissed her, hard and fierce. "We can kiss as much as you want to, baby. You sure you want to stay here, though? Won't your cat be lonely?"

"Not half as lonely as I'll be if I go home alone."

"I'll go with you," he offered.

"You will?" Layla looked so surprised.

"Of course. You have all the good sports networks."

An expression of astonishment crossed her face, and then she smacked his chest lightly. "You're incredibly naughty."

"And that sounds far too filthy when you say it like that."

"Maybe I meant for it to sound filthy." She slid her arms around his neck, giving him a soft look. "Maybe I like kissing you so much that I'm willing to say all kinds of filthy things just to get your lips on mine again."

"You don't have to say anything at all," he murmured. "All you have to do is look at me like that."

"Like how?"

"Like you are right now." And he slanted his mouth across hers. Layla let out a little gasp that he swallowed up, and then she moaned as his tongue swept into her mouth. She tasted so sweet, her mouth so perfect against his that he lost track of time. Nothing existed outside of the feel of Layla in his arms, her tongue teasing against his as they kissed.

When he finally broke the kiss, she stumbled a little against him, and he caught her around the waist to steady her.

"That . . . was a really good kiss."

"You can have as many of them as you want. I have it on good authority that the owner's a very generous man."

She chuckled and impulsively flung her arms around him. "Thank you."

Puzzled, he rubbed her back. "Why are you thanking me?"

"Because when I came here, I wasn't sure what you'd think. I wasn't sure if you'd still want to be with me."

That crazy woman. "I love you, remember?"

"Gonna need to hear it at least . . ." She tapped her chin, pretending to consider. "Four more times."

He mock-growled at her and pulled her in close. "How about I just show you instead?"

They didn't leave for Layla's place for a good half hour, too busy kissing.

CHAPTER THIRTY-THREE

After a week of sheer hell and worry that she was going to lose everyone important to her, Layla felt positively effervescent. She watched Jack pack an overnight bag of clothing and held Oscar close. He was coming over to her house. To spend the night. Just to be with her because she didn't want to be alone. Just to hold her.

Because he loved her.

It made Layla want to cry all over again, but it was good crying this time. It was crying of sheer happiness, of disbelief that she was so darn lucky to have Jack. He hadn't told her that she was a terrible person for threatening the law on family. He'd understood. He'd understood everything and had never doubted her for a moment. She felt . . . awed by him. All her life, Layla had only felt valued for what she could do for other people. Jack loved her for . . . her.

That feeling of awe continued even as they took separate cars back to her place. He had to work early, he explained, and didn't want to wake her up when he left at four in the morning. It was humbling to think he was making so much room in his life for her, just because she didn't want to be alone. She really was the luckiest woman alive.

She pulled up to her house and, once inside, some of the giddy feeling left. The stacks of paperwork were still on the dining table, her desk covered with documentation, her mother's signature visible. It was a sobering reminder of how today had gone.

Layla was more than ready for today to be over. When Jack's car pulled up behind hers in the driveway, she was even more glad that she'd invited him over. Being around him centered her.

As long as he had her back, nothing else mattered.

Even though Jack had been over several times and there had been that one drunk sleepover, he'd never stayed the night like *this* before, and it made Layla feel a bit shy and awkward. Sure, she was a grown woman, but she'd never been through this particular scenario before. Did she just head straight for bed? Insist on watching some television first until they relaxed, what?

Jack must have sensed her unease. He put his bag down by the door and moved to her side. He put his arms around her and gazed down into her face. "I can leave, if you're uncomfortable."

"No, I'm glad you're here. I'm just being weird."

"If you weren't weird, would you be you?"

She poked him in the stomach. "Very funny."

"I am quite a catch," he agreed.

She rolled her eyes, chuckling. Jack and his corny jokes always made her smile, and some of her tension eased. "Did you . . . want to watch some television?"

He shook his head. "I have to get up pretty early and you look beat. Okay if we just go ahead and go to bed?"

She was fine with that. Bed seemed like a great idea, and even as she thought about it, a yawn rose in her throat. "Okay."

"First we should probably get our son settled," Jack joked. "Where does Oscar sleep?" He glanced over at the dog curled up on the couch.

"With Sterling, surprisingly enough. He'll be fine in the living room and Sterling's bed is in the corner. If I try to separate them, Sterling gets mad and looks for Oscar. I think the cat thinks Oscar is a helpless kitten. He's always grooming him and bossing him around."

"Oscar probably loves it."

She suspected he did. The dog meekly put up with Sterling's authoritative attention and even sought it out. Layla suspected that Oscar just liked any attention, be it from a cat or a human. And Jack was good to humor the spoiled dog, she thought affectionately as her boyfriend scooped up the dachshund and settled him in the cat bed. Sure enough, Sterling jumped in after him and immediately started licking Oscar's flanks. The dog got more attention from her cat than she did lately.

Maybe Layla wasn't the only lonely one.

"Come on," Jack said, taking her hand in his and tugging on it. "You look wiped. Let's get you to bed."

He retrieved his overnight bag and she let him lead her up the stairs and into her bedroom. The moment they got into her room, though, she cringed at the state of things. Her laptop was on one corner of the bed, cords everywhere. More paperwork was scattered and there were dirty clothes and old chip bags all over the dresser. An empty carton of ice cream sat on the nightstand. "I . . . ah . . . wasn't expecting company."

"My place looked similar," he offered. "I cleaned up when you said you were coming over."

She started to pick up the trash when her phone buzzed with an incoming text. Layla froze in place, her stomach clenching.

"Don't answer it," Jack warned. "You know it's not important."

"It's late, though. What if it is important? What if something bad has happened?"

"Or what if it's just your mother guilting you?"

Layla was pretty sure it was, but it felt awful to ignore it. Her phone buzzed with two more texts and she pulled her phone out of her pocket and handed it to Jack. "I can't look. Just tell me if it's an emergency."

She watched his face as he read the texts. After a moment, he rolled his eyes. "Not an emergency. Just an emergency guilt trip."

"Okay."

"You don't want to read it. She's sending you pictures of how much she's crying."

Layla blanched.

"She's just trying to make you feel bad because you stood up to her, Layla." Jack tossed her phone down on the bed and moved to her side. He cupped her face. "I'm proud of you, though. Land aside, my involvement aside, you stood up to a woman that uses you and put your foot down. Of course she's mad. But I couldn't be prouder."

"Hearing that makes things a little easier." Layla put her hands over his and looked up at him, hoping he'd kiss her. She desperately wanted one of those deep, intense, drugging kisses that made her forget the entire world.

But Jack only smiled at her. "Why don't you get ready for bed. I'll change in the bathroom downstairs."

"Sure." Maybe he'd kiss her when they'd gotten into bed. Right now, she wanted kisses and cuddling far more than she wanted a good night's sleep. She'd told him tonight was going to be chaste, though, so she didn't want to send him the wrong signals.

Ugh. Why did she have to overthink everything?

Layla grabbed a pajama set, changed, brushed her teeth,

and got into bed. She'd deliberately picked a loose-fitting T-shirt and a pair of cotton pajama shorts and skipped underwear and a bra. Wearing so little and knowing she was about to crawl into bed with the best-looking man she'd ever met made her feel sexy and a little scandalous. Would he notice she wasn't wearing a bra? Would it make him want to touch her?

Why did she feel like such a giggly teenager right now? Good lord.

She crossed her legs and waited for Jack, because getting under the covers would have felt too weird. Layla played with a piece of lint on the hem of her worn shirt and tried not to think about her mother. Her phone was at the corner of the bed where he'd left it, and she deliberately didn't touch it. Tonight was all about her and Jack. No one else. She'd let the real world intrude again tomorrow.

There was a light knock at her door.

"Come in," Layla said, feeling nervous and giddy at the same time.

Jack poked his head in, grinning at her. "Ready for bed?"

"More than ready." Layla shifted on the bed. "Which side do you want?"

"Doesn't matter. I'm gonna hog the blankets and put my hands all over you either way."

She blushed, chuckling. "Then you get the right." She watched him as he entered the room, and her mouth went dry. Jack moved with a mix of graceful confidence and masculine swagger. He wore nothing but a pair of black sleep pants, and it showed off his glorious abdomen and muscles. Her hands itched to touch him, and a low curl of heat started in her belly.

She wasn't the only one feeling the heat, if Jack's expression was an indication. His eyes were heavy-lidded in that sexy way that made them look so very dark and sultry. He sauntered toward the bed and sat down across from her. "In all seriousness, how do you want me?"

Layla's mouth was suddenly dry. "W-what?"

"On the bed." He grinned, and she knew that *he* knew there was a double entendre there. "Under the covers? Over the covers? Across the room?"

A chuckle escaped her. "Something tells me that wasn't very serious at all. And I didn't ask you to come over so you could sleep on the floor."

"I know, but I'd do it for you if you needed me to."

Her heart squeezed. "I'd like you under the covers. With me. Can we . . . cuddle?"

"I love a good cuddle," he assured her and got under the blankets, then opened his arms for her. "Come on over."

A shy smile on her face, Layla set her glasses down on the nightstand. She scooted under the covers herself, then moved over to his side. She settled in, resting her cheek against his shoulder as his arms went around her. Her hand went to his bare, warm chest, and it felt . . . nice. Like home. Layla closed her eyes and sighed. "Thank you."

"Don't thank me. I'm greedy for every scrap of attention you give me." One of his hands drifted lazily up and down her shoulders, rubbing. "I'm happy to do this as often as you want."

"What if I said I wanted it every night?" She burrowed down lower against him, loving the warmth of his skin, the scent of him, his big presence.

"Then I would say I need to bring a toothbrush and leave it here," he teased. "Because my morning breath is utterly outrageous."

Somehow, she doubted that very much. Everything about Jack was . . . well, it was pretty close to perfect in her eyes. He didn't have a temper, he was easygoing and fun, and he was gorgeous. They had great conversations and she enjoyed every moment she spent with him. "If your morning breath is your biggest flaw, I'm the luckiest girl ever."

"I think my biggest flaw is that I'm a clingy, needy sort,"

he teased. His other hand went to her bare arm, his finger-tips skating lightly up and down over her skin. It sent prickles of arousal through her belly, and her nipples pricked in awareness.

"You? Clingy? Doubtful."

"You think so? Because I seem to recall declaring love for a girl I've been dating for about two weeks."

"Well, the girl declared it first. So what does that make her?"

"Equally clingy?"

Layla poked him in the side. Hard.

"I see nothing wrong with you being clingy, baby. As long as you're clingy to me." Jack rubbed her arm and pressed a kiss to her forehead.

It was a sweet kiss. A tender kiss. A kiss that was not nearly enough, not in the slightest. Had she said she wanted to just cuddle tonight? Clearly she was off her rocker. Because having Jack's big body pressed against hers, half naked and so close she could eat off his flat abdomen? It was doing all kinds of things to her.

All kinds of very not-chaste, not-virginal things.

Experimentally, Layla let her hand glide over his stomach, caressing down the trail of hair that disappeared when it got close to his belly button. Layla watched her finger trace along his sun-darkened stomach, and then she leaned in, pressing her mouth against his pectoral.

Jack groaned and shifted against her. The blankets had pooled at his waist, but she wondered if he'd be hard if she lifted them up. She wanted to see.

She wanted to touch.

Her hand slid lower, even as she tilted her face against his pectoral a bit more, kissing again, and then letting her tongue glide over his skin.

Arms tightened around her. Jack's hand strayed lower, playing just at the waist of her T-shirt, as if he wanted to rip it off of her. She wanted that, too, but wasn't brave enough to say it. "Thought you wanted to keep things above the belt tonight," Jack murmured. "Because you are definitely heading south of mine."

She chuckled, the thrill of anticipation racing through her body, mingling with arousal. "I was just thinking . . . maybe you help me with this virginity thing after all?"

He went still against her.

Uh-oh.

Jack sat up, and Layla did, too, feeling awkward and somewhat foolish. Before she could say anything, he reached out and took her hand in his. "I don't want you to feel like you need to do this tonight because you need to keep me or some nonsense like that."

"What? No—"

"You've had a hell of a day. A hell of a week, actually. Both of us have. And I don't mind going as slow as you need to, Layla. I don't want you to rush anything on my account." He lifted her hand to his mouth and kissed her knuckles, grinning. "I'm in it for the long haul."

Layla shook her head. "I'm not doing this because of anything other than the fact that I like looking at you." She reached out and put her hand on his chest, tracing her fingers down the hard slabs of muscle. "I like touching you." She glanced up at him, biting her lip. "And I like kissing you. And being here next to you makes me want more of all of it."

Jack's eyes seemed to grow darker. He groaned and then pulled Layla against him. Before she could say anything else, he was kissing her, his mouth hot on hers. It was everything Layla wanted, and she sighed with utter pleasure. She shifted on the bed, crawling toward him until they were wrapped around each other, mouths connected and bodies touching.

He shifted his weight and then Layla was underneath him on the bed, his weight pressing her into the mattress. It felt good to have him over her, the pressure of his body a new experience and one she liked so, so much. It didn't feel crushing; it just added to her pleasure.

"Love you," he murmured between kisses. "Want you. Want you so badly."

"I want you, too, Jack," Layla breathed.

"I can give you pleasure," he continued, mouth hot on hers as he devoured her. "But I didn't bring condoms. I meant it when I said I wasn't gonna pressure you. We can make tonight all about you."

She smiled at his offer and kissed him again, letting her tongue play against the seam of his mouth before drawing away. "Jack, when I said I want you, I mean I want all of you. I'm fine with no condoms. In fact, I'm already on the pill."

"You are?"

She nodded. "It helps with hormones and making my period regular, which might be a little too much information, but yes. I've been on the pill since I was sixteen."

He kissed her fiercely, sucking on her lower lip so hard that she trembled. "How is it that you're telling me about your period and it's the sexiest damn thing I've ever heard in my life?"

"Because I'm telling you I want you inside me?"

"That'll do it." Jack's mouth slanted over hers again, and then she was lost in the feel of his mouth, the rasp of his beard stubble against her softer skin. His tongue was hard and demanding, as if he was realizing that she wanted this just as much as he did, and so he was going to take them to another level. Layla loved it, loved the way he branded her with a kiss, loved that she could taste just how much he wanted her. The heat that had been curling in her body was threatening to turn into an inferno, but she loved it.

And she wanted so much more.

"Tell me what you want," Layla whispered between kisses, nipping at his upper lip. He really did have the most unfair mouth, full lips just perfect for biting. "Because if you want to wait—"

He groaned against her. "God, no. I've had blue balls since the day of the auction. If you're ready, I am more than ready, baby."

She chuckled, feeling a heady sense of power at his words. He wanted her that badly? Had wanted her that badly all this time? It was crazy to think that awkward accountant Layla Schmidt could do that to a man that exuded so much raw sensuality that it took her breath away. It was a little amazing . . . and it made her bolder.

She took one of his hands and pressed it to her breast. "I want you, Jack. I want this. I want all of this. I want us."

His mouth was fierce on hers. "I want us, too." His thumb moved over her nipple, rubbing in that familiar way that drove her absolutely crazy and felt so, so good. "You're not wearing a bra, sweetheart. I can feel your nipple through your shirt. Were you planning on making a move on me this entire time?" He gave her nipple a tiny pinch, just enough to sting and make her pulse deep between her thighs.

Her breath caught at the little shock wave of sensation. "M-maybe. Is that so bad that I want you?"

"Not bad at all. It's perfect. You're perfect." He punctuated each word with a fierce little kiss. "I'm going to make you come so hard."

"I know." Oh, she knew. If this was anything like that glorious Saturday afternoon when he'd made her feel so good, he was going to make her come until she saw stars, and she couldn't wait.

Jack's tongue was hot and insistent as he licked at the seam of her mouth. She moaned, wanting more of that insistent push from him, more of the sweep of his seeking tongue into her mouth, more of everything. His fingers grazed her nipple again and she ached so badly that it coiled in her belly and made her feel hollow in places she'd never felt hollow before.

It was the best of feelings, and she wanted more.

"My pretty Layla," he murmured, lightly nipping at her lower lip before giving her another deep, claiming kiss. "Been dreaming about touching you again for days. One time is not enough. It's never going to be enough. I'm going to need to keep my hands all over you until I'm old and gray."

She whimpered as his mouth moved to her throat, kissing downward. His hand cupped the entirety of her breast and it was so warm, so heavy. It felt so right, too.

"I love touching you," Jack continued, seducing her with words as much as he was with his touch. "I love the way you react. Love the way you push into my hand when I caress you. Love those little noises you make. I can't stop thinking about how you looked when you came. I want to see that again. Want to see you lose yourself in my arms when I'm deep inside you."

Could she orgasm from words alone? Because he was making her so hot and achy. "Jack," she panted. "More."

"Don't worry. I'll give you more." He buried his face against the curve of her throat and sucked on her skin, until she was positive that she was going to have a mark there, branding her as his. He lifted his head and licked the spot, then continued to move lower, kissing her through the thin fabric of her shirt.

He sucked on her skin at the collar of her shirt, one big hand kneading her breast. "Want to take this off?"

Oh god, did she ever. Layla nodded jerkily, squirming under him in a silent indication that she wanted to sit up. He didn't let her, though. He kept looming over her, kissing, and his hand snaked to the hem of her shirt and he began to pull it up. She wriggled, helping along, until her breasts were bared to him.

Jack paused, gazing down at them, and groaned. "Look at how pretty you are."

She felt a little silly, with her old sleep shirt hiked around her neck and her boobs hanging out, but when Jack lowered his head and began to kiss the valley between her breasts, she forgot all about feeling silly and gave herself over to the pleasure of it. Her hands threaded in his short hair as he kissed a pattern over her skin, his mouth light and flirty against her flesh. Layla wanted him to go right for her sensitive nipples, but he seemed determined to draw the sensations out, to tease her until she was aching and needy. Which, really, wasn't all that hard to do. She was practically panting and steering his head the moment he moved closer to her left breast.

When his mouth finally closed over her nipple, she let out a little keening sigh. The sensation of him was just too good, the flare his mouth sent through her body too much to keep silent over. Jack's tongue scraped over her nipple, teasing the sensitive underside and toying with it until she was aching. The tips of her breasts felt like diamond points, she was so aroused, and the need racing through her was intense.

"Look at these pretty nipples," Jack murmured. "So eager for my tongue." He nipped at one, gazing up at her as he did, and, oh god, that was so sexy it took her breath away. "You like my mouth on you here?" he asked, his breath hot on her skin as he moved over to her other breast. He hovered there, waiting, and she realized he wanted an answer.

"Yes," she managed to whisper. It made her feel bold and reckless, joining in his dirty talk. "I like your mouth everywhere, Jack."

"That's my girl." He nipped her breast again, one hand covering the other, and teased both her nipples at the same time. "My gorgeous, sexy accountant."

That made her giggle.

"What, you don't think accountants can be sexy?" He

glanced up at her, grinning, before pressing another kiss to her skin. "Tell that to my fantasies. I think about you working all the time."

"You . . . do?" she panted, mystified at this confession. It was hard to concentrate with his mouth doing such erotic things to her aching nipples.

"Oh, fuck yeah." He tongued her nipple again, dragging over the peak with exquisite slowness. "I think about you sitting on your couch with your laptop, in just a little pair of panties, wearing nothing but those and your glasses and your hair's up in one of those pencil buns. Gets me hard as a rock every damn time I think about it."

Layla giggled again. "I don't work like that."

"Shhh. Let me enjoy the fantasy."

"Mmm, whatever you say." As long as he kept touching her, he could imagine her any way he wanted. Her hands slid from his hair to his shoulders, and, oh, he was warm to the touch, his tanned skin hot and smooth under her fingertips. She ran her hands all over his arms, loving the feel of him over her. She'd imagined what sex would be like so many times, but the reality of Jack and the sheer physicality of his presence as he loomed over her, tasting her skin and his mouth everywhere—it was more than she had ever dreamed. It filled her with hot longing and aching need that demanded a release.

When she squirmed under him again, he chuckled and began to kiss her stomach. "You want me to move lower?"

Oh god, did she ever. "You have to ask?"

"Seems polite to ask," he teased, kissing down to her belly button. "May I lick that gorgeous pussy of yours, Layla?"

She whimpered, because his words were so filthy and yet so very erotic. "Yes. God, yes."

"Lift these hips for me, baby, so I can get your shorts off." He pressed another kiss to her stomach. "Not that they aren't cute, but they're in the way."

Layla did as he asked, arching as he tugged the shorts down her thighs and tossed them to the ground. He made a sound of pleasure in his throat at the sight of her, a sound that made her quiver.

"Look at how pretty you are. I can't wait to get my tongue on you again. Been thinking about this for days."

"Oh god, me too." Layla squirmed again, practically wriggling with need. "Jack, I want you so badly."

"I'm here. I'm not going anywhere," he promised her. He kissed lower on her belly, his big body moving down over hers. He kept kissing his way down until his mouth rested atop the curls of her mound, and then he pushed her thighs further apart. "Tell me if I do anything you don't like."

As if there was something he could do that she wouldn't like? She liked all of it. Craved all of it. Wanted his mouth everywhere. She moaned when she felt his breath over the folds of her sex, and when he pushed one thigh over his shoulder, her body clenched in response.

"You're so wet," he murmured. "Just for me."

It was true. Something about being with Jack seemed to make her ten times wetter than she'd ever been before. He turned her on like crazy, and her body responded. Just being around him made her panties permanently soaked, and tonight was no exception. She was slick with heat and arousal, her body aching for his touch.

Then Jack put his mouth on her and everything went to a new level. She keened, her hands flying to his hair. Her nails dug into his scalp as he gave her a long, slow lick that made her want to come out of her own skin. It was so damn good.

"I've got you, baby. Let me lick this pretty pussy of yours." He lapped at her folds and continued to whisper filthy things as he touched her. His mouth was everywhere, exploring and hot, and Layla couldn't stay still. She shivered when he licked her. She twitched when his tongue flicked against a sensitive spot. Her thighs jerked when a new wave of pleasure would wash over her. And through it all, Jack kept devouring her as if she was the best thing he'd ever tasted. His mouth was ravenous on her, hot and wild and needy, and he never let up, never let her catch her breath.

Then his mouth closed over her clit and he sucked, and Layla let out a little cry. He pushed a finger deep inside her even as he teased her clit again, and she bucked against his hand. The elusive orgasm was creeping closer, everything building inside her, and a whispered little "please" escaped her.

Jack murmured a sound of pleasure, pumping his finger in and out of her in a way that felt good but did nothing to ease that hollowness inside her. His finger felt big, and yet it wasn't enough. Then he pushed a second one into her, thrusting, and sucked on her clit again.

She cried out once more, the breath sobbing out of her throat. "Jack, I'm so close—"

"I've got you," he told her, working her with his fingers. His words were ticklish against her sensitive skin, and he flicked his tongue over her slit again. "Want you to come so hard for me, baby. Can you do that?"

Layla moaned. "Need your mouth."

No sooner had she said the words than his lips were on her again, his tongue flicking against her clit before he sucked on her once more, and she felt him push a third finger into her. It felt tight and almost painful, but the sensations were so sharp that it felt strangely good. She bucked against his mouth but he didn't let up, just kept teasing her even as he worked his fingers in and out in a steady pumping motion that felt as if it was going to break her.

Then it was there. Hot sensation coiled in her belly, and she whimpered once, arching, as the orgasm broke over her. Everything in her body locked up, her muscles clenching with the sheer force of it, and the world exploded into a supernova of pleasure as Jack nuzzled and worked her with his mouth, never letting up.

His fingers slid free from her and she waited for him to lift his mouth, but he never did. Instead of letting her ride the sensations down peacefully, he continued to lick and nibble at her clit, teasing her and making her squirm. It was too much, and her whimpers took on a new level as everything began to tense again. "Jack, I can't . . . I can't . . ."

One of his big arms locked around her hips and he kept his face buried against her, his tongue seeking and teasing, and her protests soon turned to cries for more. He was dragging her back up the edge toward another orgasm, determined to pull it from her no matter how much her body thought she was done.

When she was on the brink, everything tightening again, Jack lifted his head and pressed a kiss to the inside of her thigh.

"Oh, nooo," Layla moaned. She tried to push his head back down. "Please, Jack, I'm so close."

"I'll make you come again," he murmured huskily. "I promise."

She whimpered another protest as he got to his feet, standing up next to the bed, and then slid his pants off. His gorgeous cock came into view, hard and erect and breathtaking, and she couldn't stop staring.

He crawled back onto the bed and moved over her, his hands planted on either side of her shoulders. Jack leaned in and kissed Layla, his mouth light and fluttering and tasting like her, and that was just as erotic as everything else. "You're so beautiful," he said again, and it made her want to preen. "Love the way you look when you lose control."

"Can I make you come?" she asked, breathless, her hand sliding down his waist in an obvious direction.

"I'm going to come inside you," he promised, giving her one last brief kiss and then tugging on the shirt still bunched just under her arms.

She lifted up and he pulled it off of her, and then Jack nudged her thighs apart, his weight sinking between them. The heat of him rested against her pussy, and Layla gasped when he rocked his hips against her, dragging the length of him through her wetness. She hadn't anticipated that feeling so good. He did it again, exquisitely slowly, the head of him brushing just up against her sensitive clit, and Layla moaned. Her hips rose to follow as he did it again, and Jack put a hand on her breast, teasing her nipple again.

Her movements took on a sense of urgency, and Layla went from needy to wild. Her fingers dug into his arms as she held on to him, panting. "Jack. Please."

"You feel so damn good, Layla. Love the way you feel. Love how hot and slick you are. You're perfect for me, aren't you? And when I push inside you, you're going to feel so good. Trust me."

"I do. Jack, please." She tried to pull him down over her. "Quit teasing."

He chuckled at that, giving her one of those lazy, breathtaking grins that made heat pulse through her all over again. "Teasing you's my favorite part, baby." He thrust against her folds, his now-slicked cock gliding against her, and she whimpered. "You look so pretty like this."

"I bet I'd look pretty with you inside me, too," she managed, gasping.

That made him groan, and he leaned in to kiss her again. This time, the kiss was harder, more demanding, and when he pumped his hips against her, he was less controlled.

She whimpered encouragement, lifting her legs and moving her hips instinctively. She needed him inside her, needed him to scratch this itch that was driving her crazy, needed him to fill this aching hollowness deep inside.

"You want me?" Jack whispered against her lips.

Layla nodded fiercely.

"Tell me if I hurt you, then." He nipped at her mouth, hot, teasing little bites that just made everything that much more erotic. "Tell me if you want to stop and I'll stop."

Stop? The problem was that he kept stopping. She wanted him to keep going, wanted that second orgasm so badly, wanted him—

Jack shifted his weight, his hand sliding between them, and then she felt him notch the head of his cock to her entrance. He pushed against her, thrusting lightly.

It felt tight and curious in a way that was impossible to explain. She gasped against his mouth and he thrust against her again, this time going in a little further and staying there. He didn't pull back out this time, just continued to push in ever so slightly, as if easing into her by the millimeter would somehow make this easier for both of them. It felt . . . well, she'd never felt anything like it before. It was like having an enormous wedge pushed deep inside her, and in a way, that was exactly what was happening. Her body stretched around him tight, and she whimpered when the sensation grew too sharp.

Jack paused, going still. "Tell me when you're ready for me to move." He brushed a lock of hair from her face, smiling down at her. "God, you're beautiful. I love you, my sexy accountant."

She laughed, because she wasn't feeling particularly sexy at that moment. He was tense over her, his cock crammed deep, and she was sweaty and awkward and holding on to his hips and she just felt . . . like a virgin. Which, she supposed, she wasn't any longer. But she loved hearing him say that. "I love you, too, cowboy."

He groaned, eyes closing as if she'd said the sexiest thing ever, and his hips twitched. It made Layla's body flare in response, but it wasn't all bad sensation. In fact, it felt kind of . . . good. Tight, yes, but an interesting kind of tightness that made her want more despite things. "I think I'm okay," she told him. "Can we go slow?"

"As slow as you want," he promised, and he gazed right into her eyes as he moved over her, pushing deeper.

Layla's breath caught in her throat—not just at the way it felt, but at the intense sensation of having her eyes locked with Jack's at such an intimate moment. She felt completely exposed and laid bare, but he was with her. He had her. And it sent a shudder of response through her body that felt so, so good.

He groaned, pushing deeper. "You're so tight. God. Never imagined you'd feel this good, baby."

"You're welcome? I think." She giggled and then cut off with a gasp because the action of laughing sent all kinds of shocking ripples through her body, especially where she felt stretched tight around him.

"You want me to stop again?" His voice was strained.

"No. Keep going." Layla put her hands to his sides and held on, her legs curled around his hips. "You feel good."

He groaned again, and then rocked forward, and oh. That time it didn't feel like trying to cram too much into her. It felt big and foreign, but hard and smooth, and the nerves that flared up in response felt really good. She made a pleased little sound in her throat and tried to move with him. It felt awkward to try and keep pace with him, but when their bodies came together and he pushed so deep into her? Oh god, that was good. Layla moaned as he rocked in and out of her, his movements growing faster.

She fell out of rhythm with him as he sped up, and her arms went around his neck as he moved over her. Jack pumped into her with such strength and speed that it made her breathless, and she hung on while he thrust. While it didn't feel quite the same as it did when he was working her clit, the pleasure in this was deeper, slower. It was still good, though, and she found herself moaning into his ear as he drove deep. Everything was good with Jack, she realized. Everything.

His breathing became more rapid, his movements erratic, and she realized he was close to coming. Her own orgasm suddenly didn't matter anymore. She wanted to see Jack come. "Are you close?" she whispered.

With teeth gritted, he answered. "You feel far too good for me to make this last. Being inside you like this, with nothing between us . . ." He groaned again. "Gonna make you come, though."

"You don't have to. This feels plenty good—"

Her words cut off as he put a hand behind one of her knees and pushed it forward to her chest. Layla let out a muffled whine of surprise when he thrust deep, and this time, the angle was changed. This time, when he rocked her forward with the force of his movements, something went from feeling good to feeling intense.

"Right there, baby?"

She barely managed to nod before he was driving deep again, and the noise that escaped her was ridiculous in its whiny tone. She couldn't help it, though. Each time he pumped into her, hitting that perfect spot that made everything light up, she made an incoherent sound of need, and that deep-seated pleasure soon turned to an urgent, clenching arousal.

"Oh," Layla whimpered as he hit it again. "Oh, Jack, I'm close. Oh god. So close."

He growled low in her ear like some sort of animal and just kept moving over her, faster and faster. Each time it felt better, and then she was tensing, her breath catching in her throat as the orgasm spilled over her again, this one deeper and rawer and far more intense. She might have cried out his name as she came; it was impossible for her to tell. She was making noises, but the rest of her wasn't responding.

She was too busy clenching and coming and orgasming into a state of bliss as he thrust into her. Then Jack hissed, his movements stilling as he rolled their hips together, and she felt the wetness of his release between them, the slide of their bodies becoming slicker by the moment even as his movements slowed.

This time, when Layla sighed with pleasure, Jack collapsed on top of her, sweaty and spent. This was a new sort of sensation, too, the feeling of her lover sated atop her. Layla played with his hair, brushing the damp locks off his brow and just touching his face. He looked so good like this, his pupils blown with pleasure, his expression drowsy. She liked the feel of him over her, too. How he was heavy but somehow perfect, as well.

Jack let out a long sigh and then nuzzled at her throat. "Was that good?"

"Are you fishing for compliments?" she teased, feeling lighthearted and exhausted all at once. "Because you know you made me come. Twice."

"Maybe a man just likes to hear that his woman was satisfied," Jack replied, a sly note in his voice. "Twice."

She laughed, because it felt so good to smile with him, to be in his arms like this. "It was perfect," she admitted.

"You're welcome," he teased, tossing back the words she'd said earlier.

Layla put a hand over his face, groaning, and pushed at him.

He mock-bit at her fingers and grinned down at her. "Seriously though, how do you feel? You don't hurt anywhere, do you?"

"I feel perfect," she admitted. "Everything's perfect."

"I love you," he told her again. "Have I mentioned that?"

"Mmm. You're welcome."

This time he was the one that snorted with laughter.

CHAPTER THIRTY-FOUR

The next time visiting hours were open at the assisted-living facility, Layla took Jack with her to visit Cora.

Really, Layla had a million things to do at work, and she knew Jack was busy, too. The cattle were getting close to calving, which meant his workload was going to explode overnight and they'd barely get the time to see each other. Hers was going to quadruple soon, too, with tax season, but they'd work it out. Even so, visiting a new friend seemed like it was something that should be on the back burner.

But Layla felt compelled to visit Cora. Like it was something she had to do. Maybe it was because her relationship with her own mother had taken a dive. Janet had sent a flurry of angry texts for a day or two, and then nothing since. It wasn't like Janet to be utterly silent, and Layla suspected that it meant Janet's hurt ran a lot deeper than she'd thought.

Which made Layla feel awful, but it was one of those things where there was no cure but time. So she'd visit Cora, because if she couldn't fix her relationship with her own family, she could at least make that old lady's day brighter.

The attendant smiled the moment Layla entered with Oscar in her arms. "Is that Cora's dog? She's been talking about him nonstop."

"This is him," Layla said cheerfully, bouncing Oscar in her arms. She'd crocheted the dachshund a bright yellow and pink turtleneck sweater and put it on him, hoping that Cora would enjoy the sight of it. "How is Cora today?"

"About as well as to be expected," the woman said. "But I imagine having visitors will perk her right up. Come this way."

That answer was a little worrying, and Layla shot Jack a concerned look. He just put a supportive hand at the small of her back and led her forward.

Cora did seem more fragile when they entered her room. She sat near the window, an afghan on her lap, and her face seemed hollow. Her hair was freshly dyed, though, and she wore a heavy amount of eye makeup as if she knew she was going to get visitors. She brightened the moment Jack and Layla stepped through the doorway, however. "You came for my birthday!"

Oh wow, was it her birthday? Layla'd had no idea. Jack shot her a look and then moved to Cora's side. "You know we did. How are you feeling, my gorgeous flower?"

Cora tittered and waved a hand at Jack. "You flirt. I'm good. I love company, and seeing you two makes this a wonderful day. Can I see my dog?" She held her arms out.

"Just for a minute," Jack told her. "He needs to go outside for a quick walk, but then we'll be back." He took the dog from Layla's arms and held him out to Cora, and the woman kissed Oscar's ear and then let Jack have him back.

Jack moved to Layla's side and kissed her cheek. "I'm gonna run down to the bakery for a cake," he murmured. "Stall."

She nodded and sat down across from Cora in the empty seat near the window. "How are things, Cora?"

The older woman shrugged, watching Jack leave with Oscar. "Looking up. You're still seeing that handsome man?" She gave Layla a sly look. "Guess that money at the auction really paid off."

Layla blushed. "It did, yes."

"You look happy." Cora gave her an exaggerated wink.

"I am." This conversation was quickly growing awkward, though, so Layla decided to steer it in a safer direction. "So how old are you turning today, Cora? Or am I not allowed to ask?"

"Oh, it's not really my birthday. I just wanted some cake. That's where your boyfriend went, right? To get cake? If he texts you, tell him I like buttercream frosting." Cora beamed. "And sprinkles. I love sprinkles."

Layla's jaw dropped. Then she laughed. "I can text him."

"That would be lovely, dear. Be sure to tell him about the sprinkles." As Layla texted, Cora just chuckled, as if pleased with herself. "I know you're thinking I'm sneaky, but when you get to be my age, you do what you can to get results. And I really wanted some cake today." Her expression grew wistful. "And sprinkles."

Layla made sure to text Jack an emphasis on sprinkles. She smiled at her phone when the answer pinged. "He says he's going to ask for the sprinkliest cake ever."

"That's a good man. Handsome, too." Cora smiled at Layla. "I'm glad everything's working out for you. Does that mean you're not going to keep coming by?"

The words sounded so sad that Layla wanted to hug her. "No, of course not. If you like the company, I'm more than happy to keep coming by. Why would we stop?"

Cora sighed. "Because everyone does. This place is depressing, you know. Some of these people cry all day long. No one comes to visit. My daughter brought me here two years ago and has visited once the entire time." She shook her head. "We're parked here because now we can be someone else's problem."

Layla's heart squeezed. No wonder Cora dressed flashy and said outrageous things to get her way. She wanted attention, just like Layla had when she was a child and Janet had spent a lot of time ignoring her and her father had disappeared. She knew what it was like to be unwanted.

Maybe this was exactly the reminder Layla needed—that just because you had family, it didn't mean that they had your best interests at heart. Maybe the family you made for yourself could be just as good, if not better, than the one genetics gave to you. "I'm not going anywhere," Layla promised her. "In fact, while we're waiting for Jack, I was hoping you could show me the crochet stitch you used on that blanket. I brought my yarn and my hook."

Cora's eyes lit up. "What size hook are you using? That's important. Here, come slide your chair closer and I'll show you."

EPILOGUE

Three Months Later

Though there was nothing officially on the schedule, Tuesday afternoons were Cora afternoons. Jack finished his chores at the ranch, checking in on a sick heifer and bottle-feeding a baby that refused to eat solid food just yet. After that, his afternoon was free, but Jack had plans. So many plans.

First, he had to get his girlfriend, though.

He drove into town and headed for Pine Grove, where Layla would be most likely crocheting and gossiping with Cora in her room, Oscar perched on the elderly woman's lap. It had become a regular thing, the Cora visits, even though neither of them were related to her. She was as good as family at this point, he figured, because she texted both of them when she needed something, and they visited her regularly. Cora was a bit of a tough nut even if she pretended otherwise, and Jack loved how sly she was and how easily she manipulated everyone around them. She didn't do it out of a malicious nature. She was lonely, and did what she could to ensure people would visit.

Well, and bring cake. Jack had learned that he needed to show up with either Oscar or cake—preferably both.

CORA: R U coming?

She spammed the message with a half dozen emojis, and he doubted she knew what half of them meant. Or she did, and she was just doing it to be a troll. You could never tell with Cora.

JACK: OMW

He was, really. There were just a few things he needed to take care of first. He picked up a half dozen fresh cupcakes at the bakery (along with a "pupcake" for Oscar) and then swung by the florist and picked up a dozen roses. A quick glance in the rearview mirror as he got back into the car showed he was sweating. Shit. He ran a nervous hand over his face. There was nothing to be nervous over. Nothing at all.

It wasn't Jack's thing to be nervous. Layla was the high-strung one, the one always obsessed with making everyone happy. Jack was the laid-back one . . . except today, he felt tense. On edge.

Cora sending him an emoji of fire, a ring, and then an eggplant didn't help things. He wasn't exactly sure what she was trying to tell him there. Taking a deep breath, Jack drove over to the senior center, hid the flowers in the back of his truck, and went inside with the cupcakes.

The scene in Cora's room was one he'd grown accustomed to seeing regularly. Cora sat by the window in the sunlight, Oscar dozing in her arms. Across from her in her regular chair was Layla, her head bent over a cross-stitch project as she chatted with Cora. He knew that this particular cross-stitch project was daisies but with curse words delicately embroidered into the center of each flower. Both his girlfriend and Cora had hooted with laughter over that one and Layla had insisted on making it for her friend.

Layla looked up at him, her glasses sliding down her nose, and beamed.

His heart clenched with pure love.

Even after months of dating and more or less living together, the sight of her still made his heart skip a beat. She was adorable, his Layla, her hair messily piled atop her head and fixed with a pencil as usual, her glasses dominating her face, and that beaming smile he loved aimed in his direction. She was the sexiest thing ever, and he thought to himself how lucky he was to have her as he moved to her side and gave her a kiss.

"Are those cupcakes for me?" Cora asked, like she always did. There was a twinkle in her eye as she looked up at him.

He went over and kissed her cheek, setting the cupcakes down next to her. "Extra sprinkles, just like you asked."

"Good man. I just might keep you." Cora winked.

Layla chuckled. "You'll have to fight me for him."

Jack straightened and put a hand over his heart. "Ladies, ladies, there's more than enough of me to go around."

Layla rolled her eyes. "On second thought, Cora, you can have him."

Cora just tittered, unwrapping the pupcake for the dog and feeding him bites. Jack settled in, leaning against the window, and listened to them talk about nothing in particular. Cora was very into a show called *The Bachelor* and so Layla had started watching it, too, much to Jack's chagrin. It wasn't his favorite, but he watched it with her because she usually watched baseball with him. As they talked, Cora kept giving him sly looks.

He nodded at her when Layla wasn't looking. Today was the day.

Cora winked again and then yawned hugely.

Layla didn't notice their deviousness. "Did you not sleep well, Cora?"

"Not really. That new pillow's too hard." For a moment, she looked old and frail and fragile. "I'll probably lie down and take a nap soon."

"Do you need a new pillow? I can drop one off tomorrow if you like," Layla offered, a worried look on her face.

"Oh no, it's just a new pillow. I'll break it in soon enough." Cora waved a hand.

Jack cleared his throat. "We should probably get going soon anyhow. Remember, we're going to go look at that land, baby."

Layla tapped her needle on the magnetic needle minder on her project, putting her things away. "Right. I told Cora all about it. How this one might be the one."

"Fingers crossed," Cora offered. "Take pictures and send them to me."

"Oh, of course." Layla got to her feet, and Jack went to get the dog from Cora. "Before I go, do you need anything for Maxwell?"

"He needs a castle," Cora said, glancing up at the betta fish in the tank atop Cora's dresser. He'd been a present to Cora last month, because Layla wanted Cora to have a "buddy" when Oscar couldn't visit.

"A castle. I'll see what I can find online." Layla grinned over at him, all sweet pleasure.

Jack couldn't help but notice that she picked up a folder of paperwork as she got her things together, and he arched an eyebrow at her.

Layla flushed. "Um, just some paperwork for one of the other residents here. He got a notice from the IRS because his kids filed a tax return for him and didn't need to and so he tried to fix it and made it worse, and it's a long story and I'm doing it for him and you can't stop me."

"Baby," Jack began warningly.

"It's just a simple amendment. It looks scarier than it is, and Clarence can't afford a CPA right now." She lifted her chin, a defensive expression on her face.

Jack just shook his head. Count on Layla to volunteer to do work for strangers. She had the most generous heart. He supposed it was just another reason why he loved her, even if it encouraged people to take advantage of her. At least she had him to keep things in check.

"Bye, you two," Cora called, pulling the box of cupcakes into her lap and waving from her seat by the door. "Remember, take pictures."

"See you next week," Layla called. "And I promise I'll catch up on *The Bachelor*!"

"You do that. You have to see what that fool Blake did to Shelby."

"Nothing good, I'm sure," Layla murmured as they left. Jack kept Oscar tucked under one arm, his other hand at the small of Layla's back as he steered her out of the building. "And I know you're irked with me, Jack, but it's just a tiny bit of paperwork, and Clarence can barely remember who he is, much less fill out a 1040-X. It's really not a big deal."

"I know. I just need to make sure no one's hogging all your time but me."

She chuckled, gazing up at him as they exited the building and moved toward his car. "You are absolutely my first priority. You know that."

He did. He worried about her sometimes, though. The last couple of months had been a wild ride. He'd been buried in calving season, with tons of births happening on a daily basis and the three Watson brothers spending nearly every waking moment in the barn or in the pastures checking up on their charges, giving shots, tagging, and when mothers wouldn't feed the calves, bottle-feeding the babies. He was used to it, though, and had expected to be busy. What he hadn't expected was just how busy Layla got during tax season. She'd worked so many long nights that she'd had dark circles under her eyes for weeks, and she'd fallen asleep through one of their date nights (a fact he loved to tease her about). He was used to working hard, but he felt protective of Layla, and he wanted her to relax, just a little, now that things were slowing down.

He opened the truck door for her and handed her Oscar.

Layla settled into her seat and immediately frowned up at him. "Do you smell flowers?"

"Someone had on some strong perfume at the bakery," he lied. And Jack began to sweat again.

If Layla noticed his nervousness, she didn't say anything, though. She seemed happy and unconcerned as he pulled out of the parking lot and got onto the highway. "My mother called," she offered.

He tensed, like he always did when she brought up Janet. "Oh?"

"Just to say hello and to ask if she could borrow some of my heels. I told her no. She told me I was selfish and I told her I had to go." She shook her head. "So the same old, same old."

He grunted. Jack was not a fan of Janet, but he knew Layla loved her despite all her (many, many) flaws. Janet was a user, but if she was in Layla's life, he was going to have to learn to tolerate her, because he loved his girlfriend. Their relationship was still strained after the bad contract, but Janet had returned the money and donated the land, just like Layla had insisted. They had fallen out of contact for about a month, and then Janet had begun trying to slowly weasel her way back into Layla's good graces, and he was proud of Layla for standing up to her. He knew Layla had been incredibly hurt by her mother's selfishness, but she was pouring some of that generous heart toward Cora, which he supported. Cora was a sneaky woman, but she loved his Layla as much as he did.

"So where's this land again?" Layla asked, glancing over at him. "This looks like the road back to the Swinging C."

He began to sweat again. "It's near."

"Oh. Really? That'll be interesting. I can't believe there's a plot of land close by that someone wants to sell to you."

"I lucked into it," he said gruffly, hoping she wouldn't pepper him with too many more questions or he'd break.

"What are we doing after we see the land?" she asked, and put her hand on his thigh. "Going back to your cabin to celebrate?"

Now he was sweating and aroused. Layla's not-so-innocent hand crept close to his cock, and he groaned. "You are the worst tease."

"I thought I was the best tease," she said with a giggle. "That's what you told me last night."

"You can be both." God, he loved her. He loved how her initial shyness had turned into sheer enthusiasm in the bedroom. Not that the shyness was bad—but an excited Layla always willing to try new things and touch him at a moment's notice? He was living the dream. She was the perfect woman, and he really was a lucky man . . .

. . . and, yeah, he was sweating like crazy now.

Her hand remained high on his leg, just enough to distract him as he pulled up to the Swinging C parking lot.

Layla looked over at him with a slight frown on her face. "Pit stop?"

"Yeah, the guy's meeting us in the barn," he lied. "Something about wanting to buy one of Uncle Ennis's horses."

"Oh. Okay. You want me to go drop Oscar off at your cabin and meet you there?"

Perfect. He'd been wondering how to get the flowers into the barn without her noticing them. "That'd be great, actually. You sure you don't mind?"

"Not at all." She leaned over and kissed him, and her hand brushed over his cock. "You can thank me later."

He groaned, because his mind went to very dirty places. "You know I will. As many times as you want."

Layla gave him a positively lascivious look. "I'm going to hold you to that. Be right back." She got out and headed off with the dog.

The moment she disappeared from sight, Jack uncovered the flowers hidden under a blanket in the back seat of his truck and raced for the barn. Waiting inside were his brothers, Uncle Ennis, and Becca and Amy. A table had been set up in the center of the barn, full of framed pictures of the two of them together and decorated with heart balloons. A heart-shaped cake was in the center of the table, and a red carpet had been rolled out over the straw.

His older brother Hank snorted at the sight of him. "You're as white as a ghost, Jack."

"Sweaty, too," Jack agreed, running a sleeve over his face.

"Does she have any idea?" Becca clasped her hands in front of her with excitement.

"She thinks we're seeing land today."

Amy pulled out her phone, prepping the camera. "I'm so excited for you two!"

"She hasn't said yes yet," Jack grumbled, and that panicky feeling began to fill his stomach. What if Layla said no? What if she didn't want to get married? What if she wanted to break up? What if—

"Relax," Caleb said gruffly. He stepped forward and held the ring box out to Jack.

Jack took it from him, nodding. He'd asked Caleb to hold on to it so Layla wouldn't find it if she picked through his clothing. He checked the ring, swallowed hard, and looked around at his family. "Keep your fingers crossed."

"It'll be fine, son," Uncle Ennis promised with a slow

nod. "She's a great girl. You've got this. Just try not to sweat on her hand when you ask for it."

Har-de-har. Everyone had to put their two cents in that day, it seemed. He wanted to comment on that when he heard the barn door open. His heart dropped when he turned and saw Layla step in, her mouth opening in astonishment as she stared at the decorations. She glanced down at the red carpet and her gaze went to Jack.

He immediately dropped down on one knee, bouquet of red roses clutched in one hand, ring box in the other.

Layla moved up toward him slowly, and everyone else was silent.

He was sweating hard now. He was the one that was all confidence, the flirty one, the fun brother, the easygoing one, and . . . he was pretty sure he was going to pass out from nerves. "Layla Schmidt," he croaked. "From the first day I met you—"

"Yes," she said immediately.

"You didn't let me finish."

"I know the answer," she told him and beamed a radiant smile in his direction. "I love you, Jack. Yes. A thousand times yes."

He got to his feet. Handed her the flowers and the ring. She looked at neither one, just gazed up at him with that soft, loving expression of hers.

"I love you," he murmured. "You sure you want to marry me?"

"Hey," she teased. "You're stealing my lines."

"Am I? Because I'm pretty sure I'm the lucky one in this," he told her as he put his hands around her waist and pulled her in close.

"All right, then," Layla murmured. "You're welcome."

He couldn't stop grinning, even as he leaned in to kiss his new fiancée.

Turn the page to read
an excerpt from

THE COWBOY MEETS HIS MATCH

Out now!

February

S ometimes it was hard to live in a town like Painted Barrel. The community was small and intimate and supportive, but it was impossible to have secrets. Worse than that, everyone seemed to think they knew what was best for you, even if you didn't agree.

Which meant Becca heard a lot of well-meaning advice daily, no matter how many times she tried to escape it.

"You really should get out there and start dating again," Mrs. Williams told her for the seventh time in the last hour. "A pretty thing like you? You don't want all your good years going to waste. If you want to start a family, you need to move fast."

And wasn't that just depressing? Becca did her best to smile as she plucked foils off Mrs. Williams's head, as if the woman's kind words weren't stabbing her in the heart. "I'm not sure I'm ready to date. I'll know when I meet the right person."

Her customer tsked. "Like I said, don't wait too long.

You don't want to be the oldest mother at the PTA meetings." She nodded into the mirror at her reflection as if this was the worst thing in the world to happen. "It's very difficult for the children."

"I'll keep that in mind," Becca murmured as she pulled the last of the foils off Mrs. Williams's head. "Let's wash now, shall we?"

The good thing about washing was that because the water was going, it meant Becca didn't have to talk—or listen to Mrs. Williams talk. Thank goodness for that, because she needed a few minutes to compose herself. Becca had always thought that two years would be enough time to mend her broken heart. Two years surely should have been enough time to get over the man that left her on the eve of their wedding. It should have been enough time to get over the bitterness that swallowed her up every time she paid the credit card bills that she still had from the wedding that had never happened.

Instead, it all seemed to just irritate her more and more.

It didn't help that everyone in Painted Barrel still asked about the Wedding That Wasn't. Of course they did. Becca being left at the altar (well, practically) was the biggest scandal that Painted Barrel had had in all of the town's uninspiring history. She'd always been popular around town. She was moderately cute, tried her best to be friendly to everyone, ran her own local business, and, for ten years, she'd dated the ex-captain of the local football team, handsome, blond Greg Wallace.

Oh, Greg.

Greg was not good at making decisions about what he wanted in life. It had taken her ten years to figure out that particular tidbit of information, but once she had, it had explained so much. It explained why Greg never finished college, and why he'd never held down a job for longer than a year or two. It explained why he'd gone back and forth on their relationship, first wanting to see other people, then wanting Becca back, then getting engaged, calling it off, getting engaged again, and then deciding a few days before the wedding that he'd changed his mind and he was in love with another woman.

She'd been a damned idiot for far too long.

Becca scrubbed at Mrs. Williams's hair, asking about the woman's grandchildren without listening to the answer. Her thoughts were still on Greg. Why had she wasted so much time with him? Was she truly that stupid?

But, no, she supposed it wasn't stupidity as much as it was a soft heart, a fear of being alone, and the fact that Greg was a terrible decision maker but a great apologizer. He'd been so sweet every time he'd come crawling back that she'd felt like the world's worst person if she said no. So she said yes . . . and yes, and yes . . .

And now look where she was. Becca Loftis still had her salon in Painted Barrel, but she was turning thirty, she was utterly single, and now she was being warned that her womb was aging with every day that passed.

For someone that had always said she didn't want to turn into her mother, she sure was doing a terrible job of breaking that pattern. Heck, according to Mrs. Williams, she was failing children she hadn't even had yet and—

"Too hot," the woman under the water cried out. "Too hot, Becca!"

"Sorry," Becca said quickly, turning the water cooler and trying not to feel too ashamed. Even now, Greg was ruining her life, wasn't he? "You were saying it was Jimmy's sixth birthday last week?" She was relieved when Mrs. Williams settled back down in the salon chair and began to talk once more.

Enough Greg. She had customers to take care of.

* * *

Becca was sweeping up underneath the chair after her last appointment of the day when the door to the salon chimed. She looked up and inwardly felt a little stab of emotion when Sage Cooper-Clements waddled in, looking like a plump penguin with her puffy jacket and pregnant belly. The new mayor was the nicest woman, and once upon a time, Becca had thought she was the loveliest, most giving person, sweet and shy and eternally single.

Then Greg had decided he wanted Sage instead of Becca.

Then Sage had turned around and married some tall cowboy and immediately gotten pregnant.

Now Sage was the mayor of Painted Barrel and the new darling of the small town. Everyone loved her. Everyone touched her belly when she walked in and asked about her new husband. They asked about her family's ranch. They gave her advice and doted on her.

And Becca didn't hate her. Not really. It wasn't Sage's fault that Greg had bailed on Becca because he'd thought he was in love with Sage.

It was just that . . . it was hard not to be envious of someone who suddenly had everything you'd always wanted. Not the mayor thing, of course, but a loving husband and a baby? God, Becca had wanted so badly to be in her shoes.

She gave Sage a wistful smile. "Hey, Sage. How can I help you?"

Sage beamed at her and lumbered forward, all pregnancy belly and layers of warm clothing. She thrust a flyer toward Becca. "I just wanted to let you know that we're having a Small Business Summit next year to promote local tradesmen. All of the shops in Painted Barrel and the neighboring towns can rent booths in the gym and we're going to make a big festival of it. There'll be food and drinks, and everyone can sell goods from their booths. I wanted to invite you personally since you're on Main Street and one of this town's mainstays. I know it's not for a while, but I want to drum up enthusiasm ahead of time."

The pregnant mayor beamed at her, and Becca did her best to take the flyer with a modicum of excitement. It was just as Sage said, a festival featuring small businesses. "I'm not sure if I can do a haircutting booth," she admitted. At Sage's crestfallen look, she hastily amended, "But I'm sure I'll think of something! Maybe quickie manicures?"

"Wonderful! Just fill out the form on the back and turn it in at city hall and I'll make sure we save you a booth, okay?" Sage glanced around the hair salon awkwardly, her hand on her belly. She looked uncomfortable, but Becca kept smiling, even though it felt frozen on her face. They'd been friends before the Wedding That Wasn't, and now it was a little tricky finding the right footing once more.

They smiled at each other for a moment longer, and silence fell.

Please don't say anything about Greg, Becca thought. *Please don't—*

"I'm really sorry about how things turned out, Becca," Sage said softly. She bit her lip, her hand running up and down the large bulge of baby belly under her sweater. "You know I had no idea that he was going to do that."

Becca somehow found it in her to keep smiling. "Don't apologize, Sage. It was all him, okay? No one should have to make excuses for Greg." That big walking human turd Greg. "He's a grown man."

"Yeah, but I feel responsible—"

"You're not." She cut the other woman off, just wanting the conversation to end. Couldn't Sage see that this was the last thing that Becca wanted to talk about? With anyone? Certainly not with the happy, glowing pregnant woman Greg thought he was in love with? "Please. Let's just not bring it up ever again, okay?"

"Okay, so, uh, I'm going to go," Sage said, thumbing a gesture at the door.

Becca held up the flyer. "I'll make sure and get this filled out, I promise."

"Great. Awesome." Sage turned toward the door, waving. "I'll talk to you later!"

"Bye." She stayed in place, clutching the broom handle in one hand, the flyer in the other, until Sage headed out of the salon and down the cold, snowy sidewalk of quaint Main Street. Once the other woman disappeared, Becca returned to calmly sweeping . . .

For all of a minute. Her hands were shaking and she gave up, setting the broom down and then walking to her small office at the back of the salon, where she kept her bookkeeping items and the tiny refrigerator with her lunch. She shut the door behind her, thumped down on a stool, and took a long, steeling breath.

She would not cry.

She would *not* cry.

Greg didn't deserve her tears. He'd had ten years of her life, keeping her on hold and promising her that they'd get married soon, soon, soon, and then soon finally had a date . . . a date he'd never gone along with. She'd given him enough of her time and energy. She wanted to move on.

Why wouldn't anyone let her freaking move *on*?

She swiped at the corners of her eyes carefully, proud that there were only a few stray tears instead of the normal deluge. Good. That meant she wouldn't have to go to extremes to fix her makeup, just a little touch-up here and there. She could end the day on a high note, in case she had any walk-ins. Of course, if she did have one, they'd probably just ask her about Greg again . . .

Her lip wobbled. Damn it.

As Becca sniffed and dabbed her face dry, the door opened in the main area of the salon, the bell chiming.

Crap. Sage had probably come back to apologize again, and that would make Becca cry even harder and ruin her evening. She'd just have to somehow tell the well-meaning pregnant woman that really, truly, she was fine and really, *honestly*, she did not want to talk about it. Gritting her teeth, she forced a bright smile to her face, pinched her cheeks so the rosiness there would hopefully distract from her red eyes, and opened the door to face Sage.

Except . . . it wasn't Sage.

The hulking man that stood in the doorway wasn't anything like the mayor. In fact, Becca had never seen this man in her life. That was something interesting in itself, considering that Painted Barrel was a small town nestled in the less populated north of Wyoming, and most of the people that lived here tended to be lifers. Becca had grown up here, and she knew everyone in the small town. It was both comfort and annoyance—and lately it had been far more of the latter.

This man was a stranger, though. She stared at him, doing her best not to gape. He wore a light jacket, and under it a faded black-and-red-checked shirt. The jacket seemed almost too tight for the massive breadth of his shoulders. He was tall, maybe six and a half feet, but more intimidating than that were his arms, which seemed like tree trunks, and his black beard, which seemed like something out of a Paul Bunyan storybook. He wore jeans and big, muddy work boots, and a dark cowboy hat covered longish, unkempt hair. It was light wear for the snowy weather they were having, really.

He really did seem like Paul Bunyan come to life if Paul Bunyan was a cowboy, but wasn't Paul Bunyan friendly? This man had a massive scowl on his face, as if he hated the world around him.

Becca blinked and tried to size the man up, thinking fast. There weren't many outsiders in this part of town right now. Either he'd gotten lost and needed directions or he was one of the new ranch hands. Not at Sage's ranch, because

Becca had met those nice gentlemen—former soldiers looking to start a new life. The only other "outsiders" in the area were the three new ranch hands at the Swinging C up in the mountains, and those were Dr. Ennis Parson's nephews. She hadn't met any of them, but rumor had it that they were from the wilds of Alaska, here to help out for a year.

This man definitely fit the Alaska stereotype. He didn't look like a typical customer. Heck, he didn't even look like he'd ever been to a salon. That beard was untamed and so was the hair under the hat. She'd bet his nail beds were rough and his hands were covered in calluses.

It was a mystery why he'd shown up in her salon. Becca was just about to open her mouth and ask if he was lost when something pink behind his massive jeans-clad thigh moved.

Then she saw the little girl.

The big cowboy was holding the hand of the tiniest, daintiest little creature. Becca's heart melted as the small face peeped around his leg and her thumb went into her mouth. The girl in the little pink parka watched Becca with big eyes, not moving out from behind her protector's leg.

Well. This must be the daddy. It was clear he was here not for himself but for his little girl. That did something to her heart. For all that he was slightly terrifying, Paul Bunyan was a dad and this little one wasn't scared of him.

"Hi there," Becca said brightly to the two of them.

The man just gazed at her with dark eyes. He said nothing, and after a long moment, he gently tugged on the hand of the little girl, leading her forward a step.

All right, he wasn't much of a talker. Ranching took all kinds, and she wasn't surprised that this one was a silent type. It was kind of ironic if he was related to Doc Parson, though, because that veterinarian was the nicest man but definitely a talker. She studied the little girl, who stood in front of her enormous father, sucking her thumb. Her cheeks were fat and rosy, and she wore the most adorable little pink coat. Underneath it, Becca could see striped pink-and-white leggings. Her hood was down and the soft golden curls atop her head looked haphazard, pulled into a high, tight knot.

"What can I help you with?" Becca asked, crouching to get to eye level with the little one.

The girl just stared at Becca, intimidated.

"Gum."

Becca looked up in surprise. The big, silent behemoth had spoken. "Gum?" she echoed.

He nodded and nudged the little girl forward again.

The thumb popped out of her mouth and the girl spoke. "I ate all of Grampa's gum and went to sleep and when I woke up my gum was all gone."

Oh. And she was here at a hairdresser. That wasn't a good sign. But Becca kept the smile on her face and put her hand out. "I bet I know where it is. Shall we take a look?"

The small, adorable creature put her hand in Becca's and gave her a triumphant look. "It's in my *hair*! And Daddy said you'd be able to get it out."

Eek, had he said that? Becca cast the man an awkward look. "Well, let's see what we can do, shall we?" She led the little girl over to the salon chair and helped her out of her jacket, then lifted her into the seat. "What's your name, sweetheart?"

"Libby." She looked on eagerly as Becca pulled out a bright pink cape and tied it under her chin.

"How old are you, Libby?"

"Three."

"Four," corrected the man gruffly.

"Four," agreed Libby, kicking her feet under the cape.

"I see," Becca said as the man sat down in the other salon chair next to Libby's, his big legs sprawling out in front of him. "Four is a great age. That means you're a big girl." She reached for the ponytail holder to pull it out of the girl's topknot, only to realize the gum was twisted into it as well. Oh dear. Normally, she'd pick through the loose hair to check for lice—because you never knew with kids—but this was going to be . . . interesting. She touched a few strands, trying to determine how it had happened. Gum really was everywhere. Long strings of it seemed to be melted into the delicate curls, and all of it was mixed in with the hair tie. The entire thing seemed to be glued together with a light brown substance she couldn't figure out. After a moment, she sniffed. "Is this . . . peanut butter?"

She looked over at the big man, but his jaw clenched and he remained silent. After a long moment, he shrugged.

"Daddy tried to help," Libby said brightly. "But I didn't tell him about the gum for two days and he said that was bad."

Two days? Well, that explained the rancid knot atop Libby's little head. "I see."

"Late night," the man said in a gruff voice. "Sick cattle."

"I wasn't judging," Becca replied gently. She moved to the counter and grabbed a large bottle of hair oil. "Sometimes it's hard to get away from work. Trust me, I know." She crooked a smile at him, trying to put him at ease. "Emergencies come up, even at a hair salon." And she gestured at his little daughter.

He just stared at her.

Right. Okay, so that was awkward. She turned back to Libby. "Daddy was off to a good start with the peanut butter," she told the little girl. "We're going to put more oil in your hair and see if we can't work some more of this gum out, all right?"

"Okay," Libby said brightly.

"Why don't you tell me about yourself," Becca continued, dousing the girl's head with oil and trying not to worry about how the heck she was going to salvage this little one's hair without shaving it down to the scalp. "You're a big girl of four. Do you have any brothers or sisters?"

"I have two uncles! They're big and hairy like Daddy."

"Two uncles," Becca repeated, grinning. This was definitely one of Doc Parson's nephews. From the rumors around town, all three had come down from Alaska. "What about your mommy?"

"I don't have a mommy," Libby said, kicking her legs some more. "It's just Daddy and Uncle Caleb and Uncle Jack and Grampa Ennis."

"I see." She discreetly glanced over at the girl's father, but the man didn't make eye contact with her. Kept his gaze on his daughter as Becca tried to work the hair tie free. Her heart squeezed with sympathy, just a little. A single dad with a young daughter? No wonder he hadn't noticed the gum in her hair until it was a disaster. She imagined that raising a child alone was hard, and with no women to lean on? He was doing a great job.

Libby rattled on and on as Becca picked and fussed at the knot on her head. Long minutes passed, but Libby wasn't much of a squirmer compared to some of the other kids Becca got in her chair, which was a good thing. She was content to talk and talk, asking about all the hair products on Becca's counter and if she liked cartoons and flowers and everything else under the sun.

"Is this your daddy's shop?" Libby asked as Becca's oily fingers worked out another strand of hair.

"No, it's my shop. I started it myself."

"So you can play with people's hair all day?"

She chuckled. "Yes, that's right. I like playing with hair. Especially little girls' hair."

"Do you have a little girl?"

Her heart squeezed. "No."

"A little boy?"

"I don't have any family," she said brightly. "No kids, no husband."

"Daddy doesn't have a wife, either."

"Libby," the man growled.

Becca chuckled. "It's fine." Her cheeks were heating, though. She peeked at the man again. He was big and brawny, and under that crazy beard, he just might be handsome. Not that it really mattered all that much—she hadn't paid attention to any man but Greg for the last while, so her radar was off. This particular guy wasn't much of a talker, but maybe he was just shy. He did have a cute daughter, though.

Maybe . . . maybe this was a step in the right direction. Maybe she should take the bull by the horns and rustle herself up a date. Then everyone would realize she was over Greg and they weren't getting back together, and they'd stop treating her like the bastion of lonely spinsterhood. She could show everyone she'd moved on.

All it would take was one date. They wouldn't even have to have chemistry. It just had to be dinner, enough to show that she'd continued on with her life and everyone should forget about the Wedding That Wasn't.

She didn't jump on the idea right away, though. She needed time to mull over it, and working on Libby's hair was the perfect distraction. The gum was so entangled that she'd spent a good half hour on the child's hair and was just now starting to work the hair tie out of the knot. She was pretty confident she could get this done, but it would take a while.

Unless he'd rather shave her head and be done with the mess.

Pursing her lips, Becca wiped her hands on a towel. "Can I talk to you for a minute, Mr. . . ."

He didn't offer his name, just got to his feet and followed her as she headed to the far end of the salon, by the front door. It was getting dark outside, the chill seeping in through the windows, and it was long past time for her to close up shop. She kept wiping her hands on the towel, her thoughts all over the place.

The man just kept watching her, waiting.

Okay, she was clearly going to have to carry the conversation. "I think I can get most of the gum out of Libby's hair, but it's going to take a while."

He grunted.

"Like, hours. I have to go slow because her hair's very fine and I don't want to pull on it. The other option is to shave her head, but I'm not sure how you feel about that."

The big cowboy looked over at his daughter, then back at Becca. He rubbed his bearded jaw. "She won't like it shaved."

"Well . . . I have time if you have time." She gave him a bright smile.

He paused. "Is . . . this an inconvenience?" The words seemed as if they were being dragged out of him.

"No, like I told Libby, I don't have anyone waiting at home for me. It wasn't how I planned on spending my evening, but that's all right."

The big man grunted again. "Appreciated."

They both paused, and Becca took in a steeling breath. This was her moment. This was the chance she should take. She could ask him out on a date and shake off the specter of Greg and the Wedding That Wasn't once and for all. So she toyed with a lock of her hair and hoped he found her reasonably attractive. "Is it true what Libby said? That you're not married?"

The dark eyes narrowed on her. Intense. Scrutinizing. He glanced at her, up and down, as if sizing her up.

Becca flushed. She charged ahead. It wasn't about this guy in particular. It was any guy, just to change how the town viewed her. She needed to change the conversation, period. "I know I'm being forward. I hope you don't mind. But . . . I figure now's as good a time as any to ask. Want to go on a date?"

He stared at her, up and down again. There was a long, awkward pause. Then he spoke a single word.

"No."

Ready to find
your next great read?

Let us help.

Visit prh.com/nextread

Penguin
Random
House